An
UNHOLY
Alliance

An UNHOLY Alliance

Judy Nedry (signature)

Judy Nedry

iUniverse, Inc.
New York   Bloomington

An Unholy Alliance

iUniverse books may be ordered through booksellers or by contacting:

iUniverse
1663 Liberty Drive
Bloomington, IN 47403
www.iuniverse.com
1-800-Authors (1-800-288-4677)

ISBN: 978-1-4401-4206-2 (pbk)
ISBN: 978-1-4401-4207-9 (cloth)
ISBN: 978-1-4401-4208-6 (ebk)

Printed in the United States of America

iUniverse rev. date: 5/15/2009

In memory of
Ian Peterson-Nedry
Son, brother, friend

Prologue

Friday Night

He waited in the half light a little drunk, a little floaty, but with that constant edge of irritation that had grown so much worse in the past couple years that he couldn't remember when he'd last been rid of it. Surely only during sleep, which was troubled now on the best of nights.

Of course she wouldn't keep him waiting. She knew better than to do that. She was the only one who could take away the edge. Still, her magic was only temporary—and it wasn't as good as it once had been. Or maybe it was just him. He didn't want to think it was him, but knew he'd have to do something about the situation, figure it out. Then he'd deal with her, sooner rather than later. For tonight, though, she'd do just fine.

He could smell the fermenting wine in the tanks below him. In fact, it was so quiet in the winery he could hear the must caps—the slight hissing and bubbling sounds of fermentation, of carbon dioxide being released through the crust of grape skins that floated atop the stainless steel tanks. The fumes could make a person dizzy. He already was dizzy.

Then he heard her. Heard the heavy door close in the distance. Heard the clack of her heels on the concrete as she drew near the catwalk. The clacking stopped. Eyes closed, he imagined he could see her step out of her heels and move her lithe body quietly as a stalking tiger up the metal stairs to the catwalk where he waited. He felt rather than heard her footfall on the metal walkway, the slight reverberation that brought her closer. He opened his eyes, pulled her into his arms, buried his face in the scent of her hair.

She grabbed a fistful of his thick white hair, pulled his head back away from her, and looked him in the eye. "You're really drunk," she said.

"Baby, I'm fine. And you shouldn't be talking." He knew he was beginning to slur his words. He'd need to exercise care when he returned to the party. The evening was only half done, and it was, after all, his event.

She turned away from him, and he watched as she opened her evening bag and removed a small envelope. This she opened it with care, then expertly tapped a line of white powder onto the metal railing. He eyed the substance, greedy little pig eyes sparkling. "Ladies first," she said as she bent over the line and snorted it into one nostril. She gathered the remaining bit of powder on her finger and licked it. Then she tapped out another line and he took his turn.

It was good. Unbelievably good. He could feel the stirring in his groin. He could feel himself begin to focus. He pulled her *to him again, kissing her roughly, shoving his tongue deep into her mouth. She moaned as if she wanted him to continue, but when he looked in her eyes he saw the revulsion, and something more. Terror? Very good. That's what really got him going.*

He grabbed her shoulders and stuck his face near hers. He nodded toward his groin. He'd already wasted enough time. "Help me out here now," he said. "Let's get this over with." She dropped to her knees.

Chapter 1

"It'll be easy," Melody said, but I knew it would not, because nothing with Melody is ever easy. The woman leads a very complicated life.

"I don't know," I told her. "I'm not real comfortable taking this on while I'm researching a book."

"But you'll be living in your research lab. You'll be right here for six weeks." Melody sounded a bit like a teenager trying to convince a parent she really needed to go away for a week with that guy covered in tattoos and pierced in places one could only imagine. "Think of the time you'll save—at least three hours a day just by not having to drive back and forth from Portland. I doubt you'll put in three hours a day for me the whole time you're here."

"How many hours a day do *you* work?" I asked her. "A whole lot more than three. What about your sister? Why can't she do it?"

"The Bolter? No, that wouldn't do." Just like "The Bolter"

in the Nancy Mitford novels, Melody's sister Aurora was not very stable. She had run off with so many men throughout her life that Melody claimed to have lost count. It wouldn't do at all.

"Of course I work more than three hours a day," she admitted, "but I'm the owner. I've also got employees to do all the big stuff. You just need to be charming, take the money, and make sure my staff gets the work done. Please, please, oh *please*! You're my last and only hope."

I didn't reply, just sat there with the telephone receiver at my ear and waited. I had learned in sales many years ago that the one who talks first loses. And as she usually does, Melody talked first. But when she did, she made me an offer I couldn't refuse.

"I'm a money whore," I later told my friend Cate. "But what can I say? At this point in life, one must focus on survival." A week later, on a sunny Sunday afternoon in late September, I closed up my small house in southwest Portland, Oregon, and began the drive south on I-5 toward Newberg and the wine country. Within a very short time I'd be involved in survival of a more serious nature, but on that bright day my mind was clear of everything save my own immediate concerns.

My name is Emma Golden. It's my maiden name. I was married once, and then I was called Emma McCourt. Were you someone who noticed such things, you may have seen my byline in the food and wine magazines back then. I wrote for all of them at one time or another—mostly about Northwest wine and food. It was my passion and I gave my life to it.

Then it was over. The life-building and learning, growing, living and writing the story of Northwest wines and the people who made them was over. When that era ended for me, I found myself overboard and floating alone in a great sea, while the ship on which I'd traveled for so many years, along with its passengers, sailed into the distance without me.

On that lovely autumn day, I followed I-5 south from Portland past the Tigard exit to one further south that connected me via less-traveled back roads to Highway 99W, and from there southwest into Yamhill County where Melody and I had met twenty years ago. When we McCourts moved to Newberg from Portland all those years ago, we had moved to the country. Then, it was but a thirty minute drive.

Now, the farmland and homes that once dotted Highway 99W have morphed into strip malls—one after another after another. From Tigard almost to Newberg, the valley floor and hillsides are covered with apartments, condos, and ugly, pop-up houses, many of them quite large, and most poorly designed. To this day, the building continues unabated—a church here, a gas station there, a school—paving over farmland far beyond what once was called the Urban Growth Boundary. In some parts of this region, wineries have been surrounded by subdivisions. There are traffic lights, and traffic—lots of traffic—all the way to Newberg, which itself is little more than another series of strip malls.

As I drove down the hill toward Newberg, the valley opened before me with its floor of green and golden squares. On the hillsides, Douglas fir forests were dotted with enormous, multi-tiered houses. Where forests once stood were many young vineyards, still green in the waning September days. The Willamette River glinted through trees to the south of town, and the paper mill belched steam. Forty miles to the west, the Coast Range and its foothills loomed in layers of deep greens, blues, and lavenders.

Even before I got to Newberg a heavy feeling hit me—heavy and sad both in heart and gut. I had avoided the place for years, even taking a different route to the coast, seeing my valley friends only if they came to Portland. All of the reasons I had left were still there. Thinking about them was not often comfortable, but it was time to get past all that.

My immediate plan was to suck up and get on with it. I was under contract to write a book about the Oregon wine industry from its beginnings through the present time. The advance was already spent to clear up what remained of my debts, and I had not yet interviewed a single person. My copy deadline was mid-February.

I passed into the valley. I passed where our children had attended middle school. I drove through downtown Newberg where 99W divides into three lanes of traffic running west and three lanes running east right through city center. On weekdays, commuters and logging trucks pour through the center of town, some going east, some going west. Save a smattering of vintage brick buildings, downtown Newberg was, and is, almost completely without charm.

The highway narrows west of Newberg, and by the time I reached the small burg of Dundee, it was down to one lane in either direction. Vehicles full of people returning from a weekend at the coast were backed up nearly a mile on the highway west of Dundee. Driving against the returning stream of cars and minivans, I watched the oncoming traffic—couples and families, mostly. Only a few people traveled alone. I imagined the families in these vehicles, their tummies filled with good food and their moods buoyed by the weekend's bright sunshine. They were relaxed, conversing, planning another trip, perhaps, before the rains set in.

This was not entirely true, my story about all those "happy" families. My brain, as it often does, was sending me erroneous information. I reminded myself that these were not television families, because real families are not like the ones we see on television. Some were happy much of the time, but just as many of them were miserable beyond endurance, dysfunctional, cruel, or sad. They all were out just trying to make it better by taking a little air.

Inside my car, the air reeked of regret and remorse that even the bright September day couldn't dispel. I could not turn around because I had signed on for six weeks to help one of my dearest friends. I would get through it and possibly even thrive. It could and would be a useful, productive, and certainly lucrative time. I would be of service, and I would complete research for the book.

The Wyatts—Melody and her husband, Dan—own the Westerly Inn, a stunningly beautiful bed and breakfast inn located four miles outside Dundee, in the epicenter of Oregon's now-renowned wine country. Once a thriving farm with fruit and nut orchards, tucked into a little southwest-facing swale in the Dundee Hills, it is now a forty-acre parcel serving wine country visitors. Much of the land was sold decades ago, and the orchards are no longer with us. In fact, they departed in the Columbus Day storm of 1962, years before Dan and Melody purchased the Westerly. They bought the property the same year we moved to the area. Dan kept his day job in Portland, and Melody used the returns from some of his more successful investments to convert the 1910 vintage farmhouse and its outbuildings into the Westerly Inn, one of the better tourist accommodations in the valley.

A couple miles west of Dundee I turned off the highway and onto a narrow two-lane asphalt road that gently curved uphill and northward into the Dundee Hills. A new vineyard—little sticks closely spaced, each surrounded by a white plastic tube—had been planted on the left side of the road. An old hazelnut orchard sporting a "For Sale" sign stood majestically to the right, forming a canopy over the bare ground underneath. Stacks of wooden totes at the edge of the orchard announced that harvest was about to begin.

I knew that the vineyards covering the hills in front of me were almost ready as well. As I drove past a mature vineyard, I recognized the black pinot noir clusters hanging from the vines. A man and his border collie walked in the red dirt along one of the rows, the man tasting grapes for ripeness and flavor. His dog bounded ahead and back, ahead and back. The man spit out skins and grape seeds. Stacks of yellow plastic totes stood at the ends of the long rows of grapevines. To me it was a familiar scene, rich and deep and real.

Despite the disconnection resulting from past years and present circumstances, I began to feel a part of it all over again, and it felt warm and right. But while my gut continued to tell me I still belonged, the facts told a different story altogether. I reminded myself that I must remember to stick with the facts and present reality. My role was to be one of a visiting journalist.

Turning into the drive at the Westerly Inn, I noticed many changes. For starters, the once-gravel driveway had been paved and was lined with sumptuous plantings of summer and fall perennials—clumps of lavender, Shasta daisies, Echinacea, and gladiolus spiked with bunches of ornamental grasses. Tall stands of dahlias bounced in a riot of joyful color. They were backed by a hedge of rhododendron bushes. A half-acre of lush lawn set off the huge Prairie four-square house with its covered porch that spanned the front of the dwelling. Ancient oak trees flanked the back of the house, forming a dramatic backdrop. Guests lounged on a porch swing, while in the flowerbed in front of it Melody leaned on a garden rake and chatted with them, her back to the driveway. At her feet rested her standard Schnauzer, Winston, who began barking frantically when he heard my car approaching. The scene brought a smile to my face.

"Oh, my God! You're finally here!" Melody shouted over the barking. She dropped the rake and ran toward the car. I pulled my aging Toyota into the visitors' parking area beside the house and switched off the engine. Then Melody was upon me, pulling open the door and grabbing my arms as I tried get out of the car. "I was afraid you'd change your mind. I would have died!" She put her hands on my shoulders and kissed me soundly on both cheeks. I kissed her back, one old sage hen greeting another.

Winston jumped and barked as we hugged each other. "When I say I'm going to do something, I generally do it," I remarked. "The place looks wonderful! And so do you."

"Oh, I'm so excited you're here. We'll get you all unpacked and I'll show you the new stuff," Melody bubbled. "Come and meet the Webbers. You'll be taking care of them while we're gone." Then under her breath she muttered, "They are a complete pain in the ass!" I laughed out loud. Some things don't change; Melody, for one. She is almost always hilarious. Plus, she loves her work, and she loves to complain about it.

The Webbers were lodged in the Carriage House, she told me as she introduced us. I met the gay couple staying in the Chicken House. Melody introduced them as "The Boys". And yes, nearly a hundred years ago their lodging really had been a chicken house conveniently located behind the old farm house. Melody had revamped it into a sumptuous little one-bedroom cottage.

We walked up the porch and through the front door, into the cool inside of the house, across thick Oriental rugs, past the open staircase, and down a hall toward the kitchen. "This all looks the same," I said. "Where's that new stuff?"

"Just you wait," she told me.

Four guest rooms were located upstairs, each with its own bath. There was a sitting room where lodgers could gather to watch television, play cards, or borrow a book from the floor-to-ceiling book shelves. It was well-equipped with a coffee maker, microwave, and a small refrigerator stocked with snacks.

Downstairs were the living room, dining room, parlor, and master suite. A powder room was tucked under the open staircase and, a solarium on the west side of the house offered a view of flower gardens, plus glimpses of the valley below and the distant Coast Range. The huge dining room was outfitted with an antique table that could sit up to twenty people, and a European sideboard adorned with sterling silver serving pieces. The Arts and Crafts built-ins of dark stained wood with glass fronts showed off the formal china and additional silver service ware.

Melody chattered nonstop as she led me into the kitchen. The original had been so inadequate for modern times that the Wyatts immediately had built a kitchen addition and deck after they purchased the Westerly property. Since I'd moved to Portland, it had been updated and expanded again, and was approximately the size of my entire living quarters. For all the quaintness of the painted wood, glass fronted cabinets, and an old wood butcher block, this room was anything but quaint when it came to equipment.

"This is some of the new stuff," Melody gushed. "What do you think?" It was impressive—a six-burner commercial range with two ovens, next to it a separate built-in convection oven. There were large stainless steel sinks, plus a separate wet bar and salad prep area. I walked to the baking station and laid my hand on a polished concrete slab. "When did you do this?"

"It took most of last winter," she said. "We had to do it when the B&B wasn't open, so Dan and I moved a few things into the dining room, and demolition started after Christmas. We'd been planning it for some time, but you wouldn't know that since you weren't talking to us."

"It's not that I wasn't talking to you," I said. "I just couldn't make myself drive out here."

"I will *try* to understand that," she said, indicating that would take great effort, then resumed her role as tour guide.

I examined pots hung from ceiling hooks and admired the oversized cooking vessels. Ceramic serving platters and bowls were stacked neatly on baker's racks against one wall.

The place was outfitted better than many restaurants. At the far end of the large kitchen were doors that led to a laundry room and a mud room, and a pantry that housed a glass-door refrigerator. Sliding doors opened onto a deck with an umbrella table and huge planters. From there, a graveled path led to the Chicken House.

"You could feed an army here, Melody."

"We're talking about doing weddings as early as next season, but I don't know. It would be like the Webbers to the tenth power, and I may be too old. Or not hungry enough." She laughed. "It's part of the new wave, though. Nobody could make any money out here twenty years ago, and now everyone wants to drink our wines and half the West Coast wants to get married in our backyards."

"Go figure."

I was happy to find the old butler's pantry still in tact after the remodel, its cabinets filled with more dinner ware, wine glasses, and drawers of silver and linens. The alcove to its side still accommodated a chalk board listing the telephone numbers of local food and wine vendors, a phone and answering machine, and Melody's large and messy oak desk.

It was a magnificent old house, and surprisingly comfortable. Melody had managed to seamlessly blend the best of its vintage charm with every convenience imaginable. Beneath it all was a large basement with a wine cellar, more storage, and access to the outside.

"I had forgotten," I began, as I scanned the kitchen again.

"Forgotten what?" Melody asked.

"I had forgotten the scale of things here, how massive it all is."

Melody looked perplexed. "Well, I never think of it that way," she said after a minute. "I guess I'm just used to it. With so many people around, every space is used eight months of the year. And then we go away for a while. And when we come back it is holiday time and we're full up with people again."

She grinned, and then pointed to a door at the end of the kitchen nearest the old part of the house. "Now for your surprise," she said, and opened the door.

From the kitchen, the wooden door looked as if it led to another, old-fashioned closet. Behind the door, however, was a stairway that ascended to a beautiful bedroom suite.

"Ta-Da! What do you think?"

"Incredible!" I gasped taking in the bright upstairs suite, complete with a queen-size bedroom set, a sitting area and desk, and a large cherry armoire. The bathroom held an oval soaking tub, walk-in shower, and linen closet. It was all striking colors, polished wood, marble tiles, and chrome fixtures. The towels were thick and fluffy. I felt I'd walked into a luxury spa.

"This is yours when you deign to stay with us," said Melody. "I designed it for you—for exactly this purpose. You have everything you need to write or relax, and you're near the kitchen—the most important room of the house!"

"I never could have imagined this. It is glorious!" I assured her, suddenly excited about my temporary job.

The three of us dined quietly that evening on the deck, and lingered at the table long after dark. Melody chattered a bit about my chores, which were regular but not difficult. Basically, I was front person for the operation, greeting and checking in guests, joining them at breakfast, helping with dinner reservations, or setting up visits at some of the wineries that were open by appointment only. Angel Lopez, her full-time kitchen help, knew everything there was to know about getting out breakfasts each morning. She also was in charge of making certain the non-English speaking staff performed their duties. Her proper name was Angelina, but Melody called her Angel, "because she is an angel."

My other primary hostess role was to set out wine and light snacks at five each afternoon. It allowed guests to mingle and relax before going to dinner. This time of year, tourists usually stayed out until the tasting rooms closed, and dinner reservations tended to be at seven or later. "They're usually ready to gobble up everything in sight," Melody warned me.

Dan, who is less a social being than his wife, was more worried about his vegetable garden. "I have the crew weeding and watering," he told me. "But things need to be picked every day." I promised to keep after the veggies, and wondered what Angel could do to work them into the breakfast menu for the Westerly guests. Vegetable frittatas perhaps.

That night I climbed the stairway with a cup of chamomile tea and my book, and slid between the cool sheets. When I turned out the light, I sat in bed for a few moments and listened to the night rustlings, the absolute absence of motor vehicle sounds. Even when I'd lived in the valley, our house was in town and the ambient sounds were different. "It's like a dream," I told myself as I crawled under the down comforter and drifted into sleep.

Chapter 2

Having slept well, I got up early and was looking pert and hostessy when I descended from my nest into the kitchen. Melody was already on duty, chatting with a very short Mexican woman. I was introduced to Angelina Lopez, and shook her floury hand despite her protestations.

Several traveling bags sat by the slider. I was to drive Dan and Melody to the airport, but not before we had breakfast with the Webbers, who indeed were a pain in the ass. While he was merely an old fart, probably about seventy, she was closer to my age and insidiously high maintenance—long suffering, loud, and allergic to everything.

First thing, she picked through the fruit course looking for walnuts. She is very allergic to walnuts, she loudly informed me. "We don't have a walnut in the house," Melody declared.

"Well, you know, just one walnut could kill me," she said. It sounded like a good idea to me. Her name is Jane. Jane

Webber. "And the scones, are they gluten-free? You know I can't tolerate gluten."

"Jane, we've been through this," said her husband. His name is Martin but she calls him Marty. "Melody has taken every precaution."

"Look at this!" Jane was speaking to me. She had removed a device from her vest pocket that looked like an oversize writing pen. "This is my epi-pen. I carry one of these with me at all times because of walnuts."

I nodded at the appliance as if aware that walnuts were lurking everywhere. Melody silently passed Jane a basket of gluten-free bran muffins *sans* walnuts. If I were Marty I would have ground up walnuts—a lot of them—and disguised them in one of Jane's vile concoctions. I would have done it twenty years ago and saved myself a life of misery. But some people don't even know they're miserable. In two days, I told myself, they'll be gone and I can relax.

Melody introduced me as a writer, and that got both of the Webbers going on all the writers they have known. It gave me the opportunity to polish off some excellent wild mushroom quiche and a couple rashers of bacon. I was nibbling a scone when they paused for breath.

"What are you writing that brings you out here?" Martin queried.

"I'm writing a book about the Oregon wine industry," I said.

Then, just as suddenly as they had written me off, I was a person of interest. And they, as they assured me, were quite the wine experts, just ask them.

"Have you been to Cougar Crossing?" Jane began. "No?

Well, you must go, because they make the best pinot noir in the United States."

Why did I not know this? Is it because I haven't had a drink in seven years? Is it because I always thought my former husband made the best pinot noir in the United States? "Good to know," I told her. "I definitely will check them out."

"Ted is the *nicest* man," she gushed. Ted who? I didn't know Ted.

"We spent two thousand dollars there yesterday," Martin assured us. Well, certainly that accounted for something.

"And they have the *caves*, you know." Jane again. "They're the only Oregon winery with *caves*." She pronounced it with a short "a"—*cahves*.

I rolled my eyes at Melody. Discreetly, of course. Dan intercepted the look but smiled slightly, then excused himself to the back porch where he lit a small cigar. I know this because I could see him from where I sat, and I wished I was out there with him but he was too quick for me. Besides, I was practicing being a hostess.

"Yes, they built those caves at great expense," Melody interjected. "I mean anybody could build some, I guess, if they thought it was justified. And their wine is somewhat controversial—although it certainly has a following."

Jane blinked at her, speechless for a few seconds, her eyes huge and bulging behind thick glasses. I guess she thought Ted had invented caves or something.

"Maxell was the first winemaker in Oregon to charge one hundred dollars for a bottle of pinot noir." This from Martin. Now at least I knew Ted's last name.

"Well, then, it must be great," I said, hoping that would end the tortuous conversation.

"When will the book be out?" Jane asked. "We can't wait to see what you write about Cougar Crossing."

"Next year about this time," I told her. "In time for the Thanksgiving weekend tastings, and for Christmas."

"We'll want several autographed copies if Cougar Crossing is in it," she clucked. They rose from the table, off for another day of keeping the Yamhill County economy afloat.

"They're probably investors, poor souls," Melody said after they were out of range.

"Why's that?"

"Ted Maxell likes to hit and run," she said as we began clearing the breakfast dishes and carrying them to the kitchen. "He spent millions on the Oregon venture, went way over budget, and his partners were furious. So he beat the bushes and found some more investors. This group isn't particularly wine savvy, although they think they are. They have money and want to be in the game. He puts on a great show for them, and hopefully the perks are worth it to them. They probably will never recoup their so-called investments, but it will probably keep them from paying taxes." She snorted. "He did the same thing in California before he came up here."

"I guess I'll have to see the place," I said. "Whatever the back story, he sounds like a big player, and people want to read about the big players. I wish you were going to be here to help fill in the blanks."

"Oh, you'll be fine," Melody said, and I drove them to the airport.

When I returned, there were several messages on the bed and breakfast business line, and one of them was from Cougar Crossing Winery.

"This is Ted Maxell calling for Emma Golden," a voice boomed. "Understand you're writing a book, and we'd love to have you up to the winery for a little get together on Friday evening. Seven o'clock, dinner. Come about five-thirty and I'll show you around." Click. He had sounded friendly but insistent, his invitation more along the lines of an order. But since I was going to have to meet him anyway I called the winery back and said I'd be there.

Then I got to work on the other messages and the bookings in the small alcove off the kitchen. It was nearly noon, however Angel Lopez was assembling a breakfast tray for the Chicken House. The boys—they were regular visitors twice a year Melody had told me—were sleeping late. This morning, they had asked that breakfast be delivered.

Breakfast is served in the dining room from eight to nine, and guests who don't like that schedule can visit the refrigerator in the upstairs lounge and eat some fruit and yogurt. However, I was told that guests seldom miss breakfast in the dining room. Those staying in the Chicken House or Carriage House can have hot breakfast delivered; or, if they prefer their privacy, we will stock the units the evening before and they can prepare breakfast for themselves in the morning. The boys liked to be waited on.

"How's it going, Angel?" I asked when I'd finished with the bookings. "Do you need any help?"

"Oh no, Mrs. Golden. I am almost finished." Her English was good, but the accent was heavy. I stood by the butcher block as she put the finishing touches on the breakfast tray—sprigs of thyme, nasturtiums, a small vase with a perfect dahlia. It was lovely. I was certain the boys would be charmed.

"Call me Emma," I said. "I quit being a Mrs. a long time ago."

"Emma. Oh, like Madame...Bovaree?"

"Yes, like Madame Bovary, but hopefully a little wiser. You've read it then?"

"My daughter, she read it to me. She is very smart."

"I'm certain she got the smart from you," I laughed. "Does she live with you?"

"Oh, no, Mrs.... Emma. She live in Newberg. She has the house. She is a winemaker."

"Really!" A Latino winemaker—this had to be a first, at least for Oregon. "What's her name?"

"She is Zephyr Lopez. She work at Tanager Winery. It is new."

"I will want to talk to her about my book," I said. "You must be very proud of her."

Angel's cappuccino-colored complexion flushed slightly as she covered the breakfast courses with a clean tea towel. "I am," she said. "She is twenty-seven now, very beautiful."

"Well, she got that from you, too," I assured her. She stood a full head shorter than I. Her jet-black hair was pulled back and braided halfway down her back. She was cute and plump, and with her smooth skin looked to be about thirty—which obviously was impossible. She laughed and blushed again.

"I take this out to the boys now," she said. "And then I leave early today. Senora Melody say it is okay. I go to the dentist."

"What time tomorrow?"

"I come at seven. Then I do the cooking." I nodded. "Adios Mrs. Emma," she said on her way out the door.

As I perused the refrigerator, checking the items on hand for tomorrow's breakfast, I congratulated myself. Two great leads—Cougar Crossing and Tanager—in one small day. And it was only noon. I grabbed the leash, called Winston from the back porch, and the two of us took a long walk around the estate.

At five o'clock I set out a bottle of lightly chilled chardonnay and some salted hazelnuts on a small table on the front porch, then sat down with a glass of San Pellegrino and waited. I didn't have to wait long. The boys showed up, tanned and gorgeous. They rubbed Winston's head, then re-introduced themselves. Frank Morgan and Henry Siu from San Francisco. Frank, a big, beefy all-American boy with thick dark hair and a gorgeous smile, was a clinical psychologist; Henry, slight and Chinese, was an interior designer. They looked to be about forty. Besides the Webbers, they were the only guests until the weekend. I was glad, as it would give me a chance to adjust to my new routine with minimal stress.

We nibbled the nuts. Winston rested his head on Henry's lap and drooled. Henry fed him a nut. They told me a bit about their lives, I told them a bit about my book project. They finished the bottle of wine. I finished the bottle of San Pellegrino. We lolled into the warm evening watching hummingbirds visit the fuchsia baskets hanging from the porch. Occasionally a hummingbird altercation broke out and we'd laugh. I was as completely relaxed as I'd been in six months.

"We're going to Tina's at seven," Frank announced. "Would you care to join us?"

"I'd be delighted," I told them. There was no sign of the Webbers, thank God. Cocktail hour was officially over and I gathered the nut bowl, glasses, and bottles onto a tray. Frank quickly relieved me of the tray and carried it to the kitchen.

When we arrived at Tina's an hour later, the first person I saw was my ex-husband Dwight McCourt. He was sitting on a bar stool eating a salmon filet, a bottle of StoneGate Reserve Pinot Noir at his left elbow. Dwight was notorious for showing up at a restaurant with his own wine. His wine glass was half-full, or half-empty, depending upon how you choose to look at it.

He nodded in our direction, sizing up the entourage. "Hi Emmy, long time no see," he drawled when his inventory was complete. I walked over to him and we exchanged a half-hearted little hug. It always felt weird, but we did it anyway. We get along most of the time. I really did like the guy, despite the things we've both pulled over the years. Dwight is big and burly, and I noticed during that quick hug that he had gotten a bit burlier around the midriff. Things were starting to sag a little here and there, but sagging is an equal opportunity nuisance to those of us in our late prime. His red hair and beard showed flecks of silver and his eyebrows had grown very bushy, giving him a fiercer then normal look. He had gotten himself a good haircut, and the beard was neatly trimmed. He was still a very handsome man.

"What brings you to wine country," he asked?

"I'm running the Westerly for Melody and Dan while they are on vacation," I told him. "And I'm writing a book."

"It's about time!" he said, and his enthusiasm was real. "When's the deadline?"

"February, and it will be out by next November."

I introduced Frank and Henry. A large group of people came in the door behind us and it was time to move out of the way. "I need to talk to you for the book," I told him. "And by the way, do you know Ted Maxell?"

"Of course I know him," Dwight sputtered. "He tried to steal a couple acres of my North Ridge property. He's an asshole. Ask anyone." He paused for breath, then jerked his head in the direction of the new arrivals. "That's him talking to Jake," he said just loudly enough that only I could hear him. "The fat bastard." I looked in the direction of Jake, the host, to see him addressing a stout man with a great mane of white hair. Ted Maxell was talking emphatically and gesturing with his hands.

Jake said something to him, then picked up menus and motioned to us. "Thanks for the heads up," I said to Dwight, then followed Jake and the boys into the dining room.

Henry and Frank were consummate entertainers, keeping my glass topped with Perrier and regaling me with gossip and tales from the City. We barely could hear each other due to the din the Maxell party created in the small dining room. I watched enviously every time one of the wait staff delivered a bottle of wine to their table. The man was sparing no expense to impress whoever his guests were.

The blonde sitting next to him was at least a generation younger than everyone else in the group. I would have guessed she was his daughter except for the fact that she wore an enormous diamond and was great with child. And he kept kissing her on the neck. Once I caught her shudder and pull away from him, but for the most part she sat stiffly at his side, a bright smile on her face.

Henry intercepted my observation and touched my arm. "That's his wife, Tara," he said, leaning into me so only I could hear. "Ted married his granddaughter."

I chuckled and allowed myself the luxury of feeling mean. Ted appeared to be in his mid-fifties, while Tara was probably early-twenties. "She may look like a cream puff, but she has some street smarts," Henry continued. "She wanted to marry money and she did. Hooked up with him down in our home town. One of my former lovers is her financial adviser. She wants to be well taken care of down the line when beauty fleets, as it always does, alas."

Interestinger and interestinger. This was not the kind of information I could put in the book, but tasty nonetheless. "I hope your friend does a good job for her," I said.

"Oh, he does."

"And the ta-tas are not her own. I know the guy who did them," Frank chimed in. These two were a fountain of information. Henry busied himself with his duck breast in green peppercorn sauce, but he wasn't missing out on the conversation. An amused smile played at the corners of his mouth.

I observed that Tara was in dire peril of bursting the part of her cocktail dress that held her enhanced breasts in bondage.

"What don't you know about the Maxells?" I wondered between mouthfuls of salmon.

"Well," Frank continued, "we know that Ted's kids had a fit when he brought this one home. His daughter Tiffany is the same age as Tara, and Axel is only a couple years older."

"Axel? Axel Maxell? That's his son?"

"It is."

"What were those people thinking?"

"Ted liked the name. And he does have his funny side."

I looked again at the table. Ted was leaning back in his chair, head tilted back, laughing. His hands were splayed across his large belly; his face had turned very red. He looked like he burst might something before his wife did. A blood vessel perhaps. His lips were full and sensuous. At one time he would have been an attractive man. But now he was not. Age and dissipation were taking their toll. I glanced toward the bar in time to see Dwight get up, toss some cash next to his half-finished bottle of wine, and walk out the door.

"Where's the ex-wife and mother of Ted's children?" I wondered this for no particular reason save nosiness. Writers are the nosiest people on earth. We clamor for details whether the details matter or not.

"Oh, she still lives in the Bay Area part of the year, but she has a place up here so she can be near the kids. They both work for Ted, poor things," Henry said between bites of duck. "We knew them when."

"So he's got the whole damn family, past, present, and future, very close at hand."

"Yes," Frank observed. "It's thoroughly nauseating. All of

it. You'd think after the things he's done they'd want to be as far from him as possible."

"And what has he done?" I was dying to know.

"Oh, you'll find out, darling." Frank patted my hand and took another sip of his wine. "Not to worry. You'll find out."

Chapter 3

Later that evening I rested in the living room in a red leather chair, a glass of San Pellegrino at the ready. Why don't we have nice mineral water from around here? I mused. Maybe there isn't any. Eau d' Willamette brought to mind sewage and agricultural chemical runoff. A bit frightening, that. And what about llama cheese? Llamas are everywhere. Millions of them. They must be good for something. I pondered these things, but mostly I thought about the past, and art.

Across the room from me was The Painting—Carolyn's painting that dated from the early 1980s. I remembered how Melody and I fell completely in love with that piece the first time we saw it. We both had wanted it, but Melody was the one who had the means to purchase it and the place to put it. I was married to a man whose sun rose and set around an infant vineyard, was pregnant with our second child, and was in no situation to even think about buying art.

Carolyn's painting was the first piece of art I ever coveted.

It was the first time I experienced a painting that had the power to move me into a different realm of experience. A landscape artist for the most part, Carolyn painted bold, gutsy, and colorful works. Rendered in large and confident strokes, they were more often abstract than realistic. My reaction to the style and subject matter, and the colors that Carolyn used, was immediate, visceral, and passionate. It was fortunate one of us had the means to buy this particular piece.

I studied it for perhaps the thousandth time. That was Carolyn's house in the lower left-hand corner, a half-timbered white stucco only partially visible, roof purple, house shadowed by trees. I say Carolyn's house, because although Michael lived there he wasn't really a part of the house. His heart and soul belonged in the vineyard.

In the painting, sun lit the vineyard in brilliant shades of green. I observed once more that the greens were not quite green, but rather variations of true green—lime, chartreuse, kelly, forest, mint, and olive. Neither were the earth tones brown, but rather russets, siennas, reds, lavenders, and purples, plus shades of grey, some warmer, some cooler.

Broad bands of yellow, gold, and chartreuse depicted the crops of various types that once dotted a landscape now comprised almost entirely of vineyards. Barns and houses were searing splashes of white with purple and black roofs fading into emerald-black forests. Though abstract, the scene was alive with the energy I always had felt for this land. I could almost hear Carolyn's deep chuckle. "That was when none of us knew what the hell we were doing," she'd once said. "That was when it was still *fuunnn!*"

Studying the painting, I remembered I had not asked Melody about Carolyn, the oldest and most daring, the leader of our once-inseparable triumvirate. Carolyn, with her deep laugh and southern drawl, had almost disappeared from my life when I quit drinking. One could hardly blame Carolyn, could one? I had become a different person. I'd had to reinvent myself or die. And yet, how long had it been? Surely not years.

Suddenly, I had to know about Carolyn. And Michael, of course, but mostly Carolyn. Were they still together? Their relationship had been a volatile one. Was Carolyn still painting? Of course she was. Painting was life to her.

Moving quickly to the kitchen alcove, I picked up the office phone and dialed Melody's cell phone number. Where would they be by now? Already on the plane or in LAX? On the fourth ring Melody answered.

"It's me."

"Oh my God, what's wrong?"

"Nothing is wrong. It is very quiet here. The vile Webbers are silent. I had dinner at Tina's with the boys, and saw my ex-husband."

"Did you speak to him?"

"Of course I spoke to him. We had children together, remember? We speak. I couldn't *not* speak to him. I called about Carolyn."

The timbre of Melody's voice changed, became guarded. "What *about* Carolyn?"

"Oh, nothing in particular. I was just sitting in your red chair looking at the painting, and I thought of her. How is she doing?"

A barely perceptible pause raced through the space between us, then Melody sighed. It was a small sigh. "Not good."

"I'm sorry to hear that."

"Well, she pretty well cut you off at the knees."

"A lot of people did. I lived through it, though. And I'm sorry."

"She's still drinking of course, and she's drinking a lot. She's lost weight and gained wrinkles, and generally looks like hell. I saw her at Fred Meyer last week and she hid her head in the lettuces to avoid talking to me. I know she saw me."

"Oh dear." I found myself unable to say more for a moment as I remembered myself seven years ago. "And Michael? Are they...?"

"They're still married, if that's what you mean. And she is still in the house. He's living in that little guest apartment above the winery, and I hear he is seeing someone. It makes me sad."

"It makes me sad too," I said, and we finished our conversation and signed off. A long time ago life had been fun, or maybe I just thought it had been fun. Once the three of us got together, I felt like I'd found myself. We'd all lived for the challenges, ups and downs, children and the growing of things, and the little dramas that made up each day, the vineyards and the wines. Now, for me at least, it was over, and I was as done with it as done could be. Yet I had ambivalent feelings about the times gone, loves lost, victories won and those forfeited, the blood on the tracks. Even though I'd screwed up a lot, there had been some great times. And here I was, back in the old neighborhood, writing a book.

"I don't even know why I am writing this damned book," I heard myself say aloud. And then I turned on the television to watch the ten o'clock news.

"You might wake up next to the wrong man," a woman I knew in rehab told me during that phase of my life, "but you'll never wake up next to the wrong dog."

I'd never thought about it since, until my second night at the Westerly. Some time during the night I drifted out of sleep just enough to feel warm breath on my face. And when I reached toward that which was nearest my face, my hand touched silky, soft hair. I was instantly awake and on Red Alert. Who had crawled into my bed?

Further hasty investigation revealed a furry ear and a wet, juicy nose, a longish sticky Schnauzer beard. Winston had nosed open the downstairs stairway door, and had crept up the stairs from his bed in the kitchen alcove. I peeked at the clock on the night stand. It was four in the morning, perfectly still. There was no moonlight that night, just a row of faint outdoor lighting along the footpath and around the flower beds beneath my bedroom that shed a faint light on the walls. The early morning air stirred slightly, bathing my face in its soft coolness. I stroked Winston's head. He emitted a contented groan and stretched his body. I sighed and stretched my body. Unfortunately, I now was wide awake.

At these times the mind wanders. What else is it to do without the distractions of noise, light, and motion? The tiniest of euphemistic mouse turds that lurk unnoticed in the recesses of our brains by day often are blown into mental Matterhorns in the night's dark stillness. And so it was with me that early morning as I lay staring upward at blackness, a dog snoring beside me.

Melody's remarks the previous night concerned me. Carolyn was killing herself with alcohol—and prescription drugs, too, for all I knew. She'd always been able to out-drink me, which is saying something. And she'd always had a fondness for Percocet. "Takes the edge off, honey," she'd roared once over the din of a party we'd staged to celebrate our birthdays. She'd popped a couple of pills and taken a swig from the bottle of Armagnac she'd carried close to her body the way a child would cradle a teddy bear. In the background of my mind I heard someone yell "Stella!" "Right here, honey!" she yelled back. Carolyn became Stella when she drank, and Stella could be scary.

And when we went on a tear together, I morphed into Ruby and Melody became Viola. If it was just the three of us, Melody was the one among us who could stay sane enough to drive. Stella, Ruby, and Viola. We counted on Viola to get us home. If we could remember the next day what had transpired the night before, Carolyn would call me and confess, "Stella was very bad last night." "Yes she was," I'd say. "And Ruby misbehaved as well."

But in those last days of my drinking, I'd have two drinks, black out, and continue to drink, remembering nothing. It got so I'd stay home to drink because going out was just too much effort, too dangerous. I never knew what would follow the first couple drinks. I could be upright and functioning, talking, and continuing to drink, but the conscious part of me would be somewhere else. I never knew when she would leave me or where she went. But I'd hear about it the next day, even though I couldn't remember a thing.

"You're a different person when you drink," Dwight would tell me on the mornings after. Sometimes he would tell me what I'd done.

"You probably like that a lot," I'd snap back. It wasn't nice, and yet it continued for a very long time. For Carolyn it continued still. For me, to think of her still doing blackout drinking and those god-awful mornings after, that taste in the mouth, the killing headache, the silent rage of the person or persons across the breakfast table, brought it all back in its real full-blown horror. The shame and guilt, the wondering what she'd said and done the night before to invite such disdain. The knowing that she was killing herself by inches. The not caring. Yes, it was all too familiar, and it brought back feelings of my own guilt and shame.

There came a time when I couldn't do it any more, when I couldn't look in the mirror at what I had become. I quit drinking, but not for myself. I was not afraid of dying. I was afraid of dying drunk, and how my children would remember me—how I had let them down. At that time, I didn't think of the other people I had hurt along the way, including and most especially Dwight.

When I quit, I knew my life would change. It was frightening at the time, but once on the path, I learned it was an all or nothing deal. Somehow during that time, and not by my own devices, I decided that I did want to live. To survive, I could never go back to drinking. I checked into rehab and ended up changing everything about the way I lived. There was the inevitable fallout. More than I ever could have imagined. There still were parts of my life that needed to be addressed. I needed to see Carolyn and make my peace with her. I could offer to help her if she was willing. I needed to do it soon, before I talked myself out of it.

My mind wandered back to the previous evening at Tina's. Henry and Frank were so much fun. Not only had they filled my mind with salacious gossip—some of it undoubtedly true—but also had picked up the tab for my dinner. Thanks to our evening together, I knew a couple more players. And with encouragement from my former spouse and the boys' enthusiastic bolstering, I was ready to attack the book project with confidence.

Writing a book about the wine industry when I had been effectively out of it for several years meant that I had a lot of catching up to do. My old files contained the life histories of all the winemakers up to the point where I'd moved back to Portland. In the meantime, however, Oregon's wine industry had taken off. Thanks to several back-to-back vintages ranging from very good to excellent, plus the increased skills of winemakers, and media attention from around the globe, Oregon had attracted a plethora of new wineries. Several local winemakers had broken from the pack of wineries that had employed them to found new, successful ventures. But the biggest changes to the Oregon wine culture were coming from outside the state.

Ted Maxell with his Cougar Crossing project exemplified some of those newcomers—the ones with tons of money who came in and believed themselves to be the CEOs of wine country, as well as of their own successful past ventures. Thankfully, not many were of his ilk. According to Frank and

Henry, who'd visited his California operation, Maxell was arrogant, mean, and dishonest. He'd made a fortune in real estate before starting a showy winery operation in Sonoma County many years ago.

Maxell also behaved outrageously on a personal level. "His favorite trick," Henry had told me, "was luring unsuspecting female journalists up to his manse for a winemaker's dinner, just the two of them. He'd always do it when his wife, the divine Pamela, was in the city for one of her endless benefits. A writer friend of mine was invited up to a dinner party. The party turned out to be a private little affair with just Ted and his Rottweilers. Four of them. She somehow managed get away without being attacked by the dogs or Ted, but it wasn't pleasant."

"How can he think that behavior would work in his behalf?" I'd wondered.

"I doubt he'd thought much about it. He probably just was hoping to get laid. He was getting pretty out of control at that point."

Maxell's fall from grace, however, had nothing to do with lechery, but instead was a result of him going too far in the financial shenanigans department. His partners and their lawyers ousted him from Mirage—his winery in Sonoma County—resulting in publicity of the worst sort. Maxell bounced right back by doing a geographic. According to the boys, within the period of a few months he had purchased vineyard property in Oregon with big plans to build another winery.

Soon thereafter, Maxell divorced his wife (or she divorced him—neither of my sources were certain on this point), and within a couple of years he was married to the blonde with the fake boobs. He and a new group of investors had built Cougar Crossing Winery. With his own fortune, he also had built a grotesque house just up the hill from the winery and named it Tara for the child bride. He then had moved to Oregon with Tara, his grown children following in his wake.

This surely was the stuff of legend and lore. I was eager to see it all. Cougar Crossing's wines were excellent by all reports. They also ranked among the most expensive in Oregon and had developed a cult following. It certainly would be a change from the old days. With Ted Maxell and all the other newcomers, this was a project that promised to be more interesting than anything I'd done in years.

Meanwhile, there was no way I could go back to sleep, so I got out of bed, went downstairs and brewed a pot of coffee. Winston and my memories of past deeds came with me. So did an abundant and growing curiosity about my upcoming research. I drank coffee and read *The Oregonian.* Winston ate his breakfast and a couple of dog biscuits. When the birds began to sing, I set the dining room table and then, to help Angel, began bringing wonderful things from the refrigerator in preparation for the boys' breakfast tray and for my final breakfast with the Webbers.

Chapter 4

The first person I interviewed during my tenure in wine country was my very own ex-husband Dwight McCourt. I probably should call him my former husband. It sounds a little softer. I had a nice breakfast with the Webbers. They really aren't so bad...in small doses. Because they talk a lot, they dispense a lot of information—much of it worthless. There is, however, the occasional nugget.

Earlier that morning, for example, I learned that they had visited Dwight's winery, StoneGate, the day before. Marty breezed through all the wines they'd tasted and I listened carefully. What he said was revealing. I could just about gauge the style of wines these folks liked—the kind that whack one up along side of the head. But that is okay, because once I know that, I can process the information accordingly. And since Dwight didn't have nearly the stature in the Webbers' eyes as someone like Ted Maxell, their observations were less effusive and therefore more useful to me.

At the tasting the previous day, Jane had been occupied with one of her many variations on the vapors while Marty tasted wine. But she spoke at length about the beautiful art in the visitors' area and the general pleasantness of the experience. Marty, after tasting Dwight's Reserve Pinot Noir, said he found it more delicate than the Cougar Crossing but still very "strong" in the Burgundian sense. Hmm. And he'd managed to drop quite a lot of money there. I didn't tell him I was Dwight's former, that I had helped found the winery. No reason to, I guess. He'd liked Dwight, who happened to be there for the tasting, and reported him to be very forthcoming with useful information. I hoped to be as fortunate when I visited.

From my perspective, it sounded like the winery had been spruced up considerably since my departure, which meant business was good. Nice for Dwight. It also told me that Dwight was sticking to his guns style-wise, and that Marty at least knew enough to compare Dwight's wine to a *grand cru* Burgundy.

Following breakfast, I spent a pleasant hour in the kitchen loading the dishwasher, yakking with Angel, and tidying up while she made a batch of biscotti for the guests' snacks. I loved the way hers turned out and was trying to pick up some pointers. During our conversation I also learned that her daughter, Zephyr, was engaged to be married to Ted Maxell's son, Axel. Now *that* was news!

I went upstairs and changed from my hostessy summer dress into jeans, hiking boots, a short-sleeved tee shirt, and linen jacket. I put on some makeup and added some bling. While I didn't want to look too fancy when I met with Dwight, I didn't want to look like a bag lady either.

Life in Lower Hillsdale Heights, my Portland neighborhood, was pretty laid back. Jeans usually sufficed when I wasn't doing business. When I came back downstairs, Angel was whispering animatedly in Spanish with a tall, gorgeous young woman.

"I'll be back in a couple of hours, Angel," I told her as I grabbed my handbag and keys from the alcove.

"Oh, Mrs. Emma, come to meet my daughter." Angel smiled broadly, but this was not the Angel I'd been laughing with ten minutes earlier. Her eyes had a stricken, wild animal look to them that told me something definitely was wrong.

I walked over to the two. "I'm Zephyr Lopez." The young woman held out her hand and grasped mine firmly. Zephyr was tall and slender, with straight black hair pulled into a thick ponytail at the nape of her neck. Her white spandex blouse and snug jeans revealed a lovely figure. Several silver bracelets jingled on her right forearm as our hands met. On her left hand was a huge diamond ring. She was cool and professional in every way except for her eyes, which were deep and dark with sadness. Her mascara was smudged as if she'd been crying.

"A pleasure. I'm Emma. I've heard so many good things about you. I'd love to interview you for my book."

Zephyr tried to be gracious, but obviously was distracted. "Yes, I would be happy to assist you in any way," she said formally. Then she turned around and grabbed the denim jacket she'd hung on a kitchen chair. "I've gotta go now, Mama. I'll call you."

"Don't leave because of me," I interrupted. "I'm just on my way out the door. Zephyr, I'll call you next week." Then I quickly took my leave so the women could give full attention to their crisis. Once in the car, I re-checked my makeup in the rearview mirror. I was a little on edge about seeing Dwight.

Pulling into the parking lot at StoneGate was something I'd done thousands of times in the past, but it looked different this time. The winery, once a funky little edifice, had doubled in size and mysteriously had become handsome. No doubt a good architect was involved in this evolution. Outside were landscaped areas with picnic tables surrounded by banks of late summer flowers and lovely vineyard views.

StoneGate was located on a hillside, with vineyards ambling up a slope behind it and running downward to the valley below—ninety acres altogether, although we'd started with a modest twenty. We'd named the winery for the six-foot-high stone pillars that flanked the drive into the property. They had been there since the early 1900s. Since all the best regional names had been taken, and I'd be damned if I was going adapt syllables from our children's names into some stupid word as a name for the winery, we'd christened our project StoneGate.

I tucked in my shirt and headed toward the winery. It was a fairly ordinary building, long and low and nestled against the hillside. The peaked roof extended out several feet to cover a raised concrete patio festooned with large planters and small tables with chairs. As I trotted up the steps, I noticed a new building out back to the right of the crush pad. Stucco with a solar panels affixed to the roof, it was more pleasingly designed and appeared more substantial than the one I was entering.

Inside I discovered that I was in a tasting room with tile floors and a floodlit bar area, rather than the former general entrance and catch-all I remembered from the past. Behind the bar, instead of the usual glasses, were hung beautiful abstract paintings by none other than my dear friend Carolyn. Each one represented a different grape variety as interpreted through Carolyn's mysterious and twisted brain. They comprised, as I already knew, the label art for StoneGate wines, and Carolyn had been paid handsomely for her commission. She deserved it. The acrylics were stunning. They also made a statement about the winery's owner.

When one looked at Dwight McCourt for the first time, what one saw was a big, burly hayseed who had grown up on a cattle ranch in eastern Montana. What one didn't see was the medical school dropout who'd always loved art. In fact, long before we met, Dwight had chosen to major in biology rather than art because he knew he probably would get farther in life as a doctor than as an artist. And, he reasoned, he could enjoy art as an avocation.

Although Dwight's life was and always had been about work, art was a close second. At least as an interest. He never had made the time for an avocation of any sort. Even before we started StoneGate and he was able to embrace his life's calling, work was paramount. For years he toiled twelve hours a day in a research lab doing work he hated.

Now his profession also was his love. I was happy for him, even though it had taken its toll on our marriage. We'd been at cross purposes most of the time we were married, me as the wife-as-victim drunk and he as the absent husband. Ultimately, when a real crisis hit us, we were both too drained from our past struggles to give each other the love and support we needed.

Dwight entered the tasting room, his tall frame filling the doorway to the left of the bar. "Hi, Emmy. I saw you drive up," he said. "Come on back." I followed him back through the door and down a corridor to his office. Along one side of the corridor were windows that looked in on a room filled with tall stainless steel tanks. At the far end of the tank room, huge double doors opened to the outside, which was a flurry of activity—workers shoveling grapes onto a conveyor belt that transported the grapes into a crusher-stemmer, hoses everywhere, a young man driving a forklift while a woman barked orders. The romance of winemaking, I thought, as the memories swept over me.

Dwight opened a door at the end of the hall and I passed through it. His office had a view to the back lot where the grape crushing activity continued. There was a desk upon which rested a computer and several perilously tall stacks of papers and magazines. On the floor were perhaps a dozen bottles of unopened wine from a variety of producers, some local, some foreign. A stack of books rested on the file cabinet. I lifted a pile of papers off one of the chairs and set it on the floor.

"The winery may look different, but nothing has changed in here," I observed.

Dwight looked pleased. "If it changed, I wouldn't be able to find anything." He sat on his desk chair.

"When the photographer comes, we won't show him this," I said, gesturing to a dead poinsettia that languished in the corner. Three of Carolyn's paintings adorned the walls. I sat down on the chair.

"Tell me about the book," said Dwight.

"It's pretty much the book the industry hasn't had up to now," I began. "I was approached by an out-of-state publisher who got my name from someone, and we put together a deal. I have a February deadline, so there is a lot of ground to cover in a relatively short time. I hope you can help me since I've been out of the circuit for a while."

"Oh, you know the important things. You just have to get caught up," Dwight said. Two hours later, I felt like I was getting "caught up". Dwight usually wasn't much of a talker, but my questions guided him through the last several vintages, the new government-approved grape growing areas, the spread of phylloxera (a root louse that attacks European grape varieties such as those grown on the West Coast, and eventually kills the plants) in Oregon, and new grape varieties that were being tested in the region

Outside I met several of the harvest workers and the new Wilmes press. We walked the steel catwalk around the stainless steel tanks and he showed me the recently erected barrel storage building I'd seen from the parking lot. I dutifully patted the press, followed Dwight, and scribbled in my notebook throughout the tour as if I was meeting with a stranger for the first time. In a way I was, and yet it was so familiar.

Back in his office, I turned the conversation to gossip. "What is this about Ted Maxell trying to steal your land?"

Dwight laughed derisively. "Oh, you mean Fat Bastard? Yes, I was up at the original vineyard with a surveyor a couple of months ago in an area where we plan to plant next spring. It's right next to a piece of property Maxell bought when he moved here, and I'll be damned if the weasel didn't go onto my property fifty feet when he built his new deer fence!"

"Maybe it was an accident."

"Ted Maxell doesn't make that kind of a mistake. There are no accidents with him. He tried the same thing with Farley Hutchins up on Parrett Mountain. He's just a greedy bastard."

"Well I guess I'll learn more Friday. He heard I was writing this book, and invited me to dinner up at Cougar Crossing."

"You and the Rottweilers?" Dwight's laugh was a borderline sneer. It reminded me of the days when everything I did was, in his eyes, cause for derision of some sort.

"I've heard that story, and it's not funny," I snapped. "He wouldn't risk pissing me off if he wants something from me. Besides, this is billed as a gathering."

"Yeah, well watch yourself. He's a snake." Dwight looked out his office window then jumped from his seat. "Oh *shit!* Gotta go!" I followed him as he dashed out the door. A large tour bus had stopped beside the winery and old people were piling off—probably on their way to the casino. Dwight rushed up to the driver, all the while talking and gesturing. The crew stopped what they were doing to see what would happen next, while the geriatrics made their way to the tasting room as quickly as they could move, heads bobbing, like tired horses heading for the barn. Someone had not told someone else that tour buses were not welcome at StoneGate during harvest!

Driving back to the Westerly, it occurred to me that

going to Ted Maxell's gathering would not be the best way to learn about the winery. My time was limited, and I would learn more if I visited the winery during normal hours and witnessed the facility during a work day. Then I could figure out the story angle and fill in the gaps at the dinner party.

Angel was just finishing the prepping for the next day's breakfast when I returned. Her mood was anything but buoyant, but whatever was going on was none of my business. I rummaged in the house refrigerator in search of something for lunch.

"Let me fix you something, Mrs. Emma," Angel said, so I let her. Nice to be cared for. I went into the alcove, called Cougar Crossing, and was connected with Ted.

"Sure Emma, anything you want. I'll send Axel down to pick you up. How does three o'clock sound?"

"That works for me," I told him, ticking one more major interview off my list.

Back in the kitchen, Angel was warming some meat in a red sauce and frying tortillas. The aromas were divine. She shredded cabbage, added radishes to garnish, plus lime wedges and some white crumbly cheese. I poured us two tall glasses of iced tea and sat down to what were the most delicious tacos I'd ever tasted.

"Thanks, Angel, you can't believe how this helps me," I told her as we tucked into the food. "These are delicious and I'm starved. I interviewed my ex-husband this morning and am going to Cougar Crossing later this week."

Angel shook her head disapprovingly. "That Ted Maxell, he is a very bad man."

"I thought your daughter was engaged to his son," I said.

"She is," she said. "But he does not like her. He does not want any Mexican in his family. He think he is too good for us." She spat out an expletive in Spanish. I think it had something to do with a man's private parts, but since I only know a few words of Spanish I couldn't be certain.

"I'm sorry," I said neutrally. "It's too bad people have to behave that way."

"He will do anything to stop the wedding. My daughter, she is so upset. He sends her a very mean letter."

"I would think his son is old enough to marry whomever he chooses," I said more to myself than her.

"That *cabarone*, he ruins his son's life. Axel can make no decisions without his father. Senor Maxell will disinherit that boy if he marries my Zephyr."

"I'm sure they can manage just fine without anything from Ted Maxell," I told her.

"Oh, exactly. They can. It is not the money. That man has said things to her. He has threatened."

This was not sounding good. "What kind of things?"

"He said that he will hurt her babies. He say this to her, not to Axel."

"That's sickening!" I shuddered. "He can't mean that. Has she told Axel?"

"She has told him. He say he will take care of it."

"Then it's settled."

"Oh no, Mrs. Emma. Senor Maxell, he will do something. He is an evil man. My daughter is afraid. And I am afraid for her."

Chapter 5

By Wednesday, things were beginning to make sense. The boys had returned to San Francisco, the Webbers to La Jolla. Two couples who had booked last minute for Tuesday had checked into upstairs rooms, planning to tour the wineries and stay through the weekend. I was ready for them. They were easy people to entertain, and I found myself doing so almost effortlessly. I had spent Tuesday afternoon setting up interviews and Wednesday conducting a couple. Angel and I had bonded. I had won a place in Winston's heart as walker, dispenser of treats, and snuggling companion. Who would have thought I'd be sleeping with a dog?

Thursday afternoon was my appointment at Cougar Crossing. I'd finally meet Ted Maxell, whose reputation had preceded him on so many fronts. At twenty minutes past three a yellow Hummer with the Cougar Crossing logo on the door cruised up the driveway and stopped in front of the house. A woman with frizzy, pale blonde hair and designer sunglasses sat at the wheel. She was not smiling. She looked straight ahead. I was out on the porch, as I'd been waiting for half an hour.

"Hi, I'm Emma Golden," I said as I climbed into the vehicle. I gave her a quick once-over, the kind women give each other when they don't want the other one to know they are doing an assessment. Of course, the other woman always knows, but we continue to go through this ridiculous posturing anyway. She was tiny, with very pale freckled skin. Her curly, hair was somewhat contained by a bandanna. She wore a short hip-hugging skirt and a low-cut tank top with nothing underneath, fine looking wedge sandals, and lots of jewelry that appeared to be real. She was smoking a cigarette of the very long, very skinny variety.

"Tiffany Maxell." Behind those expensive sunglasses she assessed me in a glance, and I got the feeling she was not impressed. She gunned the engine and threw some gravel. Then she tossed what was left of her cigarette out the window and into the flower beds as we sped down the drive.

"Whoa!" I yelled. "Stop the car!"

She braked, jerking us forward in our seats. "What?"

"You forgot something."

"*What*?" She clearly was impatient with me. From the look on her face, I'd already ruined a perfectly good afternoon. Tough noogies.

"You left your cigarette butt in Melody's asters. That's not done around here."

"What the *hell*." She put the car in gear and we started moving forward again.

"Stop, and I mean it!"

"For chrissakes, it's a *cigarette*."

"You need to pick it up."

"Are you *nuts*?"

"Please stop the car, I'm getting out."

"Go ahead, and fuck you." She rolled her eyes, but stopped the monster car and I opened the door. I sat there for a few seconds saying nothing.

"Now what?" she demanded.

"Now I am going back to the house and you can go back to your house. And tell your dad something has come up, and I won't be visiting the winery after all."

"Jesus," she muttered. I said nothing, but stepped from the Hummer and calmly shut the door.

I walked back up the drive. The Hummer sat in the driveway with the motor running. I was almost to the front porch when I heard tires in the gravel and looked over my shoulder. She was backing up. I walked up the steps and turned around to see what would happen next. She stopped the car where she had tossed the butt. She turned off the motor and stomped into the asters, breaking several stems. It took her three minutes to find the butt, bent over with her rear in the air. It was not a pretty sight. I'm guessing she had on thong underwear, but from where I stood I couldn't be sure.

She walked toward me, holding the totem pinched between her fingers. "I hope you're satisfied," she snapped when she neared the porch. I held out my hand and she dropped the butt into my palm. I walked into the house, disposed of it, and came back out. She was still standing there in the sunshine, wind riffling her rambunctious blonde hair. If it hadn't been for her sour, bored-to-death expression she would have been an attractive young woman.

"Can we go now?"

"Yes, I think we should," I said, and started down the stairs. We got back into her yellow Hummer and rode down the drive and up through the hills to Cougar Crossing Winery in silence. When we reached the winery and she'd stopped the car, I sat for another moment. She looked over at me.

"Anything else?"

"Sure," I said. "Someone should give you a good bare-butt spanking, but I'm afraid at this juncture it's probably too late to do you much good."

She uttered a squawk, jumped from the car, and stormed into the winery. I sat another minute to make certain she was well out of the way before entering myself. I didn't want to see Tiffany Maxell again if it was at all possible.

"I have an appointment with Ted Maxell," I told the woman at the bar. She looked like another termagant.

"I'm sorry, Mr. Maxell is not available."

"I'm Emma Golden. I have a three o'clock appointment with him."

The woman stared at me for a full five seconds. Then she slowly, deliberately looked at her watch. "It's three-thirty-five," she said. She was about my age and obviously not in love with her job.

"Yes, I am aware of that. Tiffany picked me up. She was a little late."

The woman rolled her eyes. "Hang on a minute," she said, and disappeared through a door to the right of the bar.

Her minute turned into five. I browsed through the visitor's book. I found the Webbers' signature. I looked around the tasting room. It was immense. There were two long tables, each bedecked with two artsy-fartsy Deruta spit buckets and surrounded by eight comfy chairs. In addition to wine, the tasting room sold monogrammed glasses, monogrammed sweatshirts and caps, and all manner of cheese platters, snack plates, wine books, and other wine gee-gaws.

Strangely, no visitors were here to enjoy the upscale ambience and purchase the expensive merchandise. Then I remembered, Cougar Crossing was not open to the visiting public unless by appointment, except on Thanksgiving and Memorial Day weekends. It was part of the mystique. Only the chosen few were invited on the premises. That meant the Webbers had gotten in by personal invitation of some sort. Or, perhaps as Melody had speculated, they were investors and thereby entitled to private tastings and quality time with His Maxellness. Why did I already dislike this guy?

Nearly ten minutes had passed when a flustered looking young man came through the door behind the bar. He walked right up to me and stuck out his hand. "I'm Axel Maxell," he said, "and I'm sorry for the misunderstanding. My father is not here. I'll be happy to show you around."

"Not here? We had an appointment." For some reason I felt the need to be difficult.

"I know," he said. He was medium height with thick, wavy blondish hair. His eyes darted desperately. Little beads of perspiration were forming on his upper lip.

"Well, I need to talk to him. He's the owner."

"We've looked all over for him, and he's not here," Axel

stammered. His voice trailed off with, "and I don't know where he went."

Clearly this young man was upset, and I could either behave myself or make it worse. "Yes, well, let's get started then," I said. I had to be back at the Westerly before five for the usual hospitality.

"Again, I am *very* sorry." He ran his hand through his hair and nodded to himself that he was indeed sorry. His hazel eyes were fringed with long, dark lashes, and with his small nose and full lips he looked a lot like his father—or what his father may have looked like thirty-five years and many pounds ago.

It wasn't his fault I was pissed off. "I'd like to tour the winery, but I need to ask you some questions first?"

"What kind of questions?" Again, the edge of nerves was palpable.

"Just normal winery questions."

Axel led me to a conference room and we both sat down. I inhaled deeply and let my breath out slowly and quietly. "I understand Josh Spears is the winemaker here," I opened.

Axel looked miserable. "Actually, he's not. He was let go last week."

"Let go?" I was incredulous. Things like this did not happen in the middle of grape harvest. "So who's doing the winemaking?"

"I am," he said with a gulp. "My dad and I are."

More regrouping was in order. My brain had received a huge jolt. "You and your dad? I guess I didn't realize you were a winemaker."

"Well, I am. I mean I was at Davis and…and…then I came

up here." Again, the sentence fizzled to nothing. He squirmed and changed position in his chair a couple times, all the while avoiding eye contact. His overall countenance reminded me of a dog who'd been naughty and was getting chewed out by its owner.

"What direction do you plan to take, now that you're winemaker?" I asked. The question seemed to confuse him.

"Direction?"

"Yeah, direction. Like, are you going to continue making the same style of wines? Do you have any plans in that arena?"

"Oh. I mean, sure. Josh was doing a great job. We'll just continue doing...whatever he was doing...."

"And that was?" I prompted him. "How would you describe Josh Spears's style of winemaking?" And what in the world was going on here?

"Ah, yes. Well, you know he favored a highly evolved style of..." Bullshit. He didn't know what he was talking about. At least not when it came to wine. It was as if he'd never thought about it. And if Spears was doing such a crack job of winemaking, why was he let go during crush? Axel either didn't know or wasn't going to tell me.

The remainder of the interview was the standard checklist—acreage, grape varieties, general industry outlook, and so on. Along with the basic information, I was always on the lookout for the pithy quote—that special little something someone says to make a written piece come to life. I didn't get it from Axel. He was going by the book, at least what he thought the book might be had he bothered to read it. One thing was certain—I'd have to talk with Ted, or someone who did know what was going on.

"How did *you* happen to get interested in the wine industry?" I asked, finally.

He looked at me for a moment, flabbergasted. "I don't know," he said at last. "I just did. It seemed like the right thing to do." His voice was flat, no passion, not even a decipherable hint of interest. I could not for one minute imagine what kind of wines he would make.

"Why don't you show me the winery," I said stuffing my pen and notepad into my tote.

His sigh of relief was audible.

Cougar Crossing was only three years old, and like many of the newer wineries in the northern Willamette Valley it was designed so that gravity did most of the work. The first Oregon winery built along these lines was the nearby Domaine Drouhin Oregon (DDO), built in the late 1980s by Robert Drouhin, head of the elite Burgundian firm Maison Joseph Drouhin.

Since it was built into a hillside, Cougar Crossing was completely suited to the gravity flow design. Trucks would deliver grapes to the topmost level of the winery, where they were dumped into the crusher/destemmer. From there, the white grapes were separated from their skins. Then, the white grape juice and the red grape must (juice that still contained the grape skins and seeds) were transferred to the next level downhill and into large stainless steel fermentation tanks.

At Cougar Crossing, the winemaker's office was located on the second level, overlooking the fermenting tanks, making it handily equidistant between the crush pad and barrel storage.

The winemaker could oversee winemaking activities in the tank room, including punch down of the reds and the press, which was done at the end of fermentation to separate the red wine juice from the skins and seeds. A lab also was located at this level.

The third level was for barrel storage and aging. Once the fermented wines were fed from the upstairs tanks through hoses downward, they were placed in barrels for rest and aging. At Cougar Crossing, the upper-end chardonnay actually was fermented in new French oak barrels. The natural flow of the gravity system eliminated the need for almost all pumping, thus saving energy costs. Further energy costs were saved as more than fifty percent of the winery was imbedded in earth.

As Axel gave me the tour I made a few brief notes. Although it had been a while, I was very familiar with the insides of wineries. What set this one apart were the caves. At the third level, filled wine barrels were moved into caves built into the hillside for that purpose. The winery space at the third level housed case goods, a bottling line, more offices, and the large tasting room.

Axel could not tell me what had possessed Ted Maxell to build the caves. They work extremely well for controlling humidity and temperature for wines as they rest in barrel, and they are green in the sense that underground temperatures remain fairly cool and steady so there is no need for heat or air conditioning.

Wines caves are all over France of course, and have been for hundreds of years—particularly in Burgundy and Champagne. In the old days, before heating and cooling tanks and centralized heating, the caves were essential to keep the wines from getting too cool in the fall, which would stop fermentation before it was complete. And they kept the wines at a cool, steady temperature during the summer.

These days, caves are not necessary, but they're nice to have. Aside from the practical applications, they're interesting and fun to talk about. And they provide a great venue for fancy dinner parties, as I'd learned on trips to the Napa Valley. I could see how they would fill a need for Ted Maxell because they impress people. They feel old and European and entitled.

Overall, it was quite the operation. On that particular day, however, my sacred inner bitch was not impressed. Since I was going to have to come back later and redo the interview with someone who knew something, all I could think of was getting out of there. At four-thirty I told Axel I needed to get back to the Westerly. He drove me in his big shiny pick-up. I left Cougar Crossing with more questions than answers, but I'd be back the next evening and hopefully could sort it out with Ted then. I told Axel not to send anyone to fetch me, as I knew the way.

Chapter 6

When Dawn's rosy fingers crept over the distant hills on Friday morning, I was already awake. It was a beautiful early October day, and I quickly gained consciousness when I remembered there was a dinner party to attend that evening and I was lacking the proper fashion statement. Actually, I had little idea what would constitute a proper fashion statement for this particular event. But, as I had no dinner party-worthy items with me, the decision could not be made without a trip to Portland to visit my wardrobe.

Angel and I had our morning visit and dispensed trays to new guests in the Chicken House and the Carriage House. Then the phone rang. Another couple wanting accommodation for the weekend. Fortunately we had one upstairs room available, and I penciled them in. After a quick hike around the property with Winston and a couple more phone calls, I drove into Portland with a list of errands for the B&B and myself.

The wardrobe was not in the best of shape. I'd been cutting back on spending as a result of sporadic employment and diminished resources. However, my little black dress purchased ten years ago still fit. I located the rope of freshwater pearls given me by Dwight when he was trying to purchase favor after a particularly bitter quarrel. I didn't wear them often, but they looked smashing with the dress. I chose some black pumps of the sensible persuasion and a black fringed cashmere scarf a friend had given me when she was cleaning out her closet. I packed some other things as well. One never knew, did one, what Fate might offer as a sequel to the little dinner party. Perhaps I would meet a man.

I checked my mail and watered the plants. All seemed quiet in Lower Hillsdale Heights. Then I made a furtive trip to the neighborhood bakery to indulge in a Gruyere and Dijon mustard croissant and a really good cappuccino. The Westerly, for all its lovely food, did not serve proper croissants. The store-bought version definitely lacked that *je ne sais quoi* one associates with those from a good bakery, where buttery, flakey, hand-made croissants are baked expertly and daily.

On the way back to Dundee, I stopped at Costco to pick up breakfast supplies as we were running low on everything. Melody had left me the company charge card. In addition to hostess duties, shopping and banking were on my to-do list while she was gone. When I arrived back at the farm, Angel was busy checking in some of the weekend guests. Assorted chores kept me busy until five, when it was time to set out the wine, nuts, and little cheesy bits and socialize. I was grateful to have found the time to spend twenty minutes on the phone to set up interviews—two each for Saturday, Monday, and

Tuesday. Guests notwithstanding, I was here to work on the book.

Our weekend guests to a person seemed like fairly normal wine tourists, with no special diets or demands or weird personality quirks. I made a couple of restaurant reservations, cleaned up glasses and napkins, and went upstairs to change, followed by the irascible Winston. He was not at all happy to find me dressing for dinner. He knew that meant he'd be without attention for several hours.

Just before seven I took Winston out for a pee, made certain all the correct lights were on, and got in my car for the drive to Cougar Crossing. I arrived on time, and was surprised to find the parking lot filled. A young man in a sports coat and tie directed me to a parking space. What Ted Maxell had billed as a little gathering turned out to be a black tie affair for fifty or so people catered by one of Portland's finest chefs. There would be no Rottweilers to contend with, and I was going to enjoy some serious food!

I followed torches that lined the gravel path to the caves where dinner was to be served. Tiffany and Axel Maxell were greeting guests as they entered the gala scene. Axel said a stiff hello and shook my hand. Tiffany tossed her curls, stuck her cute little nose in the air, and pretended to be occupied with someone else. She was attired in a beautiful albeit flimsy cocktail dress and metallic sandals with four-inch heels. Again, no bra was perceptible. I wondered if no one had ever explained to her about under garments.

Inside, the tasting room troll from the previous day handed me a table assignment and I began to explore the cave. Barrels of wine stacked two deep lined the walls. Aside from a clustering of candles on each table, the only lighting was provided by terra cotta wall sconces. As I drew close to examine one, I realized it depicted a craven Bacchus, eyes and mouth glowing eerily, his face distorted in a lascivious grin. He looked like a creature from Hell. Inspection of the other sconces revealed variations on this garish theme. In almost ridiculous contrast, a spotlight chamber quartet at the far end of the room played a fluffy, festive little Baroque something. Behind the quartet was the ladies' room and darkness.

Since he had invited me personally, and since we had never met, I scoured the room to locate Ted Maxell before threading my way toward him through the candlelit tables laden with silver, crystal, floral arrangements, and beautiful china. Normally, the barrel-lined caves would be quite roomy, large enough to drive a forklift and perform normal winery functions. With the large round tables and wait staff bearing trays filled with hors d'oeuvre and glasses of sparkling wine, it was difficult to move through the throng. Ted was talking animatedly with a man of about his height that carried a girth of equal proportion to his own. With acres of belly between them, it was a wonder they could hear each other. As I drew closer, I realized the men were arguing.

"We had a deal," the unknown man shouted above the din. Dim light reflected off his bald head. "You're locked into this legally; you can't just walk away from me on this. I need that wine now. I've got people waiting for it."

"There is nothing more to be said about it," Maxell roared back. "I'm done with you. You can take it or leave it."

"I'll leave it then," said the other man, and turned on his heel. Then he stopped and turned back toward Ted. "You *will* regret this!" He stabbed his finger through the airspace, and then retreated toward the cave's entrance.

Frowning, Maxell took a sip of wine. Then he spotted me staring. "Yes?" He treated me to an oily smile, his face still florid with rage.

I walked up to him and extended my hand. "I'm Emma Golden. So sorry we missed each other yesterday. Thank you for inviting me to your lovely party."

"Emma Golden! What a pleasure!" He shook my hand and stared at my bosom, beady little eyes sparkling in his porcine face. It had been a great while since anyone had stared at my bosom. "Missed each other?"

"Yes, we had an appointment yesterday. Your daughter picked me up and you weren't here."

"Not to worry. We can talk at dinner. You're seated at my table. But now, enjoy. Where's your wine glass?"

"I'd really prefer some sparkling water," I said. Not to worry indeed!

"No, you must try my bubbly." He reached for a glass from a passing tray and shoved it into my hand. I held it like the proverbial hot potato, all the while reminding myself that I'd had very good reasons for moving back to Portland. "This is the best domestic sparkling wine you'll ever taste," he assured me

Instinctively I raised the glass and sniffed its contents. The alluring aromas of ripe fruit and toasted bread rose from the glass. If the flavors delivered what the nose promised, his winery indeed had produced a winner. He smiled. I smiled. "Lovely," I said. "Excuse me. I need the ladies' room." I turned abruptly and walked toward where the darkness began behind the band. There I sidled up to a barrel and discreetly poured the best domestic sparkling wine into a floor drain. Beads of perspiration had broken out on my forehead. What in God's name was I doing here? Kidding myself, that's what!

Fifteen minutes later the din subsided somewhat as we were seated for dinner. I found myself at the host's table, which was set for eight. Ted sat to my immediate left, presumably so we could talk. A reporter from the local newspaper sat to Ted's left, looking vaguely out of place in a sports coat and slacks. His name was Robert Grimes—"Call me Rob!"—an enthusiastic sort who appeared to be about forty with sandy, thinning hair. Next was an empty chair, followed by Axel, a vacant expression on his face. He nodded at me in greeting but said nothing. I wondered if the vacant seat had been intended for his fiancée, Zephyr Lopez.

Next in the lineup was Ted's wife Tara. Ted introduced us. Her handshake was lifeless. The dress she wore once again revealed abundant cleavage stuffed into too small a space. She looked to be about eighteen years old, seven months pregnant, and grumpy. But she probably was not happy to be at an event that would just be winding up around ten. All that bursting flesh crammed into such an inadequate vessel could not be comfortable. A middle-aged and prosperous looking couple from southern California—Paul and Adriana Bishop—filled the seats to my right. And there was I, delighted to be seated among the best in the land.

Following introductions, Ted stood and clapped his hands. The Baroque music faded and the cave around us glowed in an otherworldly light—the candles, the sconces, the reflections, and the faces, some beautiful and some wretched, alternately illuminated and shadowed as they faced the host.

"I want to extend a warm welcome to all of you gathered with us tonight," Ted began. He referred us to the individual menus at each place and gave a brief recitation of the chef's considerable credentials. "There will be a little surprise at the end of the evening," he promised, "so don't be in a rush to leave."

I looked around the table. Tara's arms were crossed. She seemed to smolder in the half-light. Rob, the newspaper reporter, was discreetly loosening his tie. Axel's expression was unreadable, but he seemed not to be tuned in to his surroundings. Next to him, a waiter discretely removed the superfluous place setting. The California couple, both tanned and handsome, leaned into each other and looked pleased with themselves. They were a smart-looking pair, he in his tuxedo and she in a lapis-colored St. John knit suit cut in the military style, with beads and crystals on the collar and cuffs and sparkling buttons down the front.

Ted said something that brought a burst of laughter from the guests and I looked up at him. The light accented his thick white hair and bushy eyebrows, deep laugh lines and full wet lips. What I saw was not the man laughing at his own silly joke, but the disturbing and distorted face of the grinning Bacchus wall sconce. I shuddered involuntarily. Aside from his reputation, this man was just plain creepy. Being near him bothered me at a gut level. It was instinctive and unexplainable.

Waiters emerged from the shadows carrying plates of *foie gras* with caramelized apples. The intoxicating aromas of browned butter and apples quickly distracted me from the monstrous image. I dived into the food.

The courses came and went like clockwork, one delicious plate after another, one fabulous wine after another, with plenty of time to enjoy each one. I sniffed all the wines, which was a stupid thing to do. Yet while it brought back memories of the good times, it also gave me perspective. If these wines were portent of Oregon's progress, this region had arrived and could only get better.

During the first course I asked a waiter for a glass of sparkling water. When he returned to present the fish course, Tara said loudly across the table, "She asked for sparkling water. I want you to *bring it now*!" The waiter, flushed with humiliation, bowed his head at her and disappeared to fetch my water. My insides roiled with shame. Tara then initiated a conversation with Adriana Bishop about—what else?—St. John suits.

"I have nine of them, but obviously I can't get into any of them now," Tara remorsed.

"I have seven, and I take at least one with me wherever I go," said Adriana. This began a discussion of the detachable collars and cuffs and how one could dress a St. John suit up or down, depending on the variety and availability of removable features.

I quietly nibbled at my fish course, all the while wondering if it had been this bad when I was drinking. It doubtless had been, but I couldn't remember because I was usually drunk. Listening to such bullshit certainly made one *want* to drink just to drown it out. Not that I had anything against St. John suits. If they didn't cost as much as my first car, it would have been nice to own one.

Suddenly a hand placed itself on my left thigh. I looked toward Ted Maxell, to whom the hand logically was attached. He looked at me, expression bland, wine glass raised in left hand, and asked, "How long have you been writing about wine, Miss Emma?" He squeezed my thigh.

"Sixteen years," I said. "And take your fucking hand off my leg." I didn't say it loudly, but the St. John suit conversation stopped abruptly and Tara glared at her husband from across the table. I resumed eating my fish.

"I hope Axel gave you an adequate tour of the winery," he continued, not missing a beat.

"We saw a good deal of it, and he was a fine guide. But I'm still unclear on a few things." I retrieved a small notebook and pen from my evening bag and launched into the list of questions I'd prepared after my tour the previous day.

That kept Ted busy through the fish, and the kiwi sorbet palate cleanser, at which time he stood again and clinked his crystal glass with a teaspoon. "Ladies and gentlemen, it's time for a seventh inning stretch. Girls, the facilities are behind the orchestra. Gents, to my left, behind the bar. Have a nice tinkle everyone, or smoke a cigarette—outside please—and we'll resume in fifteen minutes." I leaped to my feet.

"I'd like you to join me in the tank room for the ten o'clock punch down after dinner," Ted told me before I could get away.

That's not something I want to do," I said. "I've seen plenty of punch downs."

"I'll behave myself, promise." He laughed at me and gave me his bad boy look. He probably thought it was sexy.

"I'll go if other people come too,"

"You're no fun," he said, then hailed Axel, who was heading toward the outside door. "We'll all meet in the tank room at ten," he said, gesturing to our table. "I want these folks to see punch down."

Tara stood glowering at me and rubbing her back.

"It must be difficult sitting through a long dinner like this when you'd like to have your feet up," I said.

She shook her head. "My husband is such a shit," she said. I shrugged. Then she turned and strode into the mass of people, heading in the general direction of the women's toilets.

On her way, she broke into Ted's conversation with another guest. He listened for a moment as she addressed him angrily. Then he started laughing, head thrown back as I had seen him in the restaurant a couple nights before. She reddened and started talking again. He leaned toward her and said something that seemed to surprise her. Then he took her arm. She shook him off, changed direction and walked toward the cave entrance as the nonplussed guest who had heard their exchange watched her with his mouth open.

I sat back down and tried to blank out the rest of the room as I scribbled several observations. The Maxell family drama clearly was the stuff of soap operas, but that was not of consequence to my book. I could ignore it. As the tables regrouped, I made small talk with the affectionate Californians. They were considering moving to Oregon—who wasn't?—but had to sell their place in Montecito first. The usual rich people stuff. And wasn't the wine industry just to die for? This from Adriana.

"I've always enjoyed the romance of winemaking," I told her in my most sincere and reasonable voice. "Cold, wet, dreary and muddy, floors slick from water and grape must. Fourteen-hour days. It gets particularly romantic when the rains start in another month and the winery is about forty-five degrees inside. Maybe you should come up here for six months and try it out before you commit to moving." I did not say this facetiously. I was telling the absolute truth as I knew it from experience. Of course, they wouldn't be doing it the way we had.

Her husband was poised to say something when Rob the Reporter returned to the table. There was no sign of the three Maxells, but we sat anyway. Wait staff were pouring the next wine. Axel arrived at the table just as the food was served. "Where's Dad?" he asked. We shook our heads. "Hold his plate," he told the waiter, gesturing to Ted's place. "He'll be here in a minute. Hers too." He gestured to Tara's place, then he bobbled and mumbled his apologies to the table in general, acting more like a servant than heir to the throne. He poked the lamb chops on his plate aimlessly, but made no attempt to eat them.

Tiffany walked over and surveyed the table, then kneeled beside Axel. "Since Dad's not here, maybe *you* should get up and talk about the wine," she told him.

He looked at her as if she were crazy. "What would I say?"

"Shit if I know, *you're* the winemaker." We all looked at her. Her pretty little face was a sneer. Axel turned his attention to his plate and began hacking at a lamb chop. He said nothing more. Tiffany looked around the table again, seemingly unsure of what to do next. She fidgeted with the beads on her handbag, then she spotted Tara's empty chair. "Where's the bitch?" she asked nobody in particular. Her eyes were unusually bright. Nobody answered her.

Rob and I exchanged glances over Ted's empty chair. It was weird, and just kept getting weirder. And where was our host? Out making some righteous big deal on his cell phone? Were we all characters in the same awful soap opera? As I was sober, I was fairly sure this was the real deal and not something made for television. The lamb chops, by the way, were excellent. I had eaten both of them, and sat quietly watching, wondering what would happen next.

"Dad said you were all to go up to the winery for punch down at ten," Tiffany said to the table in general. Her words came out quickly, and she did not make eye contact with any of us. "Will you be going with them Axel? Dad wanted you to go."

"Yeah, I guess so. Yes. You can all follow me." Axel mumbled. His eyes were downcast, and he hacked earnestly at his second lamb chop. Paul and Adriana laughed nervously.

"I, for one, will not be joining you," Tiffany announced, then giggled pointlessly and retreated to her own table nearby.

Dessert arrived—some sort of lovely little fig napoleon with caramel sauce. And with it more wine, for those who were drinking. Then a lovely selection of cheeses. And more wine. And finally, thank God, the coffee. I looked over at Rob, my comrade in the Fourth Estate. "Did you get everything you needed while Ted was here?"

"I think so." He looked dubious. "I normally cover police and school district news for the paper."

"I lived out here for fifteen years and wrote about wine," I told him. "If you don't see Ted later on, and still have questions, I'll help you if I can."

He nodded and handed me his card. I scribbled the Westerly's telephone number on the back of mine. "I'm out here for another five weeks," I said. "Call any time."

"Should we go with Axel for the punch down?"

"If you haven't seen one, you definitely should. I can tag along too. Remember, Ted said there would be a surprise." Maybe he'd be out there in a tank doing *pigage* in the nude. If that was his surprise, I didn't want to miss the expressions on the other guests' faces. I glanced at my watch. Nearly ten straight up. I was tired, and torpor undoubtedly would be setting in soon.

"Some of us need to get going pretty soon, Axel," I prompted across the table, ever the mother. "Could we go take a peek at the tanks now?"

"Oh sure." Like a reluctant teenager, he lumbered to his feet.

Chapter 7

Outside, the early autumn air was chilly. Little electric lanterns lit the gravel path, but with the absence of overhead lighting in the parking lot, combined with the relative isolation of the winery site, the stars seemed oversized and magical as the five of us trudged uphill toward the tank room. The Douglas firs that surrounded the winery were silhouetted in the night light. A pale crescent moon glowed to the south. We walked up the path in a small cluster.

As we entered the building, the fruity, yeasty aromas of fermenting grapes hit us head on. To me it smelled enticing, and I was struck once again by the ambivalent feelings that had engulfed me periodically since arriving in Yamhill County. It was one thing to joke about the so-called "romance" of winemaking. It was damned hard work. But wine is an art as well as a science, and therein lies the romance. I needed only to walk into a winery during crush and the Sirens called to me, always just out of reach, always seductive.

On the far side of the room, on a catwalk eight feet above us, two *estagiers*, a man and a woman in their twenties, pushed wooden paddles into the tops of a tank. They were chattering and laughing, but the rap music that blared from a small stereo far below them drowned out anything they might have been saying. They waved at us and continued their work.

We crossed the room, Axel in the lead, and started up the steep metal staircase. When we reached the catwalk, we proceeded in the direction of the young workers, awkward though we were, in evening dress, groping our way and holding onto the rails. Behind me Adriana uttered vehement curses as her spike heels repeatedly got caught in the metal grating. Paul held her elbow and tut-tutted. Ahead of me, Rob seemed to be asking questions of Axel.

Axel attempted to introduce us to the apprentices, both from France, but couldn't remember their names. They introduced themselves as Charles and Avril. Nobody could hear very well anyway with the loud music.

I huddled near Rob and explained the must cap—the grape skins and seeds that float to the top of the vats during the active fermentation of red wines—and how it must be kept moist so that the fermenting juice continually extracts flavors from it. I was fairly certain Axel wouldn't be talking about it. In the bigger tanks, pneumatic devices would be used to moisten the cap by pumping the liquid over the must; however, with the mid-size tanks, such as the ones we overlooked, Cougar Crossing still preferred the punch down method.

Looking miffed at being upstaged, Axel grabbed Charles's

flat-bottomed paddle and petulantly began poking it into the tank in front of us.

"Hang onto the rail," I warned Rob. "The carbon dioxide fumes released during punch down can make you giddy enough to lose your balance." Then I challenged Axel, "Come on, show us how it's really done!"

He grabbed the paddle with both hands and shoved it down several times, pushing the must cap into the fermenting liquid a bit at a time, and then finally, enthusiastically keeping beat with the music. We all laughed, even Axel.

Suddenly he pulled back, a surprised expression on his face. "I've hit something!"

He gave another tentative poke with the paddle. "There's something in the tank."

The French interns came to his side, and Charles seized the paddle. "This is weird. There can't be no-thing in the tank," he muttered in heavily accented French. He shoved the paddle down again, and I could see the paddle resisting as it connected with something solid under the cap. He frowned and jabbed again, then gave several short pushes.

"I will get it! Avril!" said Charles. As he found the object once more and hooked the paddle under it, he directed Avril to find the other side and hook her paddle underneath. Then they began dragging the object upward and toward the side of the tank.

"He is very heavy," said Charles. *He*! A chill went through me. Oh God, please no, I prayed. And at that very second a human hand rose up slowly through the must. Avril screamed something in French. Adriana screamed "Oh my God!" As she back-stepped away from the horrible sight, her heel caught in the grate and she went down on her butt with a thump and a moan. The room whirled around me and I gripped the railing, fixated on the rising hand, which, as the grape skins slid off it revealed a thick gold wedding band. Voices on either side of me registered horror and shock.

Avril had dropped her paddle and withdrawn against the far railing, one hand over her mouth. She groaned softly. I grabbed the handle of her paddle and worked with Charles to pull the person toward us—a person who may still be alive, I thought, although my rational mind knew otherwise.

Grape skins and juice ran to either side as a head appeared through the cap. A man. And yes, it was the only man it could have been, our recently absent host, Ted Maxell. He was floating on his back now, hair floating out to the sides of his skull, still in his tuxedo shirt and jacket. Both his hair and the white shirt had gone to purple and were dotted with grape seeds and skins. His face was distorted, eye bulging and running with purple liquid, mouth twisted in the monstrous grimace of his Bacchus wall sconce.

Axel fell to his knees, face in hands, whimpering "Dad, Dad! Oh, no, Dad!"

"Fock!" yelled Charles. "Fock *et merde!* The wine! She is ruined!"

Chapter 8

The wine was ruined, no doubt about that. More than five tons of it.

We stood on the catwalk and argued, those of us who still had our faculties. Paul Bishop and Charles wanted to haul Ted out of the vat immediately. I said we should leave him be and not disturb scene. He was very dead, no question in my mind, and there was nothing we could do for him. Paul announced it was bad form to leave him floating. Axel, still on his knees, rocked and keened in complete shock. Rob stood there speechless, nothing in his previous journalistic experience having prepared him for something like this. And I lost the argument.

Adriana struggled to get on her feet, badly shaken from her fall. I asked Avril to please help her downstairs and into the tasting room, where she could sit comfortably and have a bottle of water. "Call 9-1-1 from the tasting room," I told her. "Tell them what happened. Talk slowly and they will understand you just fine. And tell them to get up here as quickly as possible with an ambulance and police."

She nodded and began helping Adriana to stand upright. "Take off those shoes," she commanded Adriana, who nodded and mutely did as she was told.

Next something had to be done about Axel. I didn't need to be there, and he needed to be gone, so I knelt beside him. "We're calling an ambulance for your dad," I began. "There is nothing you can do right now, so let's go sit someplace quiet and I'll get you something to drink. Would you like that?" He looked at me blankly and I took his arm. "C'mon Axel, we'll go sit down, and when the paramedics get here they will help your dad. Just come with me. We'll find your sister. Everything is going to be okay here without us."

With help, he stumbled to his feet. We walked to the end of the catwalk and I preceded him down the narrow stairway, holding the railing firmly. If he stumbled at least I could break his fall. We made it to the bottom safely.

Guests were in the parking lot, wandering toward their vehicles, some of them obviously quite drunk. I guided Axel in the general direction of the tasting room, where I knew he could sit comfortably. In the tasting room, Avril was ministering to Adriana, who was recumbent on one of the sofas sipping from a bottle of water. "Did you get through to someone?" I asked her.

"Yes, she ask me was he dead. I say he look dead. She ask more questions. I say send help, and then I hang up." Typical. All hell is breaking loose, somebody is desperately waiting for help, and some dispatcher wants to keep the caller on the line and blabbing instead of getting the help part going.

I directed Axel to another sofa, my mind racing. "Can you find him some water? I need to locate his sister." Avril nodded, and I headed across the parking lot toward the caves. The lot was nearly empty now, but lights still played through the open double doorway to the cave. A few die-hards were hanging in there, hoping to finish off the bottles that still had wine in them. A few years ago, I would have been hanging in there with them.

Tiffany was holding court with the handful of remaining guests, mostly men, most of them quite drunk, from the looks of them, and thinking about getting in her pants. She was laughing, and in the interplay of lights and shadows she bore little resemblance to the brat I'd met the day before. Her features were softer. Her shimmery little dress exposed her décolletage and otherwise floated gossamer around her tiny body. Her makeup and hair were perfect. Diamonds glimmered in her ears and at her throat. She was enjoying every bit of the attention, oblivious to the catering crew who hovered in the background waiting to clear the room and go home.

I approached the table and she looked up at me. "What?" was all she said. The brat was back.

"I need to talk to you outside."

"I'm busy."

"Please, Tiffany. Your father needs you right now," I said and turned around and walked toward the door."

"Be back in a minute," she told her drinking buddies, then trotted outside after me. "If he wants me so badly, why didn't he come himself?" she demanded before I could turn around.

"There's been an accident in the tank room. We've called 9-1-1." She started to turn, but I grabbed her by the arm. "You need to know that whatever happened is very serious. You may just want to wait here with me."

She looked me in the eye, her mouth open in a little O. My hand was still on her arm watching her face as she processed the information. Disbelief was replaced by denial and she shook her head. Then terror. "Is he alive?"

"I don't know. Paramedics are on the way. Let's go wait with your brother in the tasting room. We'll know more in a few minutes."

"Did he do something? That little fucker! I'll kill him!"

"Tiffany," I said gently. "I don't think anyone did anything."

She jerked away from me. "The little fucker. He was so mad at Dad. If he did anything, I'll kill him!"

She dashed across the parking lot in the near darkness. I heard her slip in the loose gravel, fall, and groan. I ran to help her up, but she waved me off as if I was an unwanted mosquito and clambered to her feet. The heel of one of her strappy little sandals was broken and both knees were bloodied from the fall. "Oh, shit!" she moaned, and pitched forward, nearly falling again. Then she righted herself and started running. I don't know how she did it. I couldn't keep up with her.

Once on the paved walk, she kicked off her sandals and ran barefoot up the path to the tank room. As I reached the door behind her I could hear sirens in the distance. She was halfway up the metal stairs when I entered the winery. And she was screaming.

On the upper deck, Paul and Charles stood with the

paddles in their hands looking somewhere between desperate and defeated. They had wedged their paddles under Ted from either side. They clung to these as if afraid he would get away. Rob, on his knees and reaching through the railing, had a grip on Ted Maxell's tuxedo jacket. They had been unable to pull the dead man from the tank. The fronts of their clothing were stained with grape juice, purple skins clinging to them.

Tiffany ran to them, looked into the tank, and let out a piercing scream that cut me to the core and reverberated off the steel tanks. She screamed repeatedly, head thrown backward, hands clenched, the wordless pain rolling out of her from deep inside. I'd heard that scream before. I cringed against the railing, holding tight, desperately wanting to retreat from the grisly scene. But I stayed, transfixed by the chain of events unfolding in front of me.

Avril must have directed the response team to the tank room. Suddenly they were there—two firefighters and two state troopers. They clambered up the stairs in full regalia and squeezed past us to look at the dead man. I peeped around them for a closer look. Due to Paul's and Charles's struggles with the paddle, Ted's heretofore unexposed lower half had floated to the top of the must. His trousers were bunched around his ankles, leaving him naked from the waist down. That's all I am going to say about *that*, except that it was nasty.

Tiffany continued to make noise, but it was more of the sobbing and moaning variety. At least she no longer was screaming. One of the firemen pulled on rubber gloves and reached through the railing to check Ted's throat. Then he tried to wiggle an arm. "This 'un's pretty dead," the fireman announced to nobody in particular. "Looks like he's been that way for a little while."

"We need to clear the scene and radio for backup," one of the state policemen said, and then turned to face the rest of us. "You've done a great job here folks, but now we need you out of here so we can help this man. Please leave the area immediately and find a place on the premises where you can relax while we get him out of the tank. Do not leave. We will need to talk to each of you.

"Jack," he directed the other officer, "go downstairs with these folks and secure a place. We'll need the coroner and a photographer, and at least two more backups to remove the body."

At the mention of "body" Tiffany began screaming. "Oh no, oh no! He's not dead. He can't be dead!" I caught Paul's eye, assuming he at least knew her through his connections with the winery. He approached her and took her arm, then began guiding her toward the stairs, the rest of us following. She leaned into him, sobbing miserably. As we left the tank room, two Yamhill County Sheriff cars pulled into the parking lot. The drivers jumped out and Charles directed them to the tank room.

We all followed Paul and Tiffany into to the tasting room. Once there Tiffany saw her brother. She broke loose from Paul, marched right over to Axel, and started screaming again. "You miserable fuck! What did you do to our father?"

Axel cowered on his settee. "I didn't do anything. It's horrible. I can't believe this."

"You did. I know you did! You were so angry."

"Not that angry, Tiff. I can't deal with you right now."

"Oh, you're such a fucking coward. So what did you do, just push him in, give him a good shove because he doesn't like your Mexican girlfriend?"

Axel buried his face in his hands and said nothing. Since no one else was moving, I put my arm around Tiffany and began walking her to the other side of the room. "You phony asshole!" she yelled over her shoulder.

"Tiffany, you need to shut up and sit down. You've had a horrible shock." Avril appeared next to me with a bottle of water. I grabbed it, unscrewed the cap and shoved it toward her. "You're saying things that make no sense. Now sit down and drink this. We'll find out what happened in a bit."

Tiffany accepted the water, took a gulp of it, and sat. The rest of us milled around for what seemed like a long while, but probably was only about twenty minutes. I walked to a window and looked outside. More sirens could be heard. More vehicles arrived in the parking lot—at least the entire Newberg Fire and Rescue, the Dundee Volunteer Fire Department, more sheriff's deputies, McMinnville, Newberg, and Dundee police cars, plus a few more state cops. Who even knew whose jurisdiction it was? I sure didn't. It had turned into quite the affair.

Soon all of us were gathered at the windows facing the parking lot to watch the officials move the body, draped in a sheet, to the ambulance. When the stretcher passed us, Tiffany again began shrieking. Various officials stood in small groups in the parking lot talking, then two state troopers and two sheriff's deputies entered the tasting room.

"This won't take long," one of them, who identified himself as Deputy Jeffers from the Yamhill County Sheriff's

Department, told us. He had assumed the duties of person in charge. "We'll need a brief statement from each of you, and then you're free to go home. Mr. Maxell is dead, and we need as much information as we can gather about his actions this evening."

Axel piped up. "What about my stepmom, his wife? Shouldn't someone tell her?"

The cops looked at each other. "Where is she?"

"I don't know. She left before dinner was over," said Axel.

"We will locate the widow as soon as we're finished here and inform her of her husband's death," Deputy Jeffers said. "Meanwhile, we are treating this as a suspicious death. I have additional forces coming to thoroughly investigate the tank room area. After daylight we'll be checking out the rest of the premises. The tank room is off limits to everyone."

"We need to do punch down every eight hours" said Tiffany. Surprising, since she was the one to mention it and not her brother, the winemaker. "We will need to finish what wasn't done tonight and be in there at six in the morning to do it again. We're in the middle of harvest. If we don't keep the process moving, all the red wines will be compromised. We've already lost a full tank."

Jeffers eyed her. "Who are you, ma'am?"

"I'm Tiffany Maxell. The dead man is my father."

"She's right," Avril spoke up. "We have three tanks remaining. We must finish this now or, as Tiffany says, the wine, she is ruined."

Jeffers looked to his cohorts. They shrugged. "We'll take your statements, and then we'll figure it out," he said.

Between the four of them, we were interviewed and excused in a relatively short time. Who are you? Why are you here? Where were you? What did you observe? Very basic stuff. Then the winery people and police huddled. Since the tanks awaiting punch down were at the far end of the tank room from where Ted's body was found, the authorities saw no harm in allowing the interns to finish their work under their close supervision. We broke up, and those of us who didn't belong there went home.

Chapter 9

Dawn's rosy fingers once again crept over the eastern mountains. Groggily I forced myself to consciousness by assuming the upright position. This was not easy since the authorities had kept us at Cougar Crossing until well past my bedtime, which is embarrassingly early most nights.

"At this time we are treating Mr. Maxell's demise as a suspicious death," Deputy Jeffers repeated before dismissing us. "Please do not share any of the details of Mr. Maxell's death that could possibly provide any insights into the exact way he died, which we don't know yet. We won't have any details until after the autopsy."

"I don't think we're dealing with a natural death here," I told Winston, once settled in my cozy bed that night. "What about those pants? How could someone get into a tank with his pants down around his ankles? And why were his pants down in the first place? It seems wonderfully deviant." Winston looked at me as if I were hopeless, and then crawled down under the covers. Within moments he was snoring like a moose.

Wide awake next morning, I continued to ponder this mystery and others as they had presented themselves during the course of the evening. Ted had not seemed like a suicidal man. I didn't know him well, but had been exposed to suicidal people. Those intent on taking their own lives tended to draw inward. They felt hopeless for whatever reason: money or relationship problems, addictions, serious mental illness, or a terminal disease. Ted, it seemed, had none of these woes. He was publicly jolly, wealthy, and had a young and attractive wife with a baby on the way. He enjoyed his food and drink with gusto, and seemed to take delight in being the big deal maker. From what I'd heard of him, he also took great delight in tormenting his neighbors. He had been successful in business, built a showboat winery, and was at the top of his game. Or so it seemed.

The trousers around the ankles suggested, to my devious mind at least, that something sexual had been afoot. A tryst on the catwalk perhaps? The appearance of a righteously angry husband? Or, maybe he'd just been standing there waving his wanker over the grape must in some bizarre harvest rite, had been overcome by carbon dioxide fumes, and subsequently had swooned into his own fermentation vat. Doubtful, and probably not even remotely possible.

The angry husband seemed more likely to me. Fat man, out of shape, full of wine, pants down, and caught in the act. *La crime passionelle*, as the French so rightly describe it. History and folklore were rife with such crimes. I probably could have shoved him over the railing and into the tank myself, given his compromised position. For a larger, stronger person, it would have been easy. The difficult part for me was trying to imagine the sort of person who would want to tryst with old Ted in the first place!

Ted had left the table during the interlude at dinner. During that brief period of fifteen to twenty minutes, fifty to sixty people were on their feet and going in every direction—restrooms, visiting, outside for a smoke, talking on cell phones. At our table alone, Axel was late returning, while Tara and Ted never returned at all. How many others had been unaccounted for, wandering in the caves or snorting a line in the bushes?

It had been very late when I first lay thinking about these things, thus my mind had been muddled. However, after a few hours of sleep and a different degree of alertness, my gut feeling remained the same. I believed Ted Maxell's death was no accidental fall into the vat. Somebody had wanted him dead.

As he was not popular in the wine community, it stood to reason that perhaps many locals wished him elsewhere. I thought briefly about the man with whom Ted had argued. Who was he? He didn't look local. Something about Ted reneging on a business deal. Based on his history, there probably were many people he'd tried to screw in the business world. However, the wine community I was familiar with was not a murderous lot. Given the hand on my knee at dinner, plus information volunteered by Henry and Frank a few nights back, one of Ted's major failings was his lecherous behavior. A vengeful husband seemed more in keeping with what I knew about that particular character trait.

It was nearly eight when I jumped out of bed. I took a quick shower, dried my hair, and dressed. I was downstairs in time to greet our guests for breakfast. In the kitchen Angel worked with her head down, lips pursed, and eyebrows drawn together as she prepared trays for the Chicken House and the Carriage House. She responded to my greeting with a grunt.

"We need to talk," I told her as I grabbed the coffee pot on my way through the kitchen and into the dining room. The four couples who had rented the upstairs rooms for the weekend already were seated and eating their fruit. I filled their coffee cups, offering cheery good mornings, and then helped Angel serve the quiche, sausage, and currant buns. Once I finally was seated, we discussed everyone's touring plans for the day. The group comprised an amiable bunch, and breakfast went smoothly. However, my mind was on other things. Once they rose to leave, I gathered the dishes as quickly as possible and burst through the kitchen door to find out what Angel might know.

"You've heard all the news," I said as I set my load on the counter.

"Oh, si, si. Zephyr, she call me at two in the morning."

"What did she tell you?" I asked as I began rinsing dishes and arranging them in the dishwasher. Is there anything nosier than a writer? Probably not. We probably became writers so we could be nosy. None of this was any of my concern, but I was on it like a duck on a June bug. Intrigue, smut, dirt, romance, life, death.... Hell, it looked like a story to me, and a very juicy one at that.

"Oh, Senora Emma, she tell me the bastard he is dead. He is dead in his tank, and all the wine she is ruined. Mr. Axel, he is very upset. He is crying. His sister is screaming at him that he kill his father. She say it is horrible. She go there after Mr. Axel call her, and she doesn't know very much. But there is much screaming."

I'd left before Zephyr arrived and Tiffany went on yet another tirade. "Zephyr wasn't at the dinner. I was sitting with the family and the place next to Axel was empty."

"No, she cannot go. Mr. Maxell call her, and say no Mexicans at his table. No Mexicans in his family. He tell Axel they cannot marry."

"Did Axel go along with that?" I knew Ted was an ass, but this was unconscionable. On the other hand, his son seemed absolutely spineless.

"They will marry, Senora. I do not know how this will happen, but they will marry no matter what. And Axel, he is a good man, a good quiet man."

Sometimes those latter were the best kind. Quiet could be good. Spineless was another issue entirely.

"What about the widow? Did someone tell her?"

"Oh yes, Senora. Then she arrive at the winery very pale. She was at home sleeping. She want to know what happened and see things. Zephyr say she look unwell." Tara obviously had not been present when all the yelling occurred.

"Will Axel run the winery now?" I wondered aloud.

"He has no interest in the winery," Angel said. "He is a musician."

I was stunned. "But he got his master's degree in viticulture and enology. He's trained to be a winemaker."

"That is not true, Senora Emma. He earn his degree in music at the university in Berkeley where he meet my Zephyr. His father force him to go to Davis and train to be a winemaker. He say it make the family position stronger. Axel and Zephyr, they fall in love, but he fail from the wine school. He say too much science. He have no passion for the science, no passion for the wine."

Angel chopped nuts on the cutting board like she was killing snakes, and then mixed them into her cookie dough. I couldn't see her face, but I could feel her anger. Ted Maxell had insulted her lovely and accomplished daughter, not to mention her people and therefore herself. His arrogance had been beyond belief, and arrogance, at some level no doubt, was responsible for his death. I thought of his angry business associate at the dinner. How could Ted Maxell have believed that he had the power to force people, no matter who they were, to do things his way? I returned to the dining room for another load of dishes.

"What does Axel play?" I asked, once back in the kitchen.

"Piano. The classical guitar. He like the jazz, too. He is very gifted. He can play many instruments. He sing sometimes too. Senora, it is wrong to try to kill the artist."

I had difficulty seeing Axel as an artist, but that was not the person I'd been conditioned to expect, either. I'd seen a winemaker who acted like a ditz for the precise reason that he knew very little about winemaking and didn't want to know. Meanwhile, he'd been living the lie because of his father's powerful stranglehold. Definitely a conundrum.

"So what happens to the winery?" Again I was pondering aloud, partly for the book but mostly for my own curiosity.

"There are the money problems," Angel affirmed. "Perhaps she will have new owners, that winery." Third-hand information, but if it came directly from Axel through Zephyr to her mother, it probably was true.

"Who knew about these problems?"

"Many people. The partners they are angry."

"Do people around here know the winery's in trouble?"

"Mr. Maxell, he does not pay his bills on time. There are stories."

"For some reason I thought Ted Maxell was a very wealthy man."

"He is very rich, but his business it is very poor. I know this is true," said Angel.

What a tangled web we weave, I told myself as I went about my morning business. This consisted of a trip to Fred Meyer—our local "one-stop shopping" chain grocery store— and the bank. For some reason, the Westerly kept running low on food. Probably because our guests, of which there seemed an endless stream, ate like wolverines. And my three hours a day tending to B&B concerns usually stretched into many more. But let's get real here. I am a procrastinator—a nosy procrastinator—and anything, even something as mundane as going to the bank, can distract me from writing when that is what I am supposed to be doing.

When I returned from the store, Angel was finishing a batch of spinach and mushroom-stuffed crepes. She covered them with a béchamel sauce and covered the casseroles with foil. All we needed to do was pop them in the oven before breakfast next day and voila, the entrée.

I unloaded the groceries and assembled dry ingredients

for a batch of scones, then wrote checks for the cleaning crew. Angel and I worked quickly and silently. "Have you heard anything more?" I asked her as I scrambled in the alcove assembling pens, notebook, and digital camera for my upcoming interviews.

"Nothing, Senora Emma."

"Then we'll just have to wait and see what happens next."

Chapter 10

That afternoon I visited two wineries. The first, Clementine, was a small, start-up venture owned by a young (to me) French winemaker—Yvick Robin—and his family. I'd met him and written about him when I lived in the area and was freelancing full time. Yvick had been in Oregon nearly ten years. He previously had worked for one of the area's pioneers, where he had gained experience and a good reputation as a winemaker, before starting his own operation. The winery's name was for his first child, a beautiful four year old girl.

For me, seeing him after six years was awkward. My problem. He was someone I'd always admired—a young man with intelligence, focus, and direction. He greeted me effusively, so we were over the first hurdle. Then he ushered me into his small conference/tasting room. I started through my list of questions. In a few minutes it was just like the old days, except for the fact that he was balding prematurely and I wasn't drinking. In this instance, I wished my situation was otherwise. Yvick was one hell of a winemaker, and I would have loved to taste his wines.

"What have you been doing Emma?" Yvick asked me when I finished with my questions.

"I moved to Portland five years ago and basically have lost touch out here since Dwight and I divorced," I said. "Then two months ago, a publisher approached me to do this book, and here I am. It helped that Melody and Dan went on vacation in the South Pacific for six weeks and wanted me to watch over their bed and breakfast."

"Ah yes, the Westerly. I wish I owned it for the pinot noir."

"It's a beautiful site," I agreed, "but Melody wants to keep it as it is."

"Somebody have to grow the vegetables I guess," he said. "And what of your life? It is good?"

"It's good enough."

"No boyfriend?"

"No boyfriend." Then I steered the conversation back onto the book track. "Now, what about the wine business out here? Where do you see it going?"

"It is unbelievable. In five years it change so much. It is little, now it is big. More money, more wineries, more good wine. And we continue to grow. In France you cannot do this. So many regulations, so many traditions. Well, you know."

I sniffed through the wines he set before me on the table. He tasted and spit into a metal bucket. "You do not taste?" he wondered.

"Not any more," I said. "I'm sorry if I offend you. It's hazardous to my health. But my nose still works."

He nodded but didn't say anything. He'd seen me when I was doing some of my best work. I inwardly cringed, remembering the last time I had seen him. It was at a formal winemaker's dinner. One of my earrings had fallen into the soup, and I am sorry to say that I used the "f" word at the table. Dwight had been horrified, and that had pissed me off for some reason. Apparently my behavior had gone downhill from that point, but I hadn't been able to remember much of anything after the second course.

"You want to see my little winery?" he asked. I did. We walked through his small, industrial building located at the edge of downtown McMinnville. It was nothing fancy, but very practical. At this point Yvick owned no vineyards; however, he had long-term contracts with several grape growers the Eola Hills, just a few miles south of his winery.

We began our tour on the crush pad, where two young men were processing pinot gris grapes, then walked through large double doors and into the winery. Underlying the simplicity was Yvick's attention to the best equipment money could buy coupled with an efficient floor plan and a wall of new French oak barrels. A batch of early pinot noir was fermenting in small vats. There were a couple of large tanks for white wine, but no catwalks.

"Isn't it hard to work with the fruit?" I asked. "Why don't you get catwalks?"

"With the catwalks there is the danger of falling into the must," Yvick said, and favored me with a sly grin.

"You've heard the news?"

"Emma, you know there are no secrets in wine country. You know how we gossip here. Everybody knows the news before it is time for coffee. Poor Ted! Thrown into the tank by a jealous husband!"

"I was there at the dinner last night."

"You were there?"

"Yes, indeed. I sat right next to the man himself. We took a break after the sorbet, and he never returned to the table." We both thought about that for a minute. "You think that's what happened? A jealous husband?"

"Perhaps. It is possible. So many people so angry with that man, anything is possible."

"Obviously you're not sorry to see him gone."

"Perhaps his daughter is sorry. Who else? I do not know. He comes here, he puts on the big show, he makes enemies. It is hard to feel sorry when he make so much trouble for everyone. Now he does not pay his bills."

"Did he do something to you?"

"You know I import the French barrels. Ted Maxell's winery owes me several thousand dollars, and he will not pay. He says to wait. And Axel, he is my friend. This makes the difficult situation. Ted Maxell belittles Axel in front of everyone. Zephyr Lopez also is my friend. We share many ideas on the winemaking. He insults her. He calls her terrible names. He says they can't marry. I say he is an asshole. He come here and make the trouble. But yes, I am sorry to see him gone because he owe me the money."

"What about his wife?"

"What about her? She wants to marry a rich man. She marries one."

"And the daughter? Tara? Do you know her?"

"She is Daddy's little girl. She makes difficulties for the

wife, for her brother. She is mean to the winery workers. She is very spoiled."

I told Yvick about my first meeting with Tara, and he howled with laughter. "Yes, that is our Tara," he said. "She is the queen. Very arrogant, like Daddy. She is not so smart as she think she is."

We wound up our conversation with me asking Yvick how large he wanted his winery to become.

"Emma, you know size is not everything. We are at five thousand cases and we will stay here. This is for my family, to make the good wine and live the good life here because we cannot do this things in France. We make enough, and that is all. Someday I would like to own the vineyard land. It is very expensive now."

"Yes it is." I thought about how cheap it had been when Dwight and I purchased our first property all those years ago, and how much of a struggle it had been for us just to do the bare minimum—make the property payments, slowly start planting, kids in diapers, unexpected bills. Had it all worked out between us, I suppose it wouldn't have seemed such a nightmare looking back now. Cancel, cancel, cancel, I told myself. Don't go there. I couldn't reinvent the past. I pulled myself back into the present and purchased some wine for the Westerly. Then we said our good-byes.

Yvick walked with me to my car. "Let me know when you learn who is this jealous husband, Emma," he told me as we parted. "I know you will find out soon who killed old Ted. I want to be the first to know." He patted my arm affectionately.

"It's a promise," I said, laughing. I had to admit the puzzle had my brain spinning. And since I had many interviews still ahead of me, who knew what might turn up. I realized that I very well might unearth a jealous husband.

After a quick snack in a quaint little deli in Yamhill, I wandered the small, turn-of-the-century downtown awaiting my appointment at the Yamhill Wine Cooperative. The tiny farming community had changed quite a lot in five years. Two other small restaurants had opened along the main thoroughfare through town. There also was a new Mexican grocery, a couple of art galleries, and an old-fashioned drugstore with a real soda fountain.

The co-op, which had opened only a couple of years earlier, was housed in a brick storefront in the center of town. It had been started by an up-and-coming young winemaker, who like many had left his original place of employment to found his own smaller venture. Finding himself short of cash—a common problem among small, independent winemakers—he had asked several of those in like circumstances to join forces with him. They had leased the building, and had combined their small business loans and other sources of funding to purchase equipment, set up a laboratory, and take care of other start-up costs that could, and often did, force the owners of new wineries to live at near poverty level.

It was a great concept, and when I met the owners—an enthusiastic group of men and women in their early thirties—I knew the co-op would be featured prominently in my book. In addition to the five original owners, four wineries rented space and used the equipment. The seasonal help, who were employed only during crush, worked wherever they were needed and were paid from a common pool of funds. Each of the wineries produced just a couple thousand cases of wine yearly. Combined, their production was about the same as a mid-size Oregon winery such as StoneGate.

Of the renters present for this year's harvest, two would stay on at least another year while the other two were in the process of putting together their own separate winery operations in time for next year's crush. During my two-hour visit I was able to meet a principal from each of the wineries. These were fresh new faces, with energy, education, ideas, and the passion to keep Oregon's wine industry on the cutting edge when the first generation was ready to retire. Without exception, they were determined to emphasize quality over quantity, and to behave in the most earth-friendly ways possible.

As expected, conversations strayed to Ted Maxell's unfortunate demise. No one offered any suggestions as to who might be the jealous husband. In fact, one scoffed at the idea. "Old sod was just pissed and fell in," said one of the winemakers, an Australian, and those present laughed.

"Who'd want to do *anything* with him?" gagged one of the females. "No woman I know would want to meet that old goat on the catwalk—or anywhere else. Trust me."

"Somebody finally got even with him," another member of the group observed. That seemed to summarize the group consciousness at the co-op. Nobody offered who the perpetrator may have been. There were so many possibilities.

While there, I again pulled out the Westerly credit card and bought several wines for the guests to enjoy. Then, armed with some solid information, I returned to the B&B.

As the hour neared five, the faithful gathered on the big front porch for our little wine social. By our normal gathering time, the news of Ted Maxell's unexplained departure from this vale of pain had spread throughout the land. Everyone loves a mystery, I guess. Portland television station vans had been all over the northern Willamette Valley capturing the ambience of the countryside, the harvest, and the previous evening's gruesome death.

What did I know about it? Everyone on the porch wondered as I opened and poured one of the recently purchased bottles of pinot gris.

"I didn't know the man well," I told them. "But I did sit next to him at dinner last night at the winery. He simply left the table and never returned." That was the truth. Nothing more needed to be said.

After the guests went their various ways for dinner and I'd cleared up the mess they'd left behind, I went inside and did what I had been avoiding since the day I arrived in Yamhill County. I called my friend Carolyn.

Chapter 11

She answered on the third ring.

"Carolyn?"

"Yes, this is she." At first I wasn't certain it was Carolyn; her smoky drawl had a faint, airy quality to it I'd never heard before. She spoke slowly and sounded almost breathless.

"This is Emma."

Silence at the other end of the line, and finally, "Emma honey. Well, well, well." A throaty little cackle. In the few seconds of silence that passed between us, I imagined her taking a drag on a cigarette, or a sip of something. "It's been a while, hasn't it. Where the hell have y'all been?"

"Yes it *has* been a while, Carolyn. And I confess, I've been hiding under a rock. I'm out here staying at the Westerly for a few weeks while Melody and Dan are on vacation. I was hoping we could get together."

Another brief silence. "What did you have in mind?" she asked. A suspicious note had crept into her voice.

"Oh, gee, coffee, lunch. Whatever works for you. I'm babysitting the Westerly so I have a couple of chores here, but I'm really pretty flexible." I sounded so cheery I was making myself sick. She wasn't particularly welcoming, but who could blame her. I hadn't talked her for at least two years, probably three. I'd quit calling her. To be fair, she hadn't called me either. I mean, who designated me head of the social committee?

"I don't know Emma. I don't get out much these days."

"I know how you feel. What if I came over there? I could bring lunch or something."

Silence. Then, "Yeah, OK, I guess that would work."

"How about tomorrow, say noon? Or, what are you doing tonight? We could go out to dinner. I'd be happy to come and get you."

"No, oh no. I don't want to do that. I've already eaten."

I didn't believe her. It was too early for Carolyn to have eaten. "Tomorrow then. I'll be at your place around noon with lunch. Will Michael be joining us."

"No, he's busy with harvest. You know."

"Yeah, I know. See you tomorrow. I can't wait."

"OK, 'bye," she croaked, and hung up before I could reply.

Not much, but it was a start. Meanwhile, it was Saturday night with nothing to do. I scrounged some leftovers from the refrigerator, heated them in the microwave, and returned to the porch to eat. Winston joined me and we dined together. He was more than willing to try anything and everything I put in my mouth. We watched a couple of red tail hawks circle over the neighboring vineyard as the sun moved low in the west and disappeared behind the Coast Range. Then I put him inside and drove to Newberg to see whatever was playing at the Cameo Theatre.

The Cameo is located on the main drag in downtown Newberg, and to its credit always offers first-run films. It is a marvelous art deco building, and inside the place hasn't changed since the 1930s. Five dollars buys a loge seat, and the theater does not admit anyone under sixteen unless accompanied by an adult. Every night at eight, three hundred and sixty-five days a year, the film starts.

I can't remember what I watched that evening, but it filled the time and provided distraction from the previous night's death and mayhem. Even to someone not directly involved, murder is very upsetting. It is such an unnatural occurrence. I was convinced Ted Maxell's death was murder. He couldn't have just fallen into that tank, and the trousers clinched it.

On my way out of the theater whom should I see but Rob the Reporter, a plump, somewhat blowsy woman at his side. "Hey Rob," I called out. He introduced me to his wife, Janine, and told me they were headed to the Coffee Cottage for a cuppa. Did I want to join them? Well, of course I did. Never pass up an opportunity to fill in a bit more background.

We walked the few blocks to the coffee shop. It was the only place open in downtown Newberg that time of night. All the other choices were out on the strip east of town and served mainly alcohol. The Coffee Cottage was jammed with George Fox University students, many on their way back to campus after the movie, but we found a table at the fringes of the outdoor patio and settled in under an outdoor heater with our decaf cappuccinos. (Heady stuff, these nights out in

Newberg!) After a few minutes of general remarks about the film and an effort on my part to learn a little bit about Janine (she was a third grade teacher for the local school district; she and Rob had two children and another on the way, plus two large dogs and a gerbil; she enjoyed historical romance fiction), Rob and I began reviewing Friday evening's events.

"I've been in touch with the sheriff's department. They have scheduled an autopsy because this falls into the 'mysterious death' category," Rob began. "Of course this isn't a usual situation. Most of the so-called mysterious deaths out here are drug overdoses or obvious suicides." Every so often, someone would show up dead alongside a road somewhere, but those usually were either drunks or transients, or there would be a murder as result of some brawl involving drugs and spousal abuse.

I could remember such incidents from when I lived in Yamhill County. Drunk falls into a creek and drowns, body with no identification is found along a road somewhere, man shoots his wife and then himself in a trailer park, that sort of thing. I couldn't recall a single rich person being murdered in my entire tenure in Yamhill County. All the murders out here generally fell into the "those people" category. Something like Ted Maxell's demise was until now unheard of in the wine community

"Do you cover the wine scene at all?" I wondered. I took a sip of my cappuccino. It was pretty good.

"Not usually. As I told you last night, I deal with school district and law enforcement issues. We don't have anyone that covers the wine industry, although at this point we should. I'm following this story because I was at the dinner last night. And, because it fits into the law enforcement side of things, of course."

"Of course. What did you think about last night overall?"

"Well, I've never been to anything like it. I'd met Ted before briefly. He's been fairly condescending to the local media since he moved up here, and everyone at the paper was surprised we got invited to the dinner. Somebody had to cover it. Since our lifestyle editor is deer hunting with her husband, I drew the assignment. I wish somebody had told me it was black tie." Rob still looked a little embarrassed about that gaff.

"Anyway, Ted didn't have much to say to me at the dinner. Axel was completely checked out, and I couldn't get two words out of him. And I don't get what's going on with the wife. If she wasn't pregnant, I'd guess she was coked up. Way too chatty and hyper, and she doesn't say anything substantive. She does all right socially, I guess. She keeps the conversation moving, but I didn't learn anything from her. She seemed really angry at her husband." I found that his assessment covered most of the bases.

"That's because he put his hand on my knee and I said something about it." This got Janine's interest. It fit right in with her penchant for historic bodice rippers.

"You did?" from Rob.

"I did. I said it rather loudly. I'm surprised you missed it."

"I was probably trying to figure out which fork to use." We all laughed and he went on. "The couple from California was pretty much what you see up here from California these days, rich people looking around for a cheaper place to retire. They'll come up and build a mc-mansion on the hillside, drive the property values up...."

"And live happily ever after?"

"And live happily ever after, so long as they don't smell any cow manure and the vineyards around them don't have sprayers out at six in the morning. They want to *live* in the country, but they don't want it to *be* in the country, if you get my drift. They come up here, spend their money, and bitch."

"Gee, and I thought I was the only one who feels that way."

"Not by a long shot. It's a double-edged sword. They do help the economy in some ways, but they drive us all nuts. Why don't they just get a fancy condo in Portland? As for the dinner, from a reporter's standpoint it would have been a complete waste of time if Ted hadn't been killed. I did enjoy the food."

"Do you think Ted was killed?"

"No doubt in my mind. Why would he even go up on that catwalk in the middle of the dinner? That doesn't make sense, especially since he was planning to take us up there after dinner. And why were his pants down? I have to tell you, the sheriff's department is having a field day with that! They don't for a minute think it was an accident." (A stifled cackle from Janine.) "Plus, someone beat the crap out of him. His upper body was covered in bruises."

"No kidding? What happens next?"

"Well, the crime beat is my territory, so I'm pretty plugged in to whatever comes to light law-enforcement-wise."

"I will be interviewing people all over the place for my

book," I told him. "If I hear anything regarding any of Ted's doings that might lead to a suspect—or a good angle on the murder—I'll be happy to keep you in the loop. Everybody in the wine biz out here knows everybody else's business, so I may hear something interesting."

"That would be great," he said.

"There's one requirement, though."

"What's that?"

"If you come up with anything really juicy you have to tell me."

He paused for a moment, thinking about it. "It can't go any farther than you," he said.

"Scout's honor."

"Oh, and one more thing."

"What's that?"

"Just for your information, the deceased's blood alcohol level was 0.22. At time of death, he was more than a little drunk. It would have been fairly easy for someone to push him over that rail into the tank."

Big surprise.

Back in my snug little suite, I settled in at the desk instead of crawling into bed. It had been a long and very busy day, and I didn't want any details of my interviews to escape. So, with a cup of peppermint tea at my side and Winston curled up on my feet, I carefully reviewed the notes from my interviews that day. And then, just for the heck of it, I pulled a spiral notebook out of my laptop bag and started a journal.

I haven't kept a journal *per se* for years and years. But that night, for whatever reason, I was moved to start writing down everything I remembered from when I had arrived in

Yamhill County up until the day just finished. Words flowed out of me and onto the page, the details about Tiffany and the cigarette butt, Ted standing me up for our appointment, and on and on. The characters and conversations, the daily details of country life, all of it came to life on the pages in front of me. I lost track of time, and when I was finished the tea was cold and so was I. I crawled into bed and noticed the time. It was a few minutes after one. I snuggled Winston close to me and together we sailed away to Dreamland.

Chapter 12

Sunday, the weather broke. It was cool, cloudy, and drizzling rain when I awakened. Angel had asked for the day off, so I needed to get moving. A shower, a nice outfit to greet visitors, some makeup, and it was downstairs to let Winston out, start a pot of coffee and try to remember what I was serving for breakfast.

I turned on the oven and added buttermilk to the dry ingredients I had mixed the day before, then kneaded and formed scones. By the time I had finished that chore and had put the scones and a filled crepes casserole into the oven, Winston was ready for his breakfast and I was ready for a cup of coffee.

"I haven't been a very good friend to Carolyn," I told him as he danced around me while I prepared his meal. "But I'm going to see her today, and I'm a little nervous." I set his bowl on the floor. "In fact, I'm a lot nervous," I said to myself aloud. As the years pass, it gets easier to talk to oneself aloud.

Thankfully, only a dog was there to hear my confession. My guts were roiling.

Breakfast went normally. It was a subdued group overall, probably hung over by the looks of them, and they ate heartily. By the time I'd cleaned up the dining room and loaded the dishwasher, they were ready to check out. The guests in the Chicken House and the Carriage House were staying through the week. Angel had filled their refrigerators with breakfast items the day before. The housekeepers showed up at eleven and got to work on the upstairs rooms.

Early in sobriety I'd found myself angry with Carolyn. Why wouldn't she—one of my two closest friends—just lighten up a bit when I was around? I could be where alcohol was served and be perfectly fine, but the way she paraded it was something I couldn't ignore. It made me crazy to watch her personality change as the booze had its way with her. It was too raw, too real, too close. Ultimately it had felt shameful. I had felt shame for her as I remembered all too clearly how it had been for me, the horrible things I had said and done to the people I loved when I was drunk.

Finally, I had managed to be "unavailable" when invited to evening events involving Carolyn. I had offered to meet her for lunch instead. It was my problem. I know that now. And, at the time, I didn't think it was obvious. But of course Carolyn noticed. She noticed everything.

In the end, I guess, she dumped me. If I wasn't having any fun watching her unravel, she was having even less fun feeling my eyes on her, my silent judgment. When we drank together in the past, we were always on the same wavelength, egging each other on. When I could no longer be her drinking buddy, she took the position that our friendship no longer worked. She wasn't the only friend I'd lost when I changed my life, but she was the one I missed the most.

It had been close to three years since I'd talked to her, longer since we'd seen each other. I'd called a couple times to set up a lunch date. At least, that early in the day, I knew Carolyn would be able to carry on a conversation. But the last few times I had talked to her, she would say she wasn't available. I'd finally quit trying. It had been one of the hardest things I'd ever done.

"If you really want to stay sober, you have to stay away from the people, places, and things that will trigger you," my Alcoholics Anonymous sponsor had told me. Carolyn had been a huge trigger. But I missed her. I was concerned for her. I had wanted her in my life then, and I did now. I wanted our old friendship back, and intended to do whatever I could to make that happen.

Melody, on the other hand, could take alcohol or leave it. She would make two glasses of wine last hours. Melody was able to control her drinking when she was around me because she never *had* to control it. That was the difference. When Melody and I were together, she seldom drank. Carolyn couldn't do that. Her compulsion, like mine, was beyond human control. When I had watched her drink like she did, my thirst had returned, and the craving had become almost unbearable. Don't ask me how that happens. After all the misery I'd caused myself and others, I found those feelings repugnant and completely unbelievable. But they were there nonetheless, and they were real. That, I had learned, was the insanity of alcoholism.

Getting a lunch together for the two of us was a no-brainer. I tossed together ripe tomatoes and basil from the garden with fresh mozzarella cheese, and mixed some balsamic vinaigrette dressing in a separate container. I packed a bottle of San Pellegrino, some of Angel's fabulous biscotti, and a couple of ripe pears. I even threw in a thermos of coffee. I'd pick up a baguette at the bakery in Dundee, and we were set.

It was straight-up noon when I pulled into Carolyn's driveway. The house, a 1920s English cottage-style stucco with steep rooflines and mullioned windows, was set back about one hundred yards from the curvy two-lane blacktop road that ran through the Dundee Hills. Where once they had stood among decrepit orchards, the house and adjoining outbuildings now were surrounded by vineyards that covered the surrounding hillsides on either side of the estate. Carolyn and Michael's original vineyard—now a mature forty acres of pinot noir, riesling, and chardonnay—was the oldest on the hill. With only a couple of exceptions, it was the oldest vineyard in Oregon. It rolled downhill southward from their home site.

Michael had found the property while Carolyn was still in Virginia finishing her senior year in college. At his urging, they had purchased it before she had seen it—an old walnut orchard that had been destroyed in the Columbus Day Storm of 1962 and never properly cleared, and a house that had sat empty for the five years after its owner died. When they'd arrived here after a hasty wedding, with their first child on the way, they had moved into the wreck of a house. While

Michael had planted their first five acres of vineyard, Carolyn had worked wonders with the house and then was delivered of a baby boy.

The work she'd done more than thirty years ago, and had continued to build on in the ensuing years, was looking tired. As I drove up to the house and parked, I noticed the place was in dire need of freshening. The roof was worn out, and paint was peeling from the boards above the stucco. The gutters were plugged and running over, I noted as I opened the car door and stood in what had become a pretty good rain storm. The weeds in the flower beds were taller than the rose bushes she had coddled over the years. They obscured anything else that might have been planted there. No matter what personal disaster was affecting their lives at the time, Carolyn always had maintained her garden. She used to say it kept her sane. Today, no dogs ran to greet me, as in the past, barking joyfully at the prospect of a guest. The silence, except for rain falling on my car and the earth, was deafening.

I gathered my goodies and walked toward the house. It felt deserted, and as I neared it I was seized with feelings of discomfort. Perhaps she had gone somewhere. Perhaps it had been better to leave things as they were. I tapped on the door. One could not revive the past, I told myself. So much had changed. It was quiet within, so I knocked again, this time more loudly. Not a sound. Had she forgotten, or was she standing me up?

I set my packages on the front porch and walked around to the back of the house. A car—Carolyn's?—was parked near the back door. I walked to the door and peeked through the window into the little mud room. I could see the kitchen beyond. I tried the door. It was unlocked. "Carolyn?" I called, and banged on the open door. Quiet. I walked through the mud room and into the kitchen. Dirty glasses filled the sink. A microwave meal sat on the counter half-eaten. I could smell the garbage. Near the back door were at least a dozen empty bottles of the wine and brandy persuasion.

Cold dread swept over me. I realized I had stopped breathing, and slowly inhaled. "Carolyn?" I exhaled. Deathly still. I walked into the living room, where the stench of urine vied for dominance over the equally vile aromas of booze and stale cigarettes. Two ashtrays on the coffee table were filled and overflowing. I closed my eyes and breathed in the stink of slow death in the process. Then I walked down the hall to the master bedroom.

Carolyn was sprawled across the rumpled bed, fully clothed, mouth open, her complexion a greyish yellow. At first I thought she was dead, but her chest moved slightly, and when I touched her arm she felt warm. The room smelled of vomit and urine, and I saw a sticky pool of vomit on the bedding near her face. It was a miracle she hadn't choked to death. "Carolyn," I said, and wiggled her arm gently. She moaned, rolled onto her side and began retching.

Lovely. So lovely, in fact, that I didn't want to touch her again if I didn't have to. I grabbed some towels from the linen closet in the hall, threw one over the vomit on the bed, and placed the other in the general vicinity of her head in hopes it would catch anything else that came out of her. When her heaving stopped she opened her eyes and looked over at me, eyes not quite focusing. "Howdy," she said with a lopsided smile. She looked old, very old. "Welcome to another day in Paradise."

"I brought lunch," were the first words out of my mouth. She pushed herself to a sitting position and looked around, genuinely confused. She looked down at herself, at the clothes she was wearing, and some sort of awareness took hold in her expression. Then she looked at me. Abject shame is the only way I can describe the look in her eyes. She flopped backward onto the bed and stared at the ceiling.

"Where's Michael?"

She didn't answer me.

"Come on, Carolyn, we need to get you out of this mess. Let's find Michael and get things straightened out." She grabbed a pillow and pulled it over her face.

I backed out of the bedroom and walked through the living room to the front door, where I retrieved lunch. In the kitchen I rinsed a dirty glass and poured Carolyn some of the San Pellegrino. Then I went back into her bedroom. "Here," I said, lifting the pillow up off her face. "Drink this. You're dehydrated. It's fizzy. I don't think it will make you sick."

She looked at me, propped herself up on an elbow and accepted the glass. Her features were etched with shame, and I could read the hopelessness in her eyes. She took a tentative sip, then another. "I'm disgusting," she mumbled.

"You're very, very sick, and we need to get some help so you can get better," I said evenly. I was disassociated from the words coming out of my mouth, running on automatic as it were. My words sounded calm and soothing. I had been in enough situations like this to know that she was dying slowly and horribly. It made me soul sick, but I kept talking. "How can I get hold of Michael?"

"I don't want Michael." She stared past me as she took another sip of the water.

"Okay, well, then I'll take care of you. Maybe we could get you into the shower and into some fresh clothes."

She sighed. "Whatever." She set her glass beside her and flopped back down onto the bed. The glass promptly tipped over, its contents joining the general mayhem of puke, pee, and what-have-you on the bed. I leaned over to retrieve the glass. Carolyn's eyes were closed. Her general expression told me she had no intention of opening them soon.

"You just rest here. I'll be back in a minute." I grabbed an afghan from a nearby chair and threw it over her, walked out of the bedroom, and closed the door. Back in the kitchen I found a telephone. Melody had told me Michael was living at their winery. I called StoneGate and Dwight picked up the phone. The crew was taking a lunch break, and I could hear chatter and laughing in the background.

"I've got a major problem here," I began, and quickly outlined Carolyn's dire situation. Dwight gave me Michael's cell phone number. "If you need me to come up there, just call back," he told me, and then signed off.

A moment later I reached Michael. "Emma, how the hell are you?" he boomed into the phone."

"We have an emergency," I told him, and once again described the situation. "She needs to go to the hospital," I concluded. "I'll have to take her if you won't." I hadn't intended to give him that full-on verbal slap, but there it was, out of my mouth before I could stop it.

He was quiet for a second. I heard him let his breath out. "Of course I'll take her, Emma. No problem. I'll be there as quickly as possible."

I went back to check on Carolyn. She had made it to the bathroom and was sitting on the toilet hunched over as the remainder of her system emptied. I couldn't believe she had walked that far, but for the moment she was functioning without me. I returned to the kitchen, found a telephone book, and called the Newberg hospital. From her house it's about the same distance between the Newberg and McMinnville hospitals, but there is a very good alcohol and drug treatment facility outside Newberg. It had helped me get on my feet seven years before. So I opted for Newberg.

Wet gravel crunched in the driveway. Looking out the kitchen sink window I saw Michael pull in behind my car. He was driving a new, black Mercedes sports utility vehicle. He hit the brakes hard, jumped out and walked quickly toward the house.

"Where is she?" he asked, ready to take charge the second he entered the kitchen. I pointed toward the bedroom and followed him down the hall. Carolyn had made it back to the bedroom and was sitting on the edge of the bed, head drooped forward, her hands in her lap. The smell was nearly overpowering. "Jesus Christ!" he said.

She lifted her head. "Asshole, get out of here."

"I'm here to help you."

"Bullshit. It's a little late for that. I don't need your help." Then she looked at me. "Did you call him?" Her voice was flat, but the look in her eye was deadly.

"I'm not leaving you here like this, and neither is Michael.

You've got alcohol poisoning, your skin is yellow. I've called Newberg Hospital and they are expecting us." Michael, thankfully, said nothing as he surveyed the bedroom. His jaw was clenched in that all too familiar way. This wife, this disaster, was not what he'd had in mind for himself.

As if reading his mind, Carolyn said, "I'm not too good for business, am I Michael?" He opened his mouth to speak, and then closed it again and said nothing.

"Do you want to hose off here, or would it be easier just to go straight to the hospital?" I asked her. In dealing with children I'd learned to offer two choices that were mutually acceptable to me.

She said nothing, looking through us, past us. Then she closed her eyes. I went into the bathroom and ran hot water onto a washcloth. When I returned to the bedroom, Michael was sitting on the bed next to Carolyn. I handed him the washcloth and he gently swabbed her face. Her eyes were still closed. I fetched her raincoat from the closet, and when I returned I could see tears running from her closed eyes.

"Let's go," I said, handing Michael the raincoat. "You drive and I'll ride with her in the backseat." Together we helped Carolyn into the raincoat, and from there to Michael's vehicle, one of us on each side of her, steadying her as she took halting baby steps through the rain.

When we arrived at the hospital that Sunday afternoon, Carolyn was immediately whisked into the emergency room for a thorough going-over. Michael and I told the nice doctor everything we knew—how I had found her, and what Michael knew of her drinking patterns and her previous health issues.

She lay there, refusing to cooperate or say a word. To do her justice, I don't think she was able. She'd been drinking, and in a blackout, and had no idea how much she'd consumed. She was confused and in withdrawal, and her coloring indicated her liver was struggling just to keep going. She probably didn't know what day it was.

We ended up seeing her settled in a room and hooked up to an intravenous drip to rehydrate her system. Another drip supplied drugs that would help her detox. With the medications flowing into her system, she quickly nodded off to sleep. A nurse told us they would feed her when she awakened. She also would be visited by a psychiatrist, a social worker, and a drug and alcohol counselor the following morning. Michael told the medical powers that he would check in on her later and, meanwhile, figure out what to do next. Then we drove back to their house.

Most of the drive was accomplished in silence, each of us entertaining our own private thoughts. He didn't say anything until we were pulling up their drive. "She needs to go somewhere. I can't take care of her."

"You mean you don't want to."

Michael unfastened his seat belt and turned toward me. "I mean I can't. I don't know what to do with that woman, and I haven't known for years."

"There are places she can go," I said. "From what you told the doctor, you're not living with her because she's drunk all the time. And she's going to be drunk all the time, whether you're there or not, so she can't be alone."

"Hell, she can't take care of herself, and if we're under the same roof we may kill each other. Or at least she'll kill me in my sleep."

Wondering which one of them was to blame was like the old chicken or egg phenomenon. Who started it? Who was first? Like all such relations, the details were messy and certainly not pretty. Nor were they ever one-sided. I'd heard mostly Carolyn's version over the years we'd been friends. Their life together hadn't been easy. They had done what we all do—pushed each other's buttons, yelled and screamed and pouted, made each other jealous. The list was endless. And then somewhere along the line it had all completely fallen apart to the point that trying just wasn't worth the trouble any more. Yeah, I knew that routine rather well.

"What are you thinking?" I asked.

"I was hoping you could help me," Michael said. "I know you went out here to Serenity Estate." It sounded like a plea. Yes, I had been a patient at the local treatment center. Neither Michael nor Carolyn had chosen to visit me while I was there.

"Yes" was all I said.

"And?"

"And it's good. It's as good a treatment center as there is anywhere in the country. I owe my life to that place."

"Do you think it's the place for Carolyn?"

"I think it would be as good a fit as any, and it's close. It's your decision, at least at this point. She'll scream her head off once she's feeling better, but it's where she needs to be. It's especially good because you can visit her easily and keep track of how she's doing."

"I don't know about that."

"Even more important, no one but you, she, and the boys need know she is there. It's completely private." I knew that part was gnawing at him. "And you can see her. Who knows, you might just fall in love again."

Michael snorted bitterly. "I think it's a little too late for that," he said.

"You never know," I said. "Inside, she's still the woman you married. She just got lost. She's very sick."

We said our good-byes and I drove back to my duties of entertaining guests with wine and snacks.

That night I lay awake wondering if Michael would have the courage to go through with checking Carolyn into Serenity Estate. Only the temporary surrendering of a sizable ego would allow him to do such a thing. I prayed he would follow through with the idea. Carolyn had run out of options.

Chapter 13

Dawn's fingers were not rosy the next morning, nor the one after that. It drizzled and spat intermittently, but the rain wasn't enough to hurt the grape harvest. Excessive rain will water down the flavors, and eventually can do considerable damage to wine grapes at harvest time. However, overall, the valley had experienced less than an inch of rain. At this time the amount of water was not a problem. The bigger issues, after three days of rain followed by more warm weather during harvest, were mildew and rot. Pinot noir grapes are especially susceptible because of their tight clusters.

Pinot noir harvest was well underway. Vineyard workers, inundated with perfectly ripe fruit, were bringing it in as quickly as the wineries could receive it. The valley bustled with activity. As always happened this time of year, I longed to be a part of it. This year, thanks to my book contract, I was present, and being here felt vibrant and exciting. Long term, of course, I'd be back tending to my own affairs in Portland.

But for now, I was grateful to be an observer. Part of my heart was still here in the valley, and forever would be. I wondered if that lost feeling, that longing to be connected to the earth and sun and the aromas of ripe wine grapes I feel every October, would ever leave me. To date it hasn't, and to date nothing has replaced it.

That Monday morning, after carrying breakfasts out to the remaining guests, I left the Westerly and drove to the Newberg hospital to see Carolyn. She was still hooked up to a tube, and her hair was unwashed and greasy. I found here glaring at the breakfast tray in front of her. As I walked into the room and set a vase of golden, rust, and red chrysanthemums on her windowsill, her glare fixed on me rather than the unfortunate breakfast tray.

"Hi," I said brightly. "Feeling any better?"

"This food is shit," she muttered, looking away from me. "They'll kill me before I get out of here."

I advanced to the breakfast tray, picked up the knife, and poked at a cold yellow wad of something—presumably scrambled eggs. It did not yield easily. "Lord," I said, "that is one scary mess." The toast was white balloon bread served with a little plastic cup of margarine. Other selections included a plastic tub of applesauce, a hermetically sealed plastic cup of orange juice, a carton of milk, and a cup of very weak coffee. Worse by far than any airplane food I'd ever encountered. Carolyn stared out the window. I flubbed around trying to think of something appropriate to say. "This is a hell of a way to get together, but I've missed you, Carolyn," was what finally came out of my mouth.

"Humph," she retorted. "You have a nice way of showing it." Obviously she was feeling more like herself.

"I moved to Portland because I couldn't do this any more, life out here, with all the memories and temptations. I thought you understood that."

"You abandoned me." She looked out the window. Being reasonable was not in her repertoire that morning.

"Carolyn, you need some decent coffee," I said. "This stuff looks like weasel wee-wee. I'm going to go out and get you a nice double latte somewhere close, and something that's fit to eat. This is your last chance. What do you want?"

Her eyes popped open. A bit of a grin played at one corner of her mouth.

"You're not a victim," I told her. "You did this to yourself. But now that you're here, we can figure out how to get you out of it."

She snorted and closed her eyes, frowning.

I left the room and drove to the nearby strip mall, where a small coffee shop offered what appeared to be decent pastry. I ordered a latte for each of us and an almond croissant for Carolyn. It wasn't the most perfect or healthy choice for someone in her condition, but it was better than what they were feeding her at the hospital. It would give her a little energy boost. I could go back to the house and pick up something really good for her lunch. Not that I had to babysit, I reminded myself.

As I had told Carolyn, she had done this to herself. But this was hardly the time for a debate. Her skin coloring told me, as certainly as any doctor, that her liver was failing. I was certain that information would be conveyed to the absentee husband before the end of the day. Hopefully he would set aside his look good long enough to get her into an alcohol treatment center—if not Serenity Estate, he could ship her off to California or Arizona, where she would be safe while he did whatever absentee husbands do in their idle hours. And I could mother her with food. It was something I could do to feel I had a bit of control where none was possible.

When I reentered the hospital room, Carolyn was being poked, prodded, and discussed by a doctor, a nurse, a woman in a suit, and Michael. I reached behind Michael and set the latte and bagged croissant on Carolyn's stand. A bouquet of long-stemmed yellow roses had joined the chrysanthemums on the window sill—a token from Michael, no doubt. "Should I leave?" I asked nobody in particular.

"Stay," Michael answered. "We need your input."

"So as I was saying," the doctor continued, looking directly at Carolyn, "you are suffering from severe alcohol poisoning. Your blood tests showed your alcohol level at 0.2 yesterday afternoon—after you'd not consumed any alcohol for several hours. The alarming thing to me is that your liver is functioning at about one-quarter normal. You show all the symptoms of chronic late-stage alcoholism, and your condition at this time puts your life in peril. Should you drink again, I have no doubt it will kill you."

Carolyn, for once, was paying attention. "It sounds like I'm a toxic waste dump," she cracked, but none of us laughed.

"That summarizes it very well," the doctor told her. "You're severely under weight, and haven't been eating properly. What you do eat isn't digested properly because your system is beginning to shut down. I want to keep you here for a couple more days to monitor your condition, and then I am sending you over to Serenity Estate for a recommended ninety-day stay. Ms. Francis here is the intake specialist from Serenity Estate. She will interview you, and we'll get things set up so that you can transition into detox over there as soon as possible."

Carolyn's eyes darted from the doctor to Michael and back again. For the first time her face registered fear. "No," she said. "No, I can't do that. I don't want to do that. I'll go home and take care of myself."

"You're following doctor's orders," Michael boomed. "I'm in the middle of harvest. I can't take care of you."

"You and those fucking grapes," she hissed. "They're more important than anything, than life itself."

"It's not that simple, Carolyn," I said, weighing in at last. "People like you and I are too addicted to this stuff to just give it up. You're going to be really sick, and when you feel that sick the only thing that makes it better is a drink. This is not the kind of thing we can do alone."

"What's this 'we' shit? You did it alone," she said.

"No, I did it without Dwight, you, and Melody, but I went to Serenity Estate and I found help there. They took care of me, and then I got out and became active in recovery programs. A lot of people helped me, including the other patients. I'd tried to quit by myself for years before that. I just couldn't do it."

"She's right." The doctor nodded in my direction. "Withdrawal is a painful process for someone as reliant on alcohol as you've become. Seizures are not uncommon, along with everything from flu-like symptoms to delirium tremens.

You're unable to care for yourself at this time, and that's why you're here. When we're sure we've got the big things under control, we can move you, but you can't go home."

The doctor left the room, followed by everyone but me. I went to Carolyn's bed and handed her the latte and removed the croissant from its bag. "Here, this will make you feel better," I said. "I'm going back to Melody's, but I'll visit you later today and I'll bring you something really good to eat."

"I can't go to that place," she whispered. "I just can't do it."

"We'll talk about it later," I told her, and placed my hand on her arm. "I love you, Carolyn. I want you to get better. So please, don't fight now. Pay attention to everything they are telling you, and don't fight now. Just rest. You're safe here."

"I won't go," she promised as I walked out of the room.

Back at the estate, all seemed to be going smoothly. The Monday garden crew were snipping, mowing, and edging in the mizzling rain. One of the crew skimmed leaves from the swimming pool while another bustled in and out of the pump house, presumably doing pool maintenance of the chemical variety. If it warmed up again, we'd have a few days left where the hardier guests could swim.

Angel was about her duties, and delicious baking smells filled the kitchen. I greeted her and poured myself a cup of coffee. "How's it going?"

"Oh, Mrs. Emma, there are many phone calls, many messages."

I told her about Carolyn, all the gory details. She didn't know Carolyn, which made it easier. She listened intently.

"My brother, he is like that," she told me. "He work, he drink. Sometimes he drink while he work. It is terrible. I tell him he needs to try harder."

"It's a disease," I said. "It eats us alive."

The phone pealed from the alcove and I answered. It was Jane Webber. "We've heard the terrible news about Ted, and we're flying up tomorrow morning for the funeral. Do you have a room available?"

I did, and booked them. I hadn't realized the funeral was on Tuesday, but it already had been three days since Maxell had died.

Rob the Reporter also had phoned. His message: "The coroner has determined foul play was involved in Ted Maxell's death. It will be in our Wednesday edition, but of course *The Oregonian* will beat us to the punch. He drowned in the grape must, but the marks left on the body are consistent with the wooden paddles used for punch down. Somebody went after him with a paddle, and thumped him pretty good while he was still alive. And, he had a gash on his head they hadn't noticed earlier. The funeral is tomorrow at two up at the winery. Call me."

Why on earth would anyone have a funeral at a winery?

The second saved message was particularly odd, as it came from Tiffany Maxell. "I wanted to let you know that my dad's funeral is tomorrow at two. I'm sorry I've been so horrible to you. I'd like to talk to you. It's important. So could you please come? And please join us after for food at the house. I'm really very sorry." She sounded like a little girl. There was a catch in her voice I couldn't quite identify. Timidity? Fear? The brat was gone, at least for the moment. She hadn't asked me to call back, so I didn't.

My mind digested the telephone messages, and then started to play with ideas of what to take to Carolyn for lunch. I glanced at my date book and remembered I had a two o'clock interview that afternoon at a new winery out by Carlton. I'd been here a week and only completed a handful of interviews. Of course there had been ample distraction. I picked up the phone and started dialing wineries in the Eola Hills. Twenty minutes later, I'd booked four appointments for Wednesday. That was the kind of schedule that would get my job done.

Saving the best for last, I dialed Rob and caught him just before he left his office for lunch. "Emma, great, you got my message."

"Yes I did. I guess I didn't notice the injuries because I was looking at other things," I remarked.

Rob chuckled. Then, "It looks like our man got quite a drubbing. He was whacked several times by that paddle, according to the coroner, and he was whacked hard, then probably pushed under the grape must and held there till he drowned."

"Any estimate how long that might have taken?"

"The coroner said a matter of minutes. What with his legs encumbered, and the other injuries, he wouldn't have been able to do much at all. He probably was unable to function after that blow to the head, plus he was fairly inebriated."

"Well, you've got yourself a high profile murder to report on out here in the sticks. I take it you're going to the funeral."

"Can't miss it. Half of the valley will be there, and probably the Portland media as well. Are you going?"

"It's the weirdest thing, Rob, but Tiffany Maxell called me and asked me to be there. She says she wants to talk to me."

"About what?"

"I don't know, because she hates my guts. Or did. I gave her quite a tongue-lashing last week when she threw her cigarette butt into Melody's English garden. Up until now, she hasn't said a civil word to me."

"She's a piece of work," Rob concluded. "Remind me to tell you about the night she got hauled in because she was dancing on the pool table at Lumpy's Landing."

We rang off and I returned to the kitchen. Lumpy's is a tavern in Dundee. When we first moved to the area, I remember the signs advertising women's jello wrestling. I couldn't even imagine Tiffany going into Lumpy's, much less dancing on the tables there. What a world!

As I rummaged around the kitchen getting lunch together for Carolyn, I brought Angel up to speed on all the gossip regarding Ted. As usual, she knew as much or more about it than I did. Of course, she was in the pipeline with Zephyr. In my opinion, they were on the A-list of people who had reason to want him gone.

"Is Zephyr going to the funeral tomorrow?" I wondered.

"She will not miss it, Mrs. Emma. She will be there for Axel."

"Who would have killed Ted?" As soon as I said it I realized that Axel probably was being looked at as a possible suspect, and that Zephyr, no doubt, would have to account for her whereabouts on Friday night as well.

"Many people disliked him." And then, as if mirroring my thoughts Angel said, "They ask my Zephyr, but why not me as well? I hated that man. So many people we know nothing about. He was very bad."

I made a ham sandwich and a small salad for Carolyn, and threw some fruit, a couple chunks of imported cheese, and a hunk of the bread into my bag for myself. As an afterthought, I added several of Angel's cookies to the tote for both of us. Winston eyed me, hoping for a walk.

"Not right now buddy," I told him. "You'll have to wait until I get back." I gave Angel a quick hug and headed out the door. I had asked her to set out the cocktail hour goodies for our remaining guests. Between Carolyn's lunch delivery and my interviews, I did not return to the Westerly until after dark that evening.

Chapter 14

By Tuesday morning the clouds were breaking up. Weather forecasters, and my former husband, who did his own weather forecast on the winery website every morning, had predicted an end to the damp fall weather. Since they were in agreement, it appeared the forecasters would be right for a change.

I played hostess to the Webbers at the breakfast table, quietly putting away a lovely omelet filled with the first chanterelle mushrooms of the season, fresh herbs, and crème fraiche, and trying to keep two new guests happy while Jane Webber filled all corners of the dining room with a litany of Ted Maxell's extensive attributes based on her own personal knowledge of the man. Clearly, she didn't know he'd been murdered. I was hoarding the daily newspaper in the kitchen alcove until I'd had a chance to read it.

I had cooked the breakfast myself, leaving Angel at liberty to do her baking. My muffins, as usual, were excellent. The ever alert Winston rested on my feet, and I slipped him the occasional bit of bacon, while part of my mind tuned into Jane's blather, hoping she would say something either interesting or useful. She didn't. I refilled everyone's coffee cups for the final time and excused myself to the kitchen.

Just as I was stealing a glance at the front page of the paper's regional news section, where an article blared the news about Ted's demise and copped to foul play, the phone rang. It was Tiffany Maxell. "Are you coming to Dad's funeral today?"

"Yes I am, but I'm a little curious as to why you want me there. I thought you didn't like me."

"I changed my mind. I have *got* to talk to you."

"Why?"

"It's important. It's about Daddy's death."

My interest was piqued, mostly because she wanted to talk to me. I wasn't even in the loop. "I'm not sure I could be of any help. Isn't there somebody else you would rather talk to?"

"No!" She sounded desperate. "No I can't. It's too awful."

"Why me?"

"You seem kind of balanced." Oh, thanks. "And you're not a family member." That too, thank God. Then she started to cry. "I think I can trust you. If I can't...." Sobs and sniffs.

"Okay, okay, take a deep breath. Would you like to come over here now? Or could I meet you someplace?" It is not in my nature to turn away the world-weary and pathetic. Whether or not I could help her remained to be seen, but if she was willing, I'd certainly give it a go. Who knows what interesting information I'd dredge up in our meeting?

"I can't. There's too much going on here right now."

"Where are you?"

"Up at the house...oh, gee, thanks Angie. See you tomor-row." Click. She hung up the phone. Which house? Hers? Did she have a house?

"The oddest thing just happened," I told Angel as I segued from the alcove into the kitchen. I repeated the conversation.

"I don't know, Senora," she answered. "I think they're all crazy. Too much of the money. Too much of everything." She shook her head and continued assembling a breakfast casserole so it would be ready to pop in the oven the next morning. "That Axel, my Zephyr loves him, but he is crazy too."

I went up the little stairway to my room, changed into my jeans, and took Winston for his walk. I owed him double. When I returned, Jane was in full vapors mode on the landing of the main stairway. By now she had seen the paper and her voice rang throughout the house. "Oh, it just couldn't be! How could such a thing happen here? He was the *nicest* man."

Her husband was fully engaged, making calming and clucking noises I couldn't quite hear. I checked the messages again, then sneaked up to my quarters and flopped on the bed. What was I going to wear to this event that I didn't even want to attend? Fortunately, Rob had offered to pick me up and I'd accepted. At least I'd not be there completely alone. Next thing I knew it was one o'clock. I had half an hour to get ready.

Imagine having a funeral service in the caves of a winery. Well, at the very least, it was original. Huge bouquets of flowers lined the main cave, and spilled out the entrance into the sunshine. Spotlights had been brought in, both to dispel the cave gloom and to allow the media free reign. It was a slow news day in Portland, apparently. Television crews were everywhere. The funeral home had brought in a small organ. It produced echoes in the cave that reminded me of the horror movies I'd attended as a child. I could not imagine who was capable of putting something like this together, but tastelessness could happen, and often did. I sat in a folding chair near the back and surveyed the crowd for people I knew. There were dozens of familiar faces.

A few minutes before two, the widow filed in on Axel's arm, followed by Tiffany and a couple of middle-aged men. I guessed they were Ted's brothers since they bore a family resemblance. The deceased had no religious affiliation, so the funeral director spoke over the urn containing his ashes, giving a glowing account of Ted deeds in life. Then came the opportunity for friends and family members to share their memories. Axel got up and mumbled a few words. Tiffany tearfully told those gathered that Ted had been the ideal father, kind and self-sacrificing. I came frighteningly close to blowing my lunch, but managed to avoid disgracing the family name. The brothers also mumbled a few words, but nothing that caught my attention.

Then a guy from California stepped to the podium and talked about Ted's contributions to the California wine industry. Either this guy lived in a bubble, or someone had paid him. It was my tacit understanding that said industry— or at least Ted's investors—is still recovering from those contributions. No one stood to talk about his contributions in Oregon. There was a solo about never walking alone, and more gothic sounding organ music, and then we dispatched ourselves to Ted and Tara's home. It was like being in a nightmare.

Located about a mile up the steep road from the winery, the Maxell home was an exact copy, on the outside at least, of Tara, Scarlett O'Hara's old plantation home in the film version of *Gone with the Wind*. In reality, it probably was much larger.

"My goodness!" I said to Rob, who drove his vehicle out of the Douglas fir forest, what was left of it, and up toward the top of the hill, which had been suitably raped to accommodate this monstrosity. "Do you think the grieving widow had anything to do with the house plans?"

"She insisted on living in what she calls 'a real mansion'," he noted. "One of our reporters attended an event they put on when they moved in, and that is exactly what Tara said. We have the county commissioners to blame for allowing such a thing to be built. It's the joke of the entire valley. And from almost any direction you can see it for miles."

He drove through the automatic gates, left open for the reception, and parked on the side of the wide driveway behind a growing row of vehicles that had overflowed from the parking area adjacent the house. We walked the remaining hundred yards or so to the house. The view in every direction was stunning. I could see Mount Rainier, Mount St. Helens, and Mount Adams to the north, Hood and Jefferson to the east, and way off to the southeast, the tops of the Three Sisters. To the west, plump, grey cumulus clouds were banking over the Coast Range, threatening another squall in the valley if they made it this far inland.

Catering vans and guests' vehicles filled the parking area between the house and a four-car garage that looked as if it housed guest quarters overhead. It was built to resemble an 1850s-era carriage house. Small oak trees lined the driveway. When they became large trees, it definitely would look like the 1939 movie set. "At any moment, I expect to see Mammy come out the door with a tray of mint juleps," I told Rob.

"I have not been invited to any parties up here, but that is exactly what happened last May on Derby Day," he responded. I groaned.

The doors to the house stood open, and people had gathered on the sprawling veranda sipping wine, nibbling canapés, and remembering the dearly departed. It was a flawless seventy-five degree afternoon, and as we approached the house we just as easily could have been attending a truly festive event. I had difficulty even imagining that someone here at this post-funeral gathering could have been doing something with Ted in his pantless state, that someone had beaten him about the head and shoulders, and then drowned him in a vat of fermenting grape must as recently as Friday night. But the deed obviously had been done by someone intimately acquainted with the deceased, so he or she likely was here, taking in the hospitality like the rest of us.

When we reached the veranda, Rob and I split up—he headed for the wine table, while I wandered off to find Tiffany and see if I could find out why she'd been so eager to talk with me. We agreed to check in with each other in half an hour. I also was hoping to network a bit and line up some more contacts for the book.

More people were walking up the drive as I wound

through the cluster of guests near the front door. It is possible that most of the people gathered at the house hadn't liked Ted Maxell, but this was an occasion not lacking in salacity. The curious had attended in droves, many just to see the house up close and personal after having made fun of it for the past two years. Any occasion that provided food and wine always had appealed to those of us in the wine community. Then, of course, there was the harvest to discuss, not to mention a murder.

Once inside, my own sense of loss swept through me with tsunami force. I stood among the people of my past, and although it wasn't such a very distant past, those of us at that certain age had changed considerably. For the most part, this was a group hands-on, artisan farmers who had spent most of their adult lives outdoors—hatless, gloveless, and without the benefits of sunscreen or a lot of conveniences—in all types of weather. Consumed as they had been with the pursuit of that Holy Grail, pinot noir, and with building their own little empires, few had bothered with such niceties as self-care.

The people surrounding me were lined and craggy from weather and age; their hair was brittle and faded, and in most cases gone to grey. Yet if they appeared a little worse for wear, they also exuded a collective air of contentment. These were not vanquished knights and ladies. These were the powers of the Willamette Valley wine industry who had gathered *en masse* for the Maxell event like mafia dons showing respect for a fallen enemy. For these pioneers, as for the mafia, the "us against them" philosophy toward the outside world still prevailed.

Despite their recently acquired recognition by the

international wine media, and the resulting widespread embrace of the wine-consuming public, despite financial security and European cars and even a vacation home or two, these folks could never succumb to the luxury lifestyle. It wasn't in their DNA. But they could now take some ease, knowing they had done their jobs well. Several had children who would work in the business with them and eventually fill their shoes. There had to be deep comfort in that.

Those who recognized me greeted me like an old friend. There were many hugs and brief conversations as I made my way toward the grieving widow, who wore four-inch spike heels and obviously was suffering from her poor fashion choice. She shifted painfully from foot to foot.

No amount of makeup could have hidden the dark circles under her eyes. I stood behind four or five people and observed her. She held a glass of red wine, from which she occasionally sipped as she listened, nodded, and addressed each guest solemnly. A handsome, dark-haired man stood close behind her watching the crowd. He was of medium height and wore a very fine looking silk suit. He appeared to be about forty, and was broad-shouldered and powerful looking. I wondered if Tara had hired a body guard in case the murderer came after her next.

"I am very sorry about Ted," I told her when my turn in the line arrived. "Obviously his presence will be missed."

"You're Emma? Yes, I remember you from the dinner." She eyed me through a hedge of false eyelashes. "And weren't you with the people who found my husband?"

"I was. It was a terrible shock to all of us who were there, and I can only imagine the shock it was to you."

"Yes, a horrible shock," she agreed. She noticed me eyeballing the body guard. "Have you met?" she asked, gesturing.

"No," I said.

"This is Josh Spears. He is resuming winemaking duties now that my husband is deceased."

"Lovely to meet you." I extended my hand to his. He nodded. His hand touched mine. It was dry and callused. I clasped it in the normal manner. Spears did not return clasp, but rather held his hand in place. Unnerved, I briefly shook the unresponsive appendage and released it. Tara had turned her attention to the guest behind me.

"While I am here," I said before moving on, "I wonder if you could tell me where I could find Tiffany. I want to offer my condolences to her as well."

"I haven't seen her," said Tara, waving her empty hand absently. "She's around here someplace." Then she turned away from me again.

Axel stood a few feet away from Tara, Zephyr by his side. I walked up to them. "How are you holding up?" I asked him. "I am truly sorry for your loss."

"Oh, Emma, thank you for coming." His smile was wan, but I was certain he'd be better soon. He'd just been relieved of his foremost tormentor. I smiled at Zephyr. She smiled back. Axel might have been off in the clouds somewhere, but she was focused and present.

"I'm looking for your sister," I told him. "She wanted to talk to me."

He looked around. "She was here a minute ago. Oh, there she is." He pointed to the open staircase.

A rope barrier across the bottom of the stairs kept the

curious from wandering upstairs. Tiffany was descending the staircase while talking on a cell phone. I walked to the bottom of the stairs and waited for her. She was wearing a very tight, very short black dress, and from the looks of things, not much in the way of underwear. I grimaced as she approached me, her expression vacant.

"You wanted to talk to me," I reminded her.

"Oh, yeah." She appeared not to register what I was saying. "Gotta go," she said to the cell phone.

"Well, let's talk." I looked into her eyes. Nobody was home.

She sighed and looked around the room like she didn't know where she was, then ran a bejeweled hand through her perfect tousled hair. "This is really hard," she said. "I can't really talk now."

"Okay, no problem. It was your idea." I barely had the words out when she toppled forward, dropping both cell phone and wine glass. The glass broke as I grabbed her, and someone shrieked. It may have been me.

I held her as she flailed to regain her balance. Suddenly Tara was by her side. "What's going on here?" She put her hand on Tiffany's shoulder.

Tiffany stiffened and pulled away. "Don't *touch* me!" She regained her footing and was able to stand unaided.

Tara withdrew, looking shocked and hurt. "All *right*. Calm down. Sorry." Tara rolled her eyes, then she turned away and walked into the crowd.

"Bitch," Tiffany muttered after her.

"If this is about your dad, as you said earlier, you need to talk to the police about it, not me," I said

"I know who did it," she hissed, looking around wildly. "I know who killed my dad." And then she stumbled again.

"We can't have a conversation when you're like this." I took her arm and steadied her. Looking around, I wondered if anyone had heard our exchange. And was she crazy? At that moment, at least, she was plenty crazy.

"Someday I'll tell you everything. You're gonna love it."

"You're not making sense," I said as I guided her to a sofa and sat her down.

"Oh, but I am." She giggled mirthlessly. I walked to the beverage table to find her a Coke. When I returned, several people her age were gathered around her. She laughed at something one of them said. I shoved the icy glass into her hand. She'd forgotten I was even there, which was fine with me.

Back in the crowd, I saw several more people I knew, including two of the winemakers I was set to interview next day. I spoke to them and confirmed our appointments. I said hello to several folks who obviously didn't recognize me. Perhaps my appearance had something to do with it. It had been six years, my hair was no longer red, and I'd shed thirty pounds. I'd also started wearing make-up—which actually did make a difference, whether I wanted to admit it or not.

Even so, my female friends and I had reached the age of invisibility. We no longer were the primary consumers, child-bearers, or lovers. We were neither seen nor heard. We blended into the crowds, the backgrounds. Sometimes I liked it—being left alone, being invisible. I told myself it was great, peaceful. Other times it just took a lot of work to get things done.

Rob stood at the front door. By the time I reached him, nearly an hour had passed and he was visiting with my ex-husband.

"What did you find out?" Rob asked when I drew near. He had a glass of wine in one hand and did not seem concerned about my tardiness.

"Nothing, really. Tiffany's drunk, stoned, or both, and basically is making no sense. I want to talk to a couple more people before we leave."

"No problem. Let's meet back here in fifteen?" I nodded in reply, and Rob headed toward the refreshments.

"What are you doing here?" I asked Dwight when Rob was out of range. "You hated Ted."

"Yeah, but I have to take in the sights." Dwight took a sip of wine while his eyes wandered the room. "What about you?"

"I'm not really certain," I said. "Tiffany called me today and wanted to make sure I'd be here so she could talk to me about her dad. But now she's wasted and it looks as if she is, or has been, having a quarrel with her step-mom."

"There's something not quite right about that kid," Dwight remarked.

"Who's that guy with Tara? Is he her bodyguard?" I asked just to see what he'd say.

"Oh, Josh Spears. He's been the winemaker here since the winery opened. He's a bit of an asshole, but that just means his management style fit with Ted's. They had a big falling out a couple weeks ago. Two stories are circulating regarding their altercation. Ted says he fired Josh, and Josh says he quit."

"Well, I was just introduced to him. Tiffany has hired him back."

Dwight raised his eyebrows. "Well, well," he said. "The plot thickens."

"Really."

"Yep. There have been rumors about him and Tara."

"Really, again."

"Yeah, it appears she was getting tired of Ted." And then Dwight turned on me. "Speaking of that, you seem to be pretty cozy with Rob Grimes, Emmy. Remember, he's a married man."

"Well, aren't you just the charming one today. You're a miserable soul if you think like that, Dwight McCourt!" In the past, Dwight had always nurtured a jealous streak. Or, perhaps he just liked making up things to torment me when I was drunk and getting on his nerves anyway. During those times, I usually was in no condition to fight back, and would always end up crying rather than turning our argument into something that may have been constructive.

Not so today. I was ready to have it out with him about whatever was on his mind.

Before we could really get going on each other, however, Rob reappeared carrying a paper plate heaped with food. "Are you ready to go?" he asked. I was. Clearly he was planning on taking all that food home with him!

I walked onto the veranda without saying another word to Dwight. It occurred to me that I'd already said too much—especially about Tiffany. What if Dwight *had* killed Ted Maxell? It was a long shot at best, but one that had gained purchase in my mind.

It was nearly seven when the Webbers returned from

the Maxell reception. They walked through the front door of the house somewhat subdued. "It positively gave me the creeps," Jane announced. "Anyone there could have been a murderer."

"It's a small community," I reminded her, as I closed the door behind them. "That's why people move here. Normally that's a good thing, but like anything else, it has its down side."

She continued to rattle on, and Martin did his usual clucking thing, which was really getting on my nerves. What would the woman do if she ever had to deal with a *real* crisis— like balancing a checkbook or raising a teenager? What if Martin were not there to protect her from the everyday vicissitudes of life? I wondered how he managed to do all the things he had to do to stay wealthy and take care of her as well. Marvelous man. I needed one like that so I, too, could be a princess.

I reminded them of their dinner reservation at Red Hills and departed to the kitchen alcove, where I called the hospital. Carolyn had checked out first thing that morning. There was no answer at her house, so I called Michael. "She's at Serenity Estate," he told me. "She is on telephone ban, and can't have visitors until Sunday."

"Thank God. Someone managed to talk sense into her."

"It wasn't easy. She just didn't have any other options. She is in bad shape, as you know, but apparently not bad enough that the hospital wanted her around any longer. She's not capable of making decisions right now, so I decided for her. They're worried about her liver, but we really won't know how bad it is until she's been off the booze for a while. Oh, and she called me an asshole for my trouble."

Nice, but to be expected. There is nothing meaner than a dry drunk, especially a detoxing one. That's why we go to nice places like Serenity Estate—so our loved ones don't have to deal with us while we are at our worst. Michael told me the visiting hours at the estate and we disconnected.

The evening loomed, and I made the best of it. I should have gone to an Alcoholics Anonymous meeting. I hadn't been to one for nearly two weeks. But the shit fairies in my brain talked me out of it. Instead, Winston and I played on the back lawn then came inside and ate toasted cheese sandwiches. I was minding my own business, reading a mystery novel, when the phone rang at nine. It was Rob. "Just so you know, Axel Maxell was arrested after the reception this evening."

"You're kidding."

"Nope. He was booked for his father's murder. Apparently there was a big argument Friday night before the dinner. Someone, I don't know who yet, overheard Axel threatening his dad."

"He doesn't seem like a killer to me." What exactly did a killer *seem* like? I had no idea.

"I've talked to Dave Jeffers. They're sure they've got their man."

"Well, good for them." I said and hung up the phone. Winston and I retired as soon as I got off the phone. Upstairs, I sipped chamomile tea and wrote of the latest events in my notebook while Winston crunched on his bone. We were asleep by ten.

Chapter 15

Morning came, and I lay in bed for a few minutes appreciating the new day's breathtaking, sun-dappled beauty. My thoughts, however, were somewhat disturbed. Axel was in jail, and downstairs Angel would be waiting to tell me all about it. Not much I could do about that one, but it was an unfortunate situation nonetheless.

Carolyn was safely ensconced at Serenity Estate, where she not only would be dealing with the personal monsters between her ears, but also with the very real pain and nastiness of withdrawal from alcohol. The big question with her had to do with survival. Could she and would she do what needed to be done to recover from her alcohol addiction before it killed her?

I realized it may already be too late. Her body could be compromised to the point of no return. However, she was as safe as someone in her situation could be, and I took comfort in knowing she was under the best of care. It remained a disturbing situation nonetheless. What could have been an upbeat, let's-bury-the-hatchet reunion with an old friend had turned into a battle for her survival. By now she probably had been sober long enough for someone to apprise her of this fact. Meanwhile, as it was Wednesday and I couldn't see her until Sunday, I had to put Carolyn on hold. When I saw her I would offer whatever help I could.

I showered and got ready to head downstairs and hear Angel's version of what was what. I assembled camera and interview notebook in my large canvas tote so I could go straight out the door after breakfast. Two couples would be checking in late afternoon, and two more on Friday, so I planned to make the most of the time available.

Angel was hard at work, focused on the breakfast trays when I finished breakfast with the Webbers. I was glad to be done with them. "Need some help?" I ventured as I brought a load of dishes from the dining room.

"I am almost finished Senora," she said, decorating a plate of sliced fruit with nasturtiums from the garden. She didn't look up.

"I heard about Axel. How's he doing? How is Zephyr taking it?" I grabbed another cinnamon roll and a cup of coffee and settled at the table for a quick chat.

"It is very sad for him. She will be all right. It is very difficult, but she has had to deal with horrible things all her life and she knows what to do. When they set a bail, he will find a way to pay the bail, and then he will be out again."

"What have they got against him?"

"The deputies say someone hear him in the tank room arguing with Mr. Maxell the night he was killed. They were yelling. They were loud. They scared the winery workers. Someone saw him running from the tank room."

I thought momentarily of Charles and Avril, the French interns at Cougar Crossing. Were they the witnesses to this alleged altercation? "When did this happen?"

"I do not know exactly, Senora. It happen Friday night. Axel could not do these things," Angel continued. "He is a very gentle man. He would not kill someone. He would work it out in his own way. He was learning."

I wondered what she meant by "learning", but as she kept talking I didn't have to wonder for long. "He was seeing someone, a counselor, to help him with his father. Zephyr tell me this several weeks ago. He needed to find his strength, to get away from his father, you see. Axel is a good man."

"I see, Angel. Thanks for the information. I too believe he's a good man. It's very difficult to go up against someone like Ted Maxell without getting twisted and angry. Somehow we'll make sense of all of this"

Angel looked at me closely. "How do you mean make sense?"

"We need to find out what really happened," I said, realizing as I said it that I was taking on a measure of involvement in something that didn't directly concern me. "It would be helpful to know when the argument occurred. For instance, was it early in the day, or closer to the time Ted Maxell was killed? Rob Grimes—a newspaper reporter I met Friday night—and I have been talking, putting our heads together. Right now we're just gathering more information, seeing what's what. I'm sure the authorities have good information, but if they have got the wrong man and are focusing all their attention on Axel, the real killer won't be found."

"It is tragic he is accused," said Angel. "It is so very unjust."

I could not disagree with that. Many things are unjust, I thought, as I headed out the door to my car.

I had four appointments that day, and the first one was with the former Mrs. Maxell. Pamela Fontaine, I'd learned the previous day—by poring through current wine industry literature and using the handy Google feature on my laptop— had purchased a beautiful 270-acre piece of property northeast of Yamhill a year after Ted had bought the site where Cougar Crossing now was located. Over the next three years, she'd planted one hundred forty acres to pinot noir, pinot gris and pinot blanc. She also had built herself a Mediterranean-style home of salmon-colored stucco that positively glowed on the hillside overlooking the lush, but now coloring, Fontaine Vineyard. Although I found the house an odd choice for this part of the country, it was a beautiful specimen.

I drove through the second security gate of the week and up a paved drive toward the house, vaguely wondering if Pamela referred to her home as Big Pink. The grounds were perfect. A couple of Latino gentlemen were deadheading in the flowerbeds, and when I turned off the car engine I could hear them chattering in Spanish and laughing. Birds sang. Less than a week ago the woman I was about to visit had lost her ex-husband. Whether that was a big deal in her life remained to be seen. For all I knew, she could have been among the seemingly endless supply of local residents who had no use for him. For all I knew, she could have killed him.

On top of that, her son was in jail. And here I was, and the show was going on, so I rang the doorbell.

Pamela answered the door herself. "Yes?" she asked. Her face was blank.

I introduced myself and stated my purpose. "I should have called ahead to remind you," I apologized. "Perhaps it would be better if I came back another time."

She looked me over and sighed. "I remember now. It's been a distracting few days." She stood aside to let me enter the foyer.

She was a petite woman, and although her hair was completely silver, her face was youthful and unlined. We were probably the same age, but she had taken better care of herself. I could see that Tiffany strongly favored her mother both in her build and fragile good looks. However, where Tiffany looked alternately like a deer in the headlights or a rebel without a clue, Pamela presented a sure and commanding presence. She had the look of someone who could put on a business suit and run a small country.

"Come this way. We can sit by the pool." Unlike Tiffany, Pamela's hair was thick and straight, worn in a short, sassy style. She was dressed in an expensive-looking ecru cardigan over matching shantung silk slacks and a russet-colored silk blouse. Several gold bangles adorned her left wrist.

She led the way through the foyer and across terra cotta tiles and expensive Native American area rugs. The house décor was in the Spanish motif. Large rooms were filled with Stickley Mission furniture, southwestern art, and artifacts. Huge windows offered panoramic views in all directions. We moved through the dining room, through large sliding doors, and out onto the pool patio. Pamela waved at someone in the kitchen and pointed me to a seat in the shade of a large market umbrella.

"What brought you to Oregon?" was my opener that day.

"My ex-husband," she said. "Tiffany had chosen to live with him after we were divorced. She always was Daddy's little girl—too much so, I thought. I wanted to be close to her. Axel was at university, but Tiff was never the academic sort. She wanted to work—or not work, as it pleased her. Ted spoiled her rotten. I thought I might be able to offer some balance in her life, some encouragement in the right direction, if you know what I mean."

"I think I do, but why get into the wine business?"

"I like it. I helped Ted get started with Mirage, his winery down in Sonoma County. It's a fascinating way of life, don't you think? And such a marriage of science and art."

A dark-skinned woman wearing an apron appeared on the patio carrying a tray. It contained a carafe of what appeared to be grapefruit juice, French press coffee, small glasses, two cups, and a plate of croissants. She set the tray on a small table between us, and returned to the kitchen. Pamela poured herself a glass of juice. "I haven't had breakfast yet," she explained. "Would you like something? Juice? Coffee?"

"I'll have some coffee, please."

She poured a cup and passed it to me. "I'm curious to know why you want to interview me. I'm new, I'm not really established. I certainly couldn't be a very interesting subject for your book."

"Part of the Oregon wine story is why people come here

from the outside," I explained. "You didn't need to plant this huge vineyard to be in close proximity to your children. You could have purchased a condo in Portland. So to me, why you're here, why you chose to do this, is very important to the book."

She nodded. "I can see that. I came up here, looked around, and decided Oregon was still a good investment. I found this property and I can afford to do things right. So this time I finally was able to do it my way instead of Ted's. I have a house I love that is not a monstrosity—unlike certain others I could name—and I live here six months of the year. Very contentedly, I might add. I can visit the children whenever I want and spend the winters in San Francisco." She looked out over the gardens and vineyard without making further eye contact with me. She took a sip of her juice.

Pamela Fontaine gave the appearance of many things, but at that moment I could not say contented was one of them. She appeared to be in the middle of a planning session with herself. Doubtless, she was thinking about Axel's incarceration. Or perhaps it was just the memories, the history that was being brought up by our conversation.

"It would be helpful if you'd give me some of your background, fill in the blanks. Who is the woman who helped Ted Maxell start a major California winery?"

"My family started a bank in San Francisco in the early 1850s. My great grandfather was an astute businessman and made millions, which in turn were invested in a variety of enterprises that made even more millions. My brother and I are the last of the clan—except for my children, of course.

My brother Nick is a very different person than I. He went his way and I went mine.

"Part of my way involved an unfortunate marriage. I met Ted at an opera benefit in the city nearly thirty years ago. He was young and handsome and on the make. I was a bit younger than he, and beautiful and foolish, and I was sick to death of society boys. He was so much fun then, so full of life. We eloped to Reno. My parents had a fit, but thankfully made the best of it. Ted made piles of money as a developer and I had two babies.

"Sometime during my second pregnancy I became aware that Ted was having relationships with other women, and I confronted him. He behaved himself for a couple of years, and then he began seeing those women again. I was busy with the children and the social scene, and I was in denial. I thought if I ignored it, it would go away. It didn't. Our marriage was no longer viable, but I didn't leave him. He seemed a good enough father when he was around. We lived in the same house and were seen together socially. That worked for a number of years. And I didn't do anything about his infidelities. They were no longer of interest to me."

If the idea is to get a subject talking, I usually can do that. She paused for a minute, took a bite of her croissant, and poured herself some coffee. "I'm probably boring you to tears," she said.

"Not at all. I guess the perception around here is that Ted was the wheeler-dealer, and that he had managed to put together quite a financial machine."

"Oh, and that I was *just* the wife." Pamela snorted. She finally looked me in the eye. "You people are so provincial.

Ted did have his share. He did very well in his real estate development business, especially when I was his business partner. But I was not interested in keeping his businesses afloat. And, being the shyster he was, when he tried to do it on his own the partners bailed out.

"There was fallout from deals gone sour, disenchanted business partners, and other costly mistakes. I never paid much attention to how much he had and when. But let me tell you this. Without me, there wouldn't have been a Mirage. And even though he lost it, the reputation of Mirage is what made it possible for Ted to find backing for Cougar Crossing. When he died, he was about to lose the winery. Meanwhile, money never has been an issue for me, and it never will be." She gave me a sweet, Botox-tight little smile.

Nice position to be in. "So how did you originally get into the wine business?" I asked.

"It was fifteen years ago. Napa and Sonoma were booming. Ted and I always had enjoyed wine, and he'd started putting together a nice cellar. Then one year, at the Napa Valley Wine Auction, he was top bidder and paid a ridiculous amount of money for a jeroboam bottle of wine. He got his face on the cover of *The Wine Spectator* and decided he had to be in the game. He found a couple of outside investors. I put in several million dollars of my own money. We bought property in Sonoma County and started Mirage."

"An impressive start," I said, remembering the reputation the winery had once enjoyed—and still did, though without the benefit of Ted Maxell's involvement.

"It was. We hired a first-rate winemaker and purchased grapes the first couple years, just as Ted did up here when he was starting Cougar Crossing. Then, when more money was required—as it always is with Ted—he found new investors to take up the slack. Ted always was a good front man.

"Meanwhile, things were deteriorating with us. He drank too much. He began using drugs. He openly chased women of the worse sort—like the one he married. It got to the point where he was no longer amusing. I was through feeding the project. And it was no longer possible to keep up the pretense of a marriage. I divorced him. It became quite vicious, but I managed to hang onto most of my personal fortune, and a good part of Mirage as well. He'd socked away millions of his own, the rat. I got custody of Axel and Tiffany. I'm sorry, I keep getting the personal mixed in with the business, but they do overlap."

"Not to worry," I assured her. "I won't be writing about personal issues in the book."

"They could *fill* a book." She grimaced and sipped some more coffee. "Anyway, at some point he had a falling out with his partners. Ted was doing what Ted always does—messing with the books, that sort of thing. He was removed from Mirage by its board of directors.

"Of course, Ted still wanted to be in the wine business. That big ego. He found some new partners, wowed them, and began the Oregon project six years ago to start over. Then three years ago, when the vineyards started producing, he moved up here and Tiffany came with him. She was old enough to be completely out of my control, and they'd always been close. Axel was at Cal-Berkeley then, and so was out of the house.

"I was heartbroken. And lonely. So I decided to move up

here and, as I said earlier, do it my way, and try to be close to my children. I made a lot of mistakes when they were growing up, but here I am. I want to be involved in their lives. And I did the best I could."

I shut my notebook. I had the facts. Plus, I had a lot of stuff I couldn't use in the book. It was time to get to my next interview. "Was Ted married to Tara before or after he moved north?"

"Ah, yes, that little piece of work." Pamela closed her eyes. I could almost imagine her horror when her former husband married Tara. "He met the lovely Tara at a strip club somewhere in the Bay Area. That must have been on one of his trips down there shortly after he started the winery here. According to Axel, they married on Valentine's Day." She made a gagging gesture. Not very patrician, but it got the point across. "Perhaps my biggest humiliation in life is that she and I were both attracted to the same man. But I was so much younger then."

Weren't we all?

"Will you stay here?" I wondered.

"Of course," said Pamela. "My children are here. I imagine eventually there will be grandchildren. Axel had problems with his father but now the father is gone. He can marry the fabulous Zephyr and get on with his musical career. As for Tiffany, once she outgrows her little angst thing I'm certain all will be well in her life."

Which opened the door I'd been waiting for? "I heard about Axel's arrest," I said. "I imagine that must be terribly stressful for you."

Pamela made an effort to appear unperturbed. "My son

didn't kill anyone. He's afraid of spiders. Now his girlfriend, that's another thing entirely. She looks sweet and beautiful, but she is tough. She comes from tough. I don't dislike her, don't get me wrong. But I'm guessing she'd do anything to get what she wants. She wants my son and she'll get him, have no doubt about that." Pamela shook her pointed index finger at me and her gold bracelets tinkled. I'd hit a nerve.

"Just being curious, has anyone questioned you about Ted's murder? I was there when they found him, you know." Before the words were out of my mouth, Pamela had collected herself.

"Of course the investigators have been here," she said, sitting back in her chaise and assuming a relaxed position. "And I told them that if I was interested in killing Ted Maxell I would have done it years ago. There were times when I was angry enough, and passionate enough, to have wanted him dead. That is no longer the case. And, fortunately, I have an alibi. I was at the opera in Portland with friends.

"Please rest assured that I am not in shock about Ted's death. He was an awful man, and he got what he deserved. It's Axel I'm concerned about. I had no interest in killing Ted. He wasn't worth it. Now, if you have no more questions, I've work to do today."

I stood and took my leave.

Chapter 16

I was back at the Westerly by four, exhausted. The other interviews had gone well, but it had been a very long day. I hate to admit it, but I'm not twenty anymore, and the schedule of juggling interviews plus the bed and breakfast duties comprised more structured activity than normal. For a single woman of a certain age—probably for a lonely person of *any* age—coming home after a day enduring the vagaries of modern life can be the most difficult time of the day. I was used to taking a nap. I was used to calling a friend and getting together to share a meal and conversation. Out here, it was long days and lonely nights.

Winston greeted me with his usual adoration, but Winston is a dog. Don't get me wrong. I would never discredit a good dog. Dogs, in my opinion, are better companions than most people. But Winston couldn't cook me dinner, draw my bath, or fluff my pillows. I needed, in short order, some delicious food, human contact, and a good night's sleep. I also wanted a big, handsome guy to give me a massage, cuddle me while I slept, and bring me coffee when I awakened. Since that wasn't going to happen, I decided to take myself to dinner.

Angel had checked in the new guests. I hosted them on the porch, checked messages, and fed Winston, and then we trundled around the yard for a bit. I picked a few late tomatoes while he ran off to do some pooping in the bushes. As dusk fell, I drove into beautiful downtown Dundee, what there is of it. Again, thoughts of an AA meeting rose like little bubbles in my mind. Again the shit fairies whacked them down. There'd be plenty of time for meetings later, they told me. I had important work to do, and I was far too important at that moment to be bothered with AA meetings.

The parking lot at the Dundee Bistro was full, so I parked on the side street. The dining room was crowded, and diners had spilled out onto the patio—mostly the young and the hardy—to enjoy the end-of-season *al fresco* dining. The Bistro is housed in the most architecturally interesting building in Dundee, and is one of the better restaurants in the valley. The terra cotta-colored stucco building, though modern in style, has the feel of an old Italian compound. It is U-shaped and surrounds a patio and pleasant landscaping. There are a gift shop, a winery tasting room hosted by the building's owners, and the large restaurant with its high ceilings, wood-burning fireplace, huge windows, and an open kitchen.

Food is fresh and local, Tuscan in style with an emphasis on the best and freshest of Northwest ingredients. I crossed the gleaming stained concrete floor and settled myself at the end of the counter where I could enjoy the open kitchen action while my mind idled for a while. I ordered an Arnold

Palmer and observed the chefs tossing delicious things in large sauté pans, flames leaping from the burners. Hunks of fresh salmon, sausages, and steaks vied for space on the grill as their mouth-watering aromas filled the air. Off in the corner, a kid who appeared to be about thirteen but more likely was in his early twenties, tossed pizza dough while another apparent child quickly assembled salads, her brows furrowed in concentration.

I relaxed and soaked up the ambience. Earlier, I had toyed with the idea of going into Portland to attend an AA meeting in my neighborhood and spend the night in my own place, but of course the reality of the situation didn't allow it. I was being paid a lot of money to mind the guests and oversee smooth operation of the Westerly during Dan and Melody's absence. We had guests currently in residence and more arriving Friday. Leaving because I was tired was not an option. I ordered the duck *confit* salad and a side of truffle fries. It wasn't a lot of food, but it was just what I wanted—good, basic, and expertly prepared. I sipped the Arnold Palmer and waited for my food.

"Emma, is that you?"

I glanced over my shoulder. Rob. I patted the seat next to me at the bar. "Have a seat. What are you doing here?"

"Janine wanted a wild mushroom pizza. I left a message for you at the B&B."

"What's up? I've been out most of the day."

"Axel's bail has been set at a million dollars."

"Good God!" I still couldn't think of a more unlikely murder suspect.

"The investigators know, from interviewing all of us

present, that he was absent from the table Friday night long enough to have lured his dad up to the catwalk and dumped him into the vat. And, I told you he and Ted had a really noisy argument on Friday night in which threats were exchanged."

"Yeah, but where was the argument, and when?"

"In the tank room, I guess." So Charles and Avril *had* overheard it.

"Did it get physical?"

"The sources say it was just yelling. But it was a lot of yelling, and Axel threatened Ted, said something about getting even."

Rob ordered Janine's wild mushroom pizza to go and a Tanqueray martini to drink while he waited. "I guess the argument provides evidence that is damning," he said. "Axel certainly had the motive, if you think about it. Ted ran his life up until he made a stand over Zephyr. And he must have done it big-time on Friday night."

"He's doubtless got some psychological issues, and maybe he snapped. But lots of people yell. Ted looked like a yeller. As for Axel, I can't picture him as a killer of anything larger than a spider." I remembered Pamela's words earlier in the day. Axel was afraid of spiders, for what that was worth.

I remembered our short interview at Cougar Crossing. He'd been nervous, evasive. Hell, he didn't know anything. And I certainly hadn't learned much about him or Cougar Crossing when I visited the place. Based on what I did know of Axel, transparent and naïve were the descriptors that came to mind. "What does he stand to gain from Ted's death?" I mused. "Other than the obvious."

Rob's martini arrived. He took a tentative sip, nodded his head in approval, and took another. Lust filled my heart as I eyed the gin-soaked olives in his glass. My mouth watered copiously, but I resisted the urge to grab them and pop them in my mouth.

"Getting rid of his father, of course." Rob said.

Just like I'd said—the obvious. He then took another tiny and well-considered sip of his drink, grabbed the toothpick holding the olives, and with his lips slid one off it and into his mouth. "From what I've heard of Ted, he was on Axel relentlessly about his choice of Zephyr as a bride. He made it public knowledge that Axel was out on his keister if he married a Mexican—out of the family, gone."

"So what?" I countered. "This is not sixteenth century Europe. Axel could tell his dad to stuff it, which no doubt is what he was doing Friday night. The fact that he has stuck with Zephyr through all the crap Ted was dishing out—that takes resolve of some kind, courage even."

The salad and plate of truffle fries appeared at my place. I pushed the fries in Rob's direction. "Have some," I said. Then I munched one. Heaven!

"That would be plenty of motive for some people," said Rob as he grabbed a fry. "Get the abusive old man out of the way, inherit some money, marry the woman of his dreams and get on with his life. I guess if the motive is strong enough, theoretically anyone can kill."

"I don't think money has much to do with motive in Axel's case. I interviewed his mother today. She's richer than God. She could buy Yamhill County if she wanted to." I filled Rob in on my interview with Pamela Fontaine, without all the personal details, of course. As long as Axel kept on her good side, money would never be a problem.

"That's interesting," Rob observed. "So, then, it *is* about Zephyr. And did he hate his father enough to kill him?"

"Seems to me that Ted must have worked Axel over pretty regularly through the years," I said. "Last Thursday, when I visited the winery, he was so nervous he could barely speak. I don't know where Ted was, but he had disappeared, and talking with Axel was a disaster. Until Friday, it seems like he was spineless when it came to Ted." I filled him in on what Angel had told me Saturday morning. "Everything about going to Davis and being trained as a winemaker was a complete sham," I concluded.

Rob reached for the plate of fries and grabbed a few more. "Except that Axel was with Zephyr at Davis," he observed. "And it looks as if that has changed him in some significant way. I guess with him we really don't know who we're dealing with."

I sipped my Arnold Palmer. A server set Rob's boxed pizza on the counter in front of him. He handed her a credit card and she disappeared.

"I really believe a woman is involved in the murder," I said, once she was out of range. "Ted had his pants down to his ankles. To me that suggests sexual activity. Even if Axel were able to kill him, he wouldn't have done the pants thing. Plus, his shock at finding Ted was credible, at least to me."

"In these perilous times, the pants do not present enough evidence to make a woman's presence definite." The waitress presented Rob's credit card chit, and our conversation was suspended while and he signed it.

"That is true," I agreed after she moved away. "But it wouldn't have been his son. Plus, Ted was heterosexual. There wasn't one gay thing about him. He liked women. Hell, he was even groping me under the table Friday night. Nobody's groped me in centuries! I think he finally just pushed someone too far. It could have been his wife, it could have been a girlfriend. Did he even *have* a girlfriend?"

"I don't know. I suppose he could have." Rob finished his martini and pushed the glass away. He stood up. "Janine is waiting," he said gallantly.

"Well, we have to find out," I said and gave him a little wave as he turned and left the restaurant.

On the way home, my mind spun like a roulette wheel. And like a roulette wheel, there was no telling where it would stop. Of the females I thought could have killed Ted Maxell, the only ones I knew about were his current wife, Tara, and his ex-wife, Pamela Fontaine. The spin landed on Pamela. Ted had used her badly, and had taken her for millions of dollars. People with that much money may act cavalier, but when it gets down to push and shove they know exactly how much they have, where it is, and what it's doing. And they hate to lose a cent of it. They don't even think they should have to pay taxes like the rest of us.

Pamela had been visibly agitated during our interview. She was shaking when she talked about Axel being in jail, adamant that he hadn't killed Ted, going so far as to implicate Zephyr—who was another unknown, not to mention a possible suspect. Pamela said Ted wasn't important anymore, but as a mother, the way Ted treated their son *was* important.

Getting Ted out of the way would have protected Axel from further abuse, not to mention a huge family meltdown.

My visit with Rob hadn't revealed much newsworthy, except for the bail. It was good to have someone with whom to process things, however. And, through his contacts with law enforcement agencies, he had access to information I couldn't hope to obtain on my own.

Abruptly my mind switched to Tara. She and Ted were practically newlyweds. Since Ted was a goat, it was possible he had been carrying on with another woman, or women. Or maybe he'd just grown inattentive. I remembered my pregnancies with all the mood swings. Inattentiveness on the part of my former spouse had driven me to rage more than once. Unfortunately, there had been no vat in which to push him. Add to that another woman, and a pretty good resentment could have been festering with Tara. The light at the end of her personal tunnel would be his money. On one level, Tara seemed rather vacuous. But, according to the boys, she also was cunning. She had noticed Ted's misbehavior with me on Friday night. I didn't know her at all well enough to gauge her temperament. But, it was certainly possible that she had reason to want him dead.

I tried to picture Tara climbing steep metal stairs onto the catwalk in her spiky heels, big baby tummy, and small cocktail dress. It challenged the imagination, but my imagination had been challenged many times in the past ten days. And a blow job on top of it to distract and render Ted sufficiently vulnerable? Sorry, that didn't work for me either—at least not with Tara. Ted having a tryst with his wife was unimaginable. It wouldn't have provided the adrenaline rush I believed someone with Ted's ego required. But somebody had lured him up there, and I was certain it wasn't his son.

If I believed Pamela, she wasn't interested enough in Ted to have murdered him. She seemed to have her life and everything around her just the way she wanted it. She had it all. Why mess with a creep like Maxell? And then there were the unknown quantity of potential male murderers, my former husband among them. In that case, the pants around the ankles could merely a distraction, intended to make a statement of scorn as well as throw investigators off the trail.

More information was needed. Pamela could have been lying her head off. That she was wealthy was obvious, but she could have made up everything else she told me. It was difficult for me to imagine that even in her craven youth she would have found Ted Maxell attractive. The fact that she had stayed in the marriage for so long spoke volumes. However, I'd learned long ago that one could never predict or hope to understand what attracted some people to one another. She had been married to Ted; that, at least, was fact. Revenge could be part of her story.

I pulled into the driveway at the farm. Winston set up a yowl as my car crunched into its parking spot near the back door. Cars and darkened windows at the Carriage House, the Chicken House, and the upstairs of the main house told me the guests were tucked in for the night. I let Winston out for his late night romp. He ran around with his nose to the ground for a couple minutes, and then came in. All was calm.

Upstairs, I changed into a nightshirt and fluffed up the

pillows. Then I grabbed my notebook and crawled under the covers, where I nursed a cup of chamomile tea with honey and added the latest information to my journal. It was past midnight when I finished, but I didn't feel sleepy. Finally drowsiness came, and I turned out the bedside light. Winston's rhythmic snoring lulled me quickly into a dreamless sleep.

Chapter 17

Thursday was noticeably cooler. The early morning air was very damp, and Winston ran through grass heavy with dew as he made his first dash outside for the day. I toweled him off when he came in.

Angel was less talkative than normal that morning. We worked quickly and efficiently in the kitchen. I presided at the breakfast table, then made a run into Newberg to purchase groceries and make a bank deposit before heading to McMinnville for a couple of interviews.

It was three o'clock when I returned to the farm. Angel had gone home, but had left me a plate of my favorite cookies. I quickly gobbled two, and chased them with a double shot of nonfat milk. The red light on the telephone was blinking, and Winston wanted a walk. I ignored them both, retired to my suite and flopped on the bed, where I acknowledged to the spirits around me that this whole hospitality business was a lot of work. I was so tired I was nearly shaking. An hour later

I awakened, ran a brush through my hair, and made ready to get on with the business of running a bed and breakfast inn.

Among the six messages awaiting me downstairs, two were interesting. Melody had called from New Zealand. "I'm in a place where I can receive calls on my cell phone," she said. "Call me when you have a chance, day or night. I want to hear your voice and find out what's going on."

The other interesting message was from Rob. "Pamela Fontaine posted one hundred thousand dollars this afternoon to get Axel out on bail. He is staying at her place until further notice. Talk to you soon." So the happy family was reunited.

I was just stuffing two bottles of white wine into the refrigerator to cool when front door buzzer rang. The remaining weekend guests had arrived a day early. Did we, by any chance, have their rooms available? We did. By the time they were checked in and had been shown the Westerly's many amenities, it was nearly five and I was ready for another nap.

Instead, I raced to the kitchen and prepared a tray with wine glasses, salted hazelnuts, the requisite cheesy bits, and cocktail napkins, carried them to the front porch, and set them out attractively. Four of the guests, all sweaty from playing tennis, were awaiting me when I returned to the porch with the wine, San Pellegrino, ice, and wedges of lime. "You do this so effortlessly," one of the women commented. I thanked her politely, went inside, and swallowed four ibuprofen. Somehow, with all this going on, I was going to complete three more interviews the next day.

When I returned to the front porch, it had turned into

a full-fledged party with ten of our twelve weekend guests talking, laughing, and drinking. I returned to the kitchen for another bottle of wine and more nuts, and then made dinner reservations for those who needed them. Chores accomplished, I excused myself to the kitchen where I poured myself a glass of San Pellegrino. I worked the daily crossword in the newspaper while I waited. Soon they would run out of wine and return to their rooms to prepare for dinner. Then I would be free to have a meal, walk Winston, and call Melody. I had much to tell her, and I fervently hoped she could help me sort out some of the characters in the local murder that was so much on everyone's minds.

By six-thirty, peace had returned. In came the empty bottles, dirty glasses, crumpled napkins. The guests had eaten everything in sight. I filled the dishwasher. It was time to think seriously about food for me. The refrigerator was overstuffed with things to eat, most of them geared toward breakfasts. I decided to go out again, and a steak at Tina's felt like just the solution to my hunger pangs. Winston and I took a quick walk before I headed down the hill to Dundee.

Tina's has been part of the Dundee landscape for so long it is like a second home to me. It opened about the time our family moved to the valley. At that time, the only other decent place to dine was Nick's Italian Cafe in McMinnville. In the years since, of course, many fine dining establishments have come into being. However, in the old days it was just those two—very different, each wonderful in its own right. They continue to be reliable places to forage a good meal.

The first few years, Tina's was simply a small dining room and a tiny kitchen. How its owners managed to turn out such fabulous food from that hell hole of a kitchen had been a mystery to all of us. Then, Dave and Tina doubled the building's size, added a beautiful bar, and expanded and modernized the kitchen. The dining room is twice its original size now, divided by a fireplace. From anywhere in the place patrons can see who's going out and who's coming in, and there always are familiar faces. It's still not a big place, and during tourist season it's often hard to get a table.

One thing I'd forgotten about living in a small town is how the same people keep showing up in the same places. Same people, different day—to paraphrase a favorite old saying of mine. I was nibbling an onion ring appetizer and relaxing at Tina's bar, when who should show up and sit down next to me but my former husband, Dwight. "Hi, Emmy. Mind if I join you?" he asked, after he took his seat. He smiled at me sheepishly.

"I guess not." I did mind, actually. To tell you the truth, I was still smarting from his remarks to me on Tuesday. I really didn't feel like talking to the man, but I sucked it up and decided to act like a big girl. I proffered the onion rings. He took one and ordered himself a local microbrew and some oysters.

"Looks like you're knocking off early tonight" I said, more to fill air space than because I felt like talking. During crush, seven-thirty was a bit early for a winery person to be dining.

"A load of chardonnay came in late and the crew is still crushing. They should be done by the time I'm finished eating. Then I have to go back and check some sugars and acids. We may be pressing the early pinots tomorrow."

"Looks like it's still a good harvest."

"Yeah."

"How are the numbers?"

"The numbers are perfect. The rain didn't hurt a thing."

"That's nice."

"Yeah."

"What do you hear from Darby?" That's our daughter, who chooses to live on the East Coast. If I asked enough questions, I'd eventually get some information.

"Not much," he said. "What about you?"

"I talked to her about a week ago."

"Oh."

Gee, this was almost as much fun as being married.

"What are you doing about the property line issue you had with Ted?"

"Oh, that. Well, he's dead now, isn't he, so it's no longer an issue. The fence is being moved back to the true property line at Cougar Crossing's expense. I've dropped the law suit." He was looking quite pleased with himself. I'd fleetingly considered my former husband as a murder suspect—not *really* seriously, mind you, but he did have a bad temper. It didn't show very often, but when it did, getting out of his way had always been my first consideration.

"Amazing."

"Yes it is." Dwight smiled a very self-satisfied smile. "He caused a lot of trouble around here, and now he's not. Somebody did us a big favor." He nodded to himself, and another prickle of anxiety ran through me. He seemed a little too pleased. He was big enough, fit enough, and quick enough to throw Ted into a wine tank without even breathing heavily.

He was smart enough to have lured him up to the catwalk in the first place. And he was sly enough to pull down Ted's pants after smacking him a good one. Fat, drunk, and out of shape, Ted wouldn't have had a chance.

Dwight's oysters arrived and he tucked right into them. I helped myself to one and squirted a little lemon juice on it. It was lightly breaded and pan-fried to perfection, a crisp buttery outer crust with a hot, soft middle, and a fresh briny aftertaste. I nearly swooned. Sitting next to him was so basic and familiar it was hard to realize we'd been divorced for six years. But we were, and for good reason. He was perceived as a good guy in the industry, but there was a side to him that was unyielding, crafty, and sometimes downright mean.

"Who did it?" I wondered out loud just to see what he would say. My salad was placed before me. I began shoveling greens into my mouth.

Dwight thought about it for a minute. "Right now, with nothing to go on, I couldn't even guess. Of course, any number of us would qualify," he continued as if he'd read my thoughts. "I had no use for the man. Axel is probably as good a candidate as any, but there also are Josh, and the ex-wife, Pamela."

"Josh Spears?"

"Yeah. He was Ted's winemaker from the get-go, but he also made about a thousand cases of his own wine each year. He likes to experiment, and eventually wants to start his own winery. Things got troublesome this season when Ted refused to let Josh make his wine at the Cougar Crossing facility—something Josh had done for the past three years, no problem. There was a big falling out. Josh says he quit, that he was tired of Ted's antics. Ted says he fired him." Again, the story that didn't jibe

"He wasn't really competing with Ted, was he?"

"Not in the wine sense. He never wanted to be at Ted's level of production. Josh would have gotten serious and started his own place in earnest within the next year or two. His Painted Pony wines have been getting great reviews. I guess he was able to lease space at the co-op at the last minute, and is processing his fruit there. He'll get it in barrel and move it to his garage to finish. Or back to Cougar Crossing, now that he's been reinstated there."

"Why do you suppose Ted kicked him out after allowing him to make a small amount of wine there for three years?"

Dwight scratched his bewhiskered chin and looked around, then lowered his voice and looked me in the eye. "Probably because Josh was screwing his wife."

Yes, he'd mentioned that rumor at the funeral. "So what? It sounds like Ted pretty much wrote the book on troublemaking," I said. "Unless you think I may have."

Dwight set down his fork and looked at me again. "Now what in the hell is that supposed to mean?"

"It means that you made a very unfortunate remark Tuesday suggesting that I was hanging out with married men in general and Rob Grimes in particular. I resent the accusation." I had not planned to say that or anything even close to it, but out it came.

"Oh c'mon. I didn't mean anything. Do we have to rehash that?"

"Some things are just too odious to ignore. That remark was more of the same old shithead behavior from you. It was mean and unnecessary. You could pull that crap on me ten years ago. It's just that then you always waited until I was drunk and didn't have the wherewithal to defend myself."

"Calm down," said Dwight. "I didn't mean anything."

"No, *you* calm down. You're the one who started this. And if you didn't mean it, you shouldn't have said it," I hissed. I could feel righteous anger boiling up inside me. I should have stopped it right then, but I was riding a wave. I was afraid of losing control, but I couldn't just stop the wave and get off. "You should have apologized on the spot. And don't *patronize* me!"

"I'm not, I'm not. Just settle down." He reached for my arm but I pulled away from him.

"Why should I settle down when I can fight with you now? You'd always attack me in the old days when I was drunk because you were too much of a chicken shit to really say what was on your mind when I was sober."

"And when would *that* have been?" Dwight sneered. "I hardly ever saw you when you were sober. Those last two years, the only time of day you were sober was when I was leaving for work, and then you were hung over."

"Points for your side. You must be proud of yourself. I was that bad, and you never once tried to help me. What did you think? That I would just get a lightening bolt up the ass one day and get better? If I was that horrible, why didn't you help—or just divorce me?"

"I don't know." He grinned at me. "Habit?"

"Great. Habit. *Habit*? How about just good old-fashioned mean-spiritedness? How about trying that on for size? You had no right or reason to accuse me of those things. Ever!

You could have just been nice once in a while. It might have made a difference!"

I burst into tears just as our server set a medium-rare steak at my place. I pushed the plate back toward her. "Box it," I said, gasping back tears. "I have to leave now." The poor young woman stared at me as if I'd just taken off my clothes in the restaurant. She grabbed the plate and scurried back into the kitchen.

I drove back to the Westerly sobbing, torn between feeling sorry for Dwight after my tongue-lashing and hating his guts. That's what happened when we fought. That part never changed. I didn't know how to fight, never had, I told myself. We were quite the pair. As usual, I had acted like a child, and he was an angry mess.

I reminded myself that we were divorced. I didn't need to make a scene in public. I didn't need to care anymore what he thought, because his thoughts were his issues and not mine. I didn't need to engage. I certainly didn't need to go around starting quarrels. But I had, and I'd said vile things. Now, not only did I feel awful, but I'd have to do something to make it right.

Back at Westerly and reunited with Winston, whom I had become convinced was the only male I could ever love, I quit blubbering and dialed Melody's cell phone. She picked up on the second ring.

"What time is it over there?" I asked.

"I just had a massage, so it's time to eat. I'm on my way to meet Dan and go to dinner. You have *got* to tell me what's going on!" With Melody, entire conversations are dotted with italicized words.

So I told her what was going on, from Ted's unscheduled departure and Carolyn's medical emergency, up through my dinner exchange with Dwight. We had such a good connection that I could hear her sucking in her breath at various junctures.

"Oh dear," she said when I'd finished.

"What does *that* mean?"

"Well, first off, you need to lighten up on dear old Dwight," she said. "He may be crazier than a shithouse goose, but he's a pretty good guy most of the time."

"Is that all you have to say about this mess you've gotten me into?"

"Being the victim, are we?" Nobody could send a zinger like Melody. It put me in my place. "I have nothing to do with you and Dwight and your problems, never have. He has his faults just like the rest of us. He was heartbroken when you left him, and probably still is. It wasn't *all* his fault, you know. He made a lot of mistakes, but you made your share too. Now that you're divorced you could probably just let it be. He's being the only person he knows how to be."

"You're right," I said. Crap, I thought. "I owe him an apology." I hated the way that felt, but I also had to admit that I wouldn't be agitated or in trouble with Dwight or in need of making an apology if I had just remembered how to behave. It occurred to me that I hadn't been to an AA meeting in nearly three weeks. I needed one badly just to keep myself balanced. Then there was my mouth. It got me into trouble faster than anything. Always could.

"What else is going on? Is there any more news on Carolyn?"

"Not really. Nobody can have contact with her until Sunday, and then I'll visit. As I told you, her liver is malfunctioning. When she gets detoxed, we'll just have to see. It depends entirely on how much damage she's done. I'm confident she is where she needs to be."

We talked a bit more, mainly speculating on whom in the wine community could have committed the murder. "It's not one of us," Melody concluded. "I just know it. It has to be someone from the outside. People here don't behave that way."

"Maybe they didn't in the old days," I told her as we disconnected with promises to talk soon. But times had changed, as anyone who had known Ted Maxell—or someone of his ilk—certainly realized. And like it or not, the new people were here to stay. Most of them were good folks just like the rest of us, but there was the occasional Ted. We'd been small, isolated, and precious, and now we weren't. Those days were gone forever.

I performed the usual evening beauty rituals and tucked myself into bed with Winston, my tea, and the notebooks. Then, with all thoughts, happenings, and conversations duly recorded, I fell into a restless sleep.

Chapter 18

Friday returned to somewhat normal. I breakfasted with the house guests and conducted one interview at a new winery in Carlton that morning, then drove down the valley after lunch to profile two wineries in the Eola Hills. Like the Dundee Hills, the Eola Hills is a designated American Viticultural Area (AVA). It's a series of ancient volcanic hills running north to south approximately between McMinnville and Salem. Although its soils and microclimates vary somewhat from those of the other AVAs in the region, the Eola Hills and its cousins all have one thing in common—the ability to grow excellent and distinctive wine grapes.

I listened to Oregon Public Broadcasting, and enjoyed the drives both down and back. While I learned a lot for the book, nothing came of my thinly veiled queries into the murder. Vintners were scrambling to bring in and process an abundance ripe fruit. They were aware of Ted Maxell demise, but were not particularly interested. Overall, I heard a couple remarks of the "serves him right" ilk, and very little more. He had been a renegade and a troublemaker, and now he was gone.

Axel had been invisible during his short tenure at Cougar Crossing. Unless one had business dealings with the winery, most of the wine people down the valley didn't know of his existence, much less his suitability as a murder suspect. One of my interviewees speculated that the winery would be on the market very soon, but it was someone who had sold grapes to Cougar Crossing the previous year and was still waiting for a check.

Back at the Westerly, I entertained the guests in the sun room, took Winston for an evening walk, and watched a movie on television. Instead of eating dinner, Winston and I had a woman and dog popcorn party—popcorn with lots of butter for both of us, and a diet root beer for me. We retired early.

Saturday dawned beautiful. I was up at sunrise, well rested and standing on the front porch of Melody and Dan's venerable house while Winston pursued a varmint at the far end of the front lawn. I sipped a cup of strong, fresh coffee and observed where the mists had settled in the valley's many swales, creating a scene at once mysterious and serene. Birds called to one another, the air was crisp, cold, and fresh. It was exquisite—the very epitome of why people want to move here in droves.

Angel putted up the driveway in her aged Honda Accord. As Winston ran to the back of the house to greet her, I went inside, poured her a cup of steaming coffee and added cream and sugar. I handed it to her as she came in the back door. "Good morning, Angel!" I announced.

"Good morning, Emma. She is a beautiful day!" It was the first time since my arrival that Angel had called my by my given name. She treated me to a huge smile.

"It's going to be a busy day," I told her. "But tomorrow everyone checks out, and we have no more guests scheduled until Wednesday."

We decided we each needed a day off. I intended to spend mine in Portland, attending to bills and other household matters, and having lunch with a friend. Angel opted for Monday, and I planned a Tuesday holiday. We agreed to resume normal duties on Wednesday morning.

The breakfast invasion came and went. Everyone was hurrying out to taste wine, enjoy the beautiful autumn sunshine, and see the wineries in full harvest mode. Following their chaotic exodus, I gathered my camera, notebook, and appropriate snacks into the car and drove south on Highway 99W to the Corvallis area, where I was expected at two wineries. My mood continued buoyant as I drove at a leisurely pace through the western Willamette Valley savoring the beauties of this autumn day.

In the vineyards visible from the highway, small tractors hauled their trailers of yellow plastic totes filled with black grapes as pickers in their blue work shirts labored in the fields bringing in the harvest. My mind burst with ideas for the book, to the point that I pulled to the highway's shoulder several times to scribble notes. Leaves were turning gold on the lower branches of the grapevines signaling the vineyards' impending dormancy. On the distant hillsides, groves of ancient, black-trunked oak trees and Douglas fir dotted the landscape, the former beginning to turn the dun brown of autumn. Tractors stirred up dust in the fields, creating a golden haze that enveloped the land, giving it a truly magical appearance. I had not seen a day so unutterably beautiful since my move back to Portland.

The interviews proceeded in a timely manner, and by three o'clock I was headed north again, my notebook filled with more information for the wine book. It was good to be back on track after so much of my time had been displaced in my imagination by the murder mystery unfolding in the valley.

Angel had departed by the time I arrived at the bed and breakfast, and I rushed to organize wine and snacks for the guests' five o'clock get-together. By this time, everyone knew each other. They greeted like long-lost friends, comparing notes on restaurants and wineries. Fortunately my presence as a hostess was unnecessary. I checked to make sure they had what they needed, then retired to the alcove to check telephone messages. As usual, there were a bunch of them.

I ticked them off, duly noting reservation requests and making notes to check back with the callers once I'd determined which prospective guests were new and which were returning. The fourth call was from Tiffany Maxell. "I need to see you," her voice moaned into the telephone receiver. "I have to talk to you *now*." Then she rang off. She had called mid-afternoon. "Now, what in the hell does she want?" I sputtered at the vile machine. I jotted down the remainder of the messages and then called her.

"What is it?" I asked, after she answered her cell phone and I identified myself.

"I *need* to talk with you." She sounded frightened.

"Can you tell me what this is about?"

"It's about my dad's murder."

"I'm not really in the loop on this one," I said. "You should talk to your mother."

"I *can't*!" she wailed. "I can't tell her any of this stuff. I've never been able to talk to her. Please. You're the only one who can help me."

"Tiffany, I frankly don't think I'm able to help you."

"You have to help. I have to talk to someone, and I can't think of anyone else."

I thought about that for a minute. "What about your stepmother?"

"Especially not her. She hates me." She started blubbering into the phone. "I know who killed my dad," she blubbered. "I'm so scared."

"You need to call the authorities," I said, sounding every bit the mother. "Call 9-1-1 and get someone from the sheriff's office to talk with you."

"I can't. I can't. I'm so scared."

"Where are you?"

"Almost home. I'm so scared. I'm so scared." Chanting, her voice sounded like a little girl's. A spoiled little girl's. More to the point, a very screwed-up brat who always needed to have her way. However, listening to her pleading, something inside me changed again—just an iota—just enough to cave in to her.

"Okay, when you get home, just stay where you are. I'll be

at your place as soon as I can." I told her it would be half an hour, maybe a little longer. Then I jotted down the directions. "You really need to call 9-1-1, because that's what I plan to do when I get there" I said in conclusion. But it was too late. She'd already disconnected the call.

The sun was just setting as I pulled onto the access road leading up the hill that led past Cougar Crossing Winery toward the Maxells' vineyards, home, and other properties. Evening light played over the vineyards and the day's golden glow had deepened and settled over the irregular rises of the hillsides. Once again, I drove slowly with the windows down, taking in the autumnal beauty and the indescribable loveliness of the landscape. What a gift, I told myself. I vaguely wondered how I could have left it for the city. But, when I played that old tape through to the end, I heard my own words echo in my head. "It has its down side, too."

In the dips and swales, long shadows produced the dark greens and purple hues that had found their way into Carolyn's paintings. I had not seen her since Monday. If Michael had attended the funeral, I had missed him as well. He was not at the reception. When I thought of Carolyn, I was filled with worry and fear. Whether she realized it or not, she was extremely fragile. I reminded myself that we would see each other tomorrow. No use to worry now.

My mind turned to Tiffany as I neared her house. She was as disquieting a soul as I'd ever encountered. Her neediness to an almost complete stranger was perhaps the most disconcerting aspect of her personality I'd encountered to date. Given her upbringing, one could expect her to be spoiled. Why not? She'd never had to think of anyone but herself, and everything she'd ever wanted had been handed to her.

It surprised me that she would not choose her mother to talk to about her father's death, or at the very least her brother. Unless she suspected him. I remembered how she'd cursed and screamed at him the night of Ted's death. Perhaps he was a viable suspect after all.

Dusk gathered, and I slowed to a crawl to locate the drive to Tiffany's house. It was there on the right, marked by a mailbox set in a stone column, just as she'd described. I turned in and drove between a vineyard and a hazelnut orchard to a small oak grove nestled on the hillside.

Her home clearly was not what I had expected because what I'd expected was garish and weird— a bit like its owner. Instead, before me stood an old and weathered log cabin with a broad, covered front porch and a new red metal roof. It was a cottage, really, a place I would have liked to call my own. Two large windows, one on either side of the door, and a porch decorated with sumptuous hanging flower baskets, faced a small lawn and a graveled area large enough for two vehicles. Native plants made up the bulk of the landscaping to the extent that I could see it in the fading light. Altogether a tasteful presentation—save for Tiffany's piss-on-you yellow Hummer, which was parked in front of the cabin.

I walked up onto the unlit porch and knocked on the door. No answer. I stood there feeling like a fool for taking her bait a second time. Still, I banged on the door again and then peeked in one of the windows. It was dark inside. I tried the door and it was unlocked, so I opened it and stepped into the cabin.

"Tiffany, it's Emma, I'm here." No answer. I stood just inside the door for a moment, closing it quietly. I stood long enough to let my eyes adjust to the near darkness. Inside it was eerily quiet. Tiffany was a very unquiet girl, and her home revealed that. I located the light switch inside the front door and flipped it. Two lamps came on in the living room.

The beautiful open living area, with a huge river rock fireplace at one end, was strewn with stuff—clothing, untidy heaps of newspapers and magazines, and a scattering of handbags and shoes left where they were dropped as their kinetic owner passed through the rooms. The dining table and countertop were covered in junk mail, a few dirty dishes, the handset of a telephone, and—of all things—underwear! On the counter adjacent the sink was an inhaler, the type used by asthmatics. Interesting.

"Tiffany?" I called again. Nothing. Not a sound, except the bells that suddenly began clanging inside my head. I realized I had stopped breathing, took a deep breath, and exhaled slowly.

I walked toward the kitchen island looking for a light switch, found one and turned it on, then gave an involuntary shriek. Bare feet protruded from behind the island near the sink. I almost had expected to find her passed out. I had not expected to find her dead, which she was. A hypodermic was stuck her thigh—an epi-pen, actually, very similar to the one Jane Webber carried. Tiffany's eyes and mouth were open; her lips and fingers a bluish hue. My brain registered overdose, but the epi-pen and inhaler suggested allergies or asthma.

She had fallen askew in a most unbecoming position, and I pulled down her skirt to the extent possible in order to cover her tight little butt. Once again, I was forced to observe that she was wearing the heinous thong underwear. I touched her leg with the back of my hand. The flesh was still warm, but not warm enough. She had died only a short while before my arrival, but she was dead beyond question, the eyes a blank, the spirit departed. I would not attempt to revive her. I cursed under my breath, then moved to her head and pondered her bluish pallor. Had she perhaps strangled on her own tongue? I walked outside to my car and dialed 9-1-1 on my cell phone.

Once assured that help was on the way, I went back inside. I looked around the living space again, slowly this time. Despite my grim surprise, I willed myself to remember everything. At the kitchen sink, I inspected the inhaler and another of the small pens without touching them. Maybe she wasn't shooting dope. Maybe the needle in her thigh was tied to a legitimate medical emergency.

With a kitchen towel, I gingerly opened the refrigerator. A couple small medicine bottles sat on an upper shelf. There were diet drinks and energy drinks, but no real food. Pathetic. A couple bottles of Stoli rested on their sides in the refrigerator's freezer. A fused glass plate sat among the detritus on the kitchen island. It was piled high with biscotti. I was so upset I almost ate one, but good sense prevailed. I had no right to touch anything in the house.

Still, I continued into the bedroom, tea towel in hand in case it was necessary to open something. I took my time and opened first one drawer in her chest and then a second. There I found what I'd been seeking—a small plastic bag of white powder. I didn't touch it. The bathroom cabinet contained several prescriptions—Xanax and Ambien were among the few I was familiar with, plus what appeared to be enough Vicodin to decommission a rhinoceros.

Satisfied, and perhaps just a little guilty, I returned to the veranda and settled onto the porch swing to await the authorities. Sitting there, I felt myself being swallowed into what felt like the heart of darkness. From all appearances, Tiffany's life had been a train wreck. But she had been young, and where there was youth were also the hopes and dreams that were part of that stage of life. Up until this day, she had been blessed with the ability to change, had she wished, and become what she was destined to become. Even given the drugs and alcohol, she could have turned it around.

Everything had been possible for her. And now, suddenly, it wasn't. I hadn't liked her particularly, but that didn't matter. I hadn't known her, much less understood her. The truth and the tragedy were her youth and her unrealized life. Hers was the needless death of someone who hadn't yet had the opportunity to learn who she was.

Sheriff's deputies arrived, and the paramedics, and within a few minutes the whole place was lit up and no fewer than six vehicles crowded the tiny parking area, including police from various locales. I got out to meet the first wave and walked with them inside to the body. Then I returned to the porch swing and waited for the inevitable questions, watching as even more vehicles came up the drive and pulled onto the lawn, or just parked themselves in the middle of the driveway. I didn't wait long.

Very shortly, a tall man of perhaps forty, with buzz-cut

blond hair and a deep tan joined me on the veranda. Doing the best I could, I recounted to Deputy Douglas Haymore how Tiffany had wanted to talk to me, had asked me over, and had told me on the telephone that she knew who killed her dad. No, there was no indication of who that might be. I hadn't gotten to her soon enough.

"When you discovered the body, did you touch it?" Haymore inquired. Yes, I'd touched her. No, I had not moved her, nor had I tried to revive her. No, I hadn't touched or moved anything in the house. I had called them immediately (or darn close to it).

"When you talked to her on the phone did it occur to you to have her call us?" Deputy Haymore sounded a bit sarcastic.

"I told her to call 9-1-1. She said she couldn't, she was scared. She got hysterical, so I told her to just wait. I got here as quickly as I could, figuring we could sort it out and call you guys if it was necessary."

Haymore shook his head in disbelief. "We could have prevented this," he said. "All she needed to do was call us."

"Well, you know that and I know that," I reasoned. "But if you'd ever talked to this woman you'd know she was flighty and temperamental and accustomed to doing things her way. Who knows what was going through her head when she called me. You would have just loved it if I'd called you out here for nothing."

We glared at each other. We both knew neither he nor anyone else would have responded to such a call just on hearsay. Meanwhile, the officials who had shown up to gawk came outside and got in their cars to return to their jurisdictions. The paramedics packed up and departed. A couple of sheriff's deputies stepped outside, nodded in our direction, then moved to the gravel where they lit cigarettes and talked quietly. A county van came up the driveway and parked on the lawn. A man and a woman got out and began removing cameras and other equipment from the rear and loading them into the well-lit premises.

I suddenly felt very tired, and for the first time in quite a while I also felt old. Haymore handed me his card and said I could go home. He reminded me not to talk about the circumstances of Tiffany's death and to call him if I remembered anything else, or thought of anything else, no matter how insignificant. I agreed. Then he looked at me again as if remembering something else. "Weren't you there last Friday night at the winery when they found Ted Maxell?"

"Unfortunately, yes, I was with the group who found him."

"We have two mysterious deaths, family members, out here within a week. How do you, a stranger, end up being at both of the scenes of death?"

"I have no idea." I sighed deeply. "When I came out here to do my work, this sort of thing was not in the contract."

Chapter 19

The first time I saw Carolyn she was seven months pregnant with her second child, Blaine. It had been the kind of blistering hot, sunny day we sometimes get briefly in May—that year it had occurred on Memorial Day weekend. Dwight and I had been invited to a picnic at the home of one of the wine country pioneers—most specifically, the Delaneys, of whom we were in awe. And, since we had recently moved out to the valley from Portland, we were eager to attend. We desperately wanted to bond with and be accepted by these people, the first generation of Oregon winemakers, who to us were bigger than life. It almost had seemed too much to ask that it would happen this quickly, this easily.

There were only a very few of us back then, and everyone was invited to every social occasion. Because there were so few of us, everyone came. Newcomers were assimilated quickly. In those days, divergent characters were able to put aside their petty differences for these events. We all hung together back then because we needed each other. It was necessary for survival.

The wine critics and experts of the day, most of them from California, had let it be known that we were crazy, that the grapes we were attempting to grow in the Willamette Valley would never produce good wines because, these wise men opined, it was too cold this far north to ripen wine grapes.

We knew they were wrong, but without mature vineyards, greater winemaking expertise, and several good vintages in the bag, it was not something we could prove. We came together to socialize, but more important, we came together to share ideas and techniques and taste each others' little triumphs and mistakes. In effect, we had to circle the wagons against those naysayers in order to keep moving forward. Lying in a cozy bed these many years later, I felt like it was an age ago, a different lifetime. For all practical purposes, it was. I just wasn't ready to feel that old yet.

More than the social occasion of that long ago day, I was in awe of Carolyn. She was so striking, so confident, as she strode across the lawn. Even her large belly and her four-year-old son Archie, clinging to her skirt as she walked, did not diminish her grandeur. She wore a billowing floral sundress constructed in the empire style. It hit her mid-calf and it flowed out behind her like a sail when she walked, sometimes obscuring Archie, who squealed and giggled as the folds engulfed him. Her broad-brimmed straw hat had flowers in the band. In one hand she clutched a bouquet of wilted dandelions—a gift from Archie—and in the other was a glass of white wine. Her thick blonde hair was cropped short. She wore a rakish expression.

Carolyn doubtless was uncomfortable in the heat—but if she was, she didn't show it. Everything about her, save her naughty grin, radiated serenity. In her presence, I felt that I may have walked onto the set of "The Great Gatsby"—at least I knew how Jay Gatsby must have felt the first time he set eyes on Daisy. Carolyn's presence dominated the event for me, and made it shine with a deep and priceless luster. I had to know that woman. I wanted to *be* that woman. Whatever she had—that magical *It*—I had to have as well.

We did not become friends that day. When we were introduced, Carolyn said hello and I seized her hand in mine and shook it. It was cool and soft. She did not return the grip, but nodded and said something appropriate and sincerely welcoming, and then she moved on. I learned at a later time that Southern ladies do not grasp when shaking hands. Years after that, when she was Stella and I was Ruby, we even laughed about it. But on that day, in my blue jeans and polo shirt, I felt as if I'd fallen off a turnip truck.

Winston poked his wet nose in my face. It was time to get going, play hostess at the breakfast table, and delight those who were conscious with my vast knowledge of wine country or a bit of salacious (albeit old) gossip. To date, each morning I'd come up with some bit of information, some funny little anecdote about one of us back then that managed to amuse. I doubted it was anything I could use in my own book. But it was interesting to see how those memories arose from the depths of my mind—long forgotten stories, some of them best left long forgotten.

Stella, Ruby and Viola. Melody, as Viola, was the least

dangerous of the three of us, simply because she was a normal drinker. She would sip her one or two glasses of wine and be designated driver on those nights when the three of us dined in Portland and then raised hell in some wine bar or other before coming back to the sticks. It certainly had seemed funny then.

Now the memories curdled, for this was the day that I was to visit Carolyn at Serenity Estate. As I had done in the past, she now was paying her dues for those nights we had found so amusing. For alcohol, we are told, is a subtle foe—all good times and laughter, until the day it quits working and fun is no longer part of the equation. It is replaced by terror and self-loathing so great that only a drink or a drug will quiet the screaming in your brain. On that day you learn that one drink is too many and a thousand are not enough.

Maybe Carolyn would be okay, I told myself as I crawled out of bed. Remembering her yellow complexion, I feared otherwise.

Angel was already working, of course, stern of expression, head down. She was vigorously kneading a ball of dough. She looked up when I entered the kitchen.

"You know," I said, reading the expression in her eyes.

"Yes, I know senora. Because Zephyr knows through Axel. He called her after he learned. It is a terrible thing."

"I found her."

"Yes, senora."

"At least we know Axel didn't kill his sister. He was with his mother, right?"

"Si." Angel's kneading had crossed the proverbial Rubicon

and declared war. She now was beating the shit out of the dough that occupied her attentions.

"And you're angry."

Angel momentarily ceased punishing the dough and looked at me. "These people, they are crazy. They exhaust me." She flung her hands upward and loose dough bits and flour flew around her head before landing on the floor where Winston quickly gobbled them up. "They have everything. Still they are not happy. They have to kill each other? They kill themselves? What is wrong with them?" She gathered the dough into a ball and soundly slapped it.

"I wish I knew," I said. "I wish I knew."

Breakfast was uneventful. I was filled with a growing apprehension as mid-day drew closer. By shortly after eleven the guests were checked out. I called Michael. He was going to visit Carolyn at noon and would leave about two, he told me. I went outside and picked a large bouquet of sunflowers to take to Carolyn. I picked tomatoes. Winston rolled in the dirt and kicked his legs in unbridled Schnauzer joy. With no cookies to bake for guests, no breakfasts to prep for the following morning, Angel went home early.

"Remember, you're off tomorrow," I told her. "I'll see you Tuesday." She waved as the old Honda putted down the drive. I wondered what she and the other workers did to keep money coming in during the slow season when work at places like hotels, bed-and-breakfast inns, and wineries was sporadic at best. I'd have to ask her when I saw her again.

Inside, I changed out of my hostess garb and into the more familiar jeans and a pullover, then took Winston for a walk. We followed the road that passed the Westerly and hiked uphill past vineyard after vineyard. All the land that had been up for grabs in the old days when outsiders believed we couldn't make wine here was now planted to a variety of grapes—predominantly pinot noir, but also pinot gris, chardonnay, riesling and a smattering of other, less familiar varieties. And land costs continued to rise. My former husband had to be laughing all the way to the bank.

However, my mind was not on grape varieties and escalating land prices. Over and over again I relived finding Tiffany dead in her kitchen. I thought about the walls she'd built around herself with drugs and alcohol. And I thought about Carolyn and how she'd done the same thing. I was eager to see her, but also dreaded our meeting.

Why is it so damned hard just to be honest with those we love? Is it the way people my age were raised? Or was it just the dynamics of our particular families? That morning I would rather have had my fingernails pulled out than go to see Carolyn and tell her face-to-face how I felt about her—the good and the bad.

I had plenty to say, of course. She had done me wrong. She had abandoned me several years ago when I needed her. She had been afraid—of me, of my situation. She wouldn't return my phone calls because I no longer was her drinking buddy. That had hurt me deeply, even as I realized she had behaved in the way she had out of fear. She had not wanted to look me in the eye and see herself. Her behavior had been rotten and she knew it. I'd been hurt, but we'd never talked about it. She, like so many other friends from my past, had simply disappeared. She had mattered more than the others.

And I had let her—them—go. That was my part. I'd

expected my crowd to rally around me, and on my terms. Not all of them did. Did I ask them? Did I talk to them? Did I do everything I could to make certain the friendships remained close?

Regrettably, I didn't. I had retreated, distrustful, hurt, and ashamed. I'd walked around that elephant that lives in so many of our homes, never spoken about but always there. While it is true I'd gotten sober, I had still behaved like I always did—like it was all about me for some reason. It had taken me a very long while to unlearn old behavior and embrace the new. I had moved to Portland and left my old life behind. And then, I had told myself it was too late. Better to just start over.

Poor me! I was just as ego-driven as ever. But I did behave a *little* better. Most of the time. I thought back to my Thursday night behavior with Dwight. That was *not* an example of shining behavior. The move, the disappearance, I now realized, was just another side of my inflated ego—the ongoing story about myself wherein I was a legend in my own mind, impossibly good or impossibly bad, given the time of day. It was two sides of the same character defect.

When I looked back over those years—from the day we moved to wine country as a family until the day I left, alone—I wondered if all those things I thought about now had indeed happened. Maybe I had imagined them—not the stories I wrote about the industry, but the people I thought would be there forever. Maybe the bonds had just existed in my mind. My brain could do that to me.

Then I had agreed to write the book and to come out here to live for six weeks. That, for better or worse, had reawakened me to the past. There was much that I had simply left behind when I moved to Portland. Now here it was in front of me again. This time I would deal with it.

For the thousandth time I told myself, "It's not *all* about *you*!" Then I went to see my friend.

I pulled into the parking lot at Serenity Estate in glorious sunshine. The burning bush shrubs, so little when I'd been in residence there seven years before, now towered as tall as I. Their leaves flamed red in the sunshine, an audacious display. As I walked across the parking lot I saw Michael leaving the women's residence hall. He walked with his hands in his pockets, head down. I waited at the edge of the parking lot watching him walk toward me, watching the families sitting in lawn chairs visiting while small children ran across the lawn.

"Hi Michael."

He looked up. "Oh, hi Emma. How's it going?"

"I'm here right on time. How's Carolyn?"

"I guess she's OK. See for yourself. It's a little awkward with us. She's so different. Withdrawn, subdued. I don't know. At least she wasn't yelling and calling me names. Her color is terrible."

"Yeah, well, it takes some time for that to go away. Her liver needs to heal."

"Well, you girls have a nice visit. I need a drink."

I laughed at his gallows humor. "So do I," I quipped. "I've been dreading this all week."

He just smiled at me, obviously not wishing to talk any more. He unlocked his Mercedes, got in, and backed out of the parking slot. I sucked up and walked toward the reception area from which he'd come.

Inside the residence hall, I signed the requisite confidentiality forms and opened my handbag to the nice lady who served as greeter. Someone tapped me on the shoulder and I turned. "Emma? Is it you?" It was Rhonda, the day nurse, dispenser of medications, and collector of urine specimens when I was there.

"Oh my God! Rhonda. You're still here!" I hugged her.

"Of course I'm here. I'll be here till I die. Are you checking in?" she joked.

"Yeah, I missed the place so much I staged a relapse. No, truly, I have a friend here. Carolyn Delaney."

"Oh, yeah, Carolyn." Rhonda's face darkened. "She's pretty sick."

"I knew that just from looking at her."

"She'll probably tell you more about it when she's ready," said Rhonda. Obviously she couldn't tell me anything. Indeed, she'd already said too much.

Having performed the necessary check-in duties, I headed to the deck off the women's residential unit where I was told I'd find Carolyn. She was sprawled in an Adirondack chair smoking a cigarette when I approached her. A bunch of fat, middle-aged males were attempting to play volleyball on the lawn not far from us. I could tell from her expression that she was not impressed with their displays of manliness. Most of them were shirtless. It was not a pretty sight. Carolyn, however, looked clean, rested—a far cry from a week ago. She wore a short-sleeved shirt and her arms, long and thin, were covered by crepe-like skin that hung loosely from her bones.

Her complexion was an alarming shade of grayish-yellow. She looked old.

"Hey, y'all!" I greeted her.

"Hey, y'all, back," she said and smiled. I walked over and hugged her, then pulled up a deck chair next to hers. We both watched the fat boys struggling in the sunshine. They were sweaty and greasy.

"You look pretty comfortable," I said.

"It's not too bad," she said noncommittally. "I probably wouldn't come here for a vacation, but I've been treated worse."

We looked at the grounds for a while. "Do you want anything?" she asked. "Cup of tea? Soda?"

"I'm fine, thanks."

The fat boys called it quits and walked past our deck toward the men's residence hall. They looked hopefully at the deck, no doubt anticipating a glimpse or two of nubile females. Alas, the nubile ones were somewhere else. It was just us two old broads. We waved at them and smiled. They waved back and sighed.

"Thank God," I said under my breath, grateful their gyrations had ended.

"We've got some catching up to do," said Carolyn.

"Yeah, I was hoping we could do that under better circumstances, but this will have to work I guess."

"I guess," she said. "You probably know I'm not long for this world."

"I don't know much of anything, Carolyn. I know you're yellow and that's usually not a good sign. But I've seen yellow people here before. The liver has amazing regenerative powers and...."

"Mine's shot," she interrupted. She never was one to mince words. "At least that's the prognosis this week. They're sending me up to Pill Hill in a couple days for further tests. If I qualify, they'll put me on the list for a liver transplant. That could take years, and I haven't got years."

I felt like I'd been socked in the gut.

"Not long ago I wanted to die," she continued. "Now I'm not so sure."

"What changed?"

"Being here. Feeling the hope. I don't believe that higher power shit for a second, and I sure as hell don't want to go to AA meetings when I get out of here. But there's hope. People are good here. They're good to me. It's different than anything I've ever experienced. I haven't had a drink for seven fucking days, Emma. Do you know what that means? That's huge!"

I knew what that meant, and it *was* huge. "You're doing great, Carolyn. Your liver will come back. Just be kind to the poor little thing."

"Oh, honey, it's big and it's hard. I've been really bad to it. And I'm scared. But shit, I've been getting some sleep and eating good food, and even ole Michael didn't look too bad today." She laughed and I laughed with her.

"He's got his faults," I said. "But I've seen worse."

"Emma, I've been listening this time. Why wouldn't I ever listen?"

"It's what we do Carolyn. It's part of the disease. You're saying good things. I'm so happy for you."

"Well, don't get too excited. I'll probably get sick of it and leave. I almost left yesterday when I got mad at one of those counselors. But where would I go? There's nowhere to go back to."

"Don't even think about leaving. Give it a chance to work. Keep an open mind and focus on today. And keep listening; some of what you hear might actually sink in."

She laughed again. She was looking her mortality in the eye and laughing. Then she went down a completely different path. "You know, I don't even know why you're out here or what you're doing or anything, I've had my head up my butt for so long. Michael said you came over to the house last Sunday, and I don't remember any of that."

So I brought her up to speed. The book, the gig at Melody and Dan's place while they were in the South Pacific, Ted Maxell's murder, and the mysterious business of Tiffany Maxell's death. I told her how she and I had set a lunch date, but I knew she was drunk, and about finding her passed out in the house. "You damn near died," I concluded.

"And you just came out here on a busman's holiday and look at all the trouble that's come up." She tsk-tsked and shook her head. "You think you're going to solve a murder mystery?"

"I'm just following the thread to see where it goes," I said. "It's so incestuous out here. I understand how it is, or at least how it used to be. Law enforcement doesn't know this culture. They may be very good at their jobs, but they are not in synch with us. We're like a big, extended, dysfunctional family. We know our dysfunctions and they don't. And I just know the murderer is somebody in the industry, horrible as that seems. It's somebody you probably see at the grocery store."

"Well, you're good at this stuff," she said, alluding to some of my adventures from years ago. "Ted Maxell was a dirty bastard, and any number of us would have loved to see him go. But it does shed an ill light on us all, doesn't it. Tell me more."

I told her every detail I could think of. We talked for two hours, and it was so good. By the end of our time together, I felt I had my friend back. She wasn't totally sharp, but I saw glimpses of the old Carolyn, the irreverent Carolyn, the Carolyn who never missed a beat.

"I wish I was out of here so I could help you solve the mystery," she told me as I readied to leave.

"Now that we can talk on the phone, I can keep you up to speed on what is happening. And I'll be back next Sunday, of course."

Carolyn walked me to the parking lot, and at my car we hugged just like in the old days. "Yo, Stella!" a woman called to her as a pack of walkers passed us. She waved at them and turned back toward the residence hall as I climbed into my car. I left Serenity Estate happy that afternoon. I believed in my heart of hearts that Carolyn would embrace recovery and live a long and happy life. Just seeing her today had seemed like a miracle to me, but I had seen miracles before. Anything was possible.

Chapter 20

Back at the farm, I walked Winston around the yard, replaced a burned out light on the back porch, then went inside and picked through leftovers in the refrigerator. I tried to read, but I couldn't concentrate. Nothing of interest was on television, as usual. It was too early to go to bed. I wandered into the dining room and perused the liquor cart. It was all so very English, in keeping with Melody's anglophilia, right down to the proper metal seltzer bottle and tiny ice bucket. Melody and Dan had good taste in cognac, too. A bottle of my favorite VSOP sat there in plain sight. It was half empty, or half full, depending upon your point of view.

I was all the things a drunk isn't supposed to be—hungry, angry, lonely, and tired. One drink. I almost could feel the instant relief, the little shudder of pleasure that always accompanied that first drink when it hit my system. It was like nothing else. I told myself that one drink would help me sleep, and that would be the end of it. And no one would be the wiser. It was a dangerous lie.

The telephone rang and I answered. It was Melody calling from Australia. "We're in Melbourne," she chirped. "This is just such a great trip. The people are wonderful."

"How's the food?" I asked her, remembering that I'd not eaten a proper dinner.

"Superb! Way better than I expected. Very fresh, smart presentations. Lovely fish—and lamb, of course. What's happening there? Have you figured out who killed Ted?"

"No, they still think Axel did it. But at least he's out on bail." And then I told her about Tiffany. There was a long silence at the other end.

"She died of an overdose?" Melody finally asked.

"I don't know. The needle in her leg looked like Jane Webber's epi-pen, and she had some sort of inhaler thingy on the counter. She had some serious medicine in the refrigerator as well. Maybe she was allergic to something."

"You *looked* in the refrigerator?"

"I used a tea towel," I confessed. "I couldn't help myself."

"You're just as bad as you ever were," Melody said, and then recanted. "Well, not *quite* as bad."

Well, maybe I was. "I also looked in her medicine cabinet," I allowed.

"Emma, no."

"Yes."

"Well, tell me."

"Lots of drugs. Lots of prescription drugs. If she mixed those up, she could have overdosed. And then there was the stuff in her drawer."

"What was *that*?"

"Contraband of some sort. White stuff in a plastic bag. I didn't touch it."

"That explains why she was batshit crazy!" Melody exclaimed. Given a bit of excitement, she could lapse into her old West Texas expressions in a heartbeat.

"That's one way to look at it," I said. "Other than those few little things, it couldn't be better. Business is booming, Winston is well, and we've bonded." I detailed the goings-on regarding the Westerly. Thanks to a good crew, and especially Angel, things were humming along. We delved a little deeper into their trip, then got back to the nitty-gritty of local doings.

"Do you know any of these people, Melody—the Maxells? Some of the other new people since I've been gone?"

"I have met the Maxells at a couple of large events," Melody told me. "The wife is a gold digger, and—if you can believe this—a former stripper. She does the dumb blonde bit, and she's not an educated person, but she is cunning. The ex-wife, Pamela is around as well, and has her own vineyard about three miles from Cougar Crossing. She loves to stick it to Tara whenever they run into each other in public."

That sounded extremely pleasant for all concerned.

"I interviewed Pamela a few days ago," I said. I filled Melody in on what Pamela had told me about her venture, the family, her life in general.

"I know very little about her" Melody said, "except that the Portland arts scene is better for her being here. In fact, I doubt it would survive without her." She chuckled. "She loves to look good. I never pictured her for the hearth and home sort of mom."

"That didn't stop her from springing Axel from jail at first opportunity."

"It would look bad, in her eyes, to have him in jail. Besides, he didn't kill Ted. Given what little I know of him, he just didn't have it in him. He just wanted out."

"Killing Ted would have accomplished that."

"He did have motive, but not enough anger to jeopardize having a life with Zephyr. She has been his saving grace.

"The daughter, though. That's another matter. Ted had some weird control thing going on with Tiffany. She was completely under his thumb. He seemed to want her around him at the winery all the time, and everyone who knew them said he was berating her all the time. She worked there, but it's up to speculation what she actually did, since he had experts to do all the important stuff. The point is, she never got away from the man, ever. She was glued to him. Axel was under his thumb, too, and put up with all kinds of verbal abuse. But at least he went away to college."

"Well, Tiffany couldn't have killed him if she was going to tell me who did."

"Don't be so sure. There is no telling what she was going to tell you," said Melody. "The woman is...was...a congenital liar. Maybe she did the deed and then killed herself out of misplaced remorse or something."

I mulled that for a moment, then asked, "Did Tiffany have a history of drug use?"

"I don't know, but then why would I? Rumors of her erratic behavior preceded her everywhere she went. She definitely had a reputation that made her stand out from her crowd of peers. She behaved desperately at times, drug-related or not.

She seemed to most of us, on the outside at least, to be more pathetic than dangerous."

"I wonder if she was strong enough to kill him."

"Who? Tiffany? How strong do you have to be to push a drunken fat man over a rail? But I don't think she would have. Toward him was…well, I'm not sure how to say this. She was more like a slave than a daughter. She groveled to him when I saw them at events, almost like she was afraid of him. It was creepy."

"Sometimes slaves revolt," I said, then added, "Pamela didn't care enough. At least she gave a convincing performance."

"Killing someone would be bad form," said Melody. "I don't think she'd do it, although I am sure that at times she wanted to. She could have hired someone, I guess."

"And what about Tara?"

"Perhaps, if there was a good enough reason. But half the county had reason to want this guy gone," Melody reminded me.

"Find the motive and you find the killer. Motive, means, opportunity. There are four potential killers just among the family—only now one of them is dead, of course."

With that we changed the subject. I gave Melody an update on Carolyn, answered a couple questions, and we disconnected.

No sooner than I had hung up, the telephone rang again. This time it was Rob. "Did you hear that Tiffany's dead?"

"Rob, duh. I was there. I found her. Do you suppose that makes me a suspect?"

"Not unless you have a good motive. Maybe you've been

holding out on me. Were you the one giving her father the blow job?"

I snorted. Then I gave him the details of finding Tiffany, including the inhaler. I did not mention my other snooping; he was just a bit too close to the sheriff's deputies for me to feel comfortable sharing that information. Plus, I am not particularly proud of my weaknesses in that arena. "It appears the 'drug paraphernalia' I thought I had discovered may have had more to do with allergies. So, alas, no helpful information," I concluded.

Rob was silent for a moment as he processed the update. "Is there a pattern here?" he asked finally.

"Perhaps the elimination of a family," I said. "Maybe the rest of the tribe ought to apply for police protection. Or leave town for a while."

"John Law is keeping them on a short leash. They're keeping an eye on everyone. Axel may be out of jail, but he's basically under house arrest. He and Zephyr were dining at Pamela's Saturday night. They were still at the table when the deputies arrived to break the news. Axel is off the hook on this one."

That was good news for Axel.

"What about Tara?" I asked.

"What about her?"

"Would she have a motive?"

"Good question. She didn't come back to the dinner table that night. She was unaccounted for, but she's also pregnant. The boys found her at home in bed when they went up there to tell her about Ted's death."

"She had plenty of time to go home and get settled," I said.

"That's true," said Rob. "But what about a motive? A lot of people had no use for Ted Maxell—people he never would have invited to a social event."

"Given the crowd at the winery the night Ted was killed, any number of people had access to the winery. This time of year everybody has their doors open. People are coming and going—and for the most part, no one pays too much attention. It would be easy for someone to slip in and wait."

I remembered the days when I'd been around StoneGate during harvest. Sometimes people just showed up to gawk. If someone had entered the winery and hidden, knowing—or suspecting—Ted had a tryst, it would have been easy. There was no end of places to hide and watch and wait.

For that matter, the winery would be a good place to have a tryst that time of night—one need only plan it around punch-down. The crush workers would be exhausted, and as far from the workplace as possible, except for those who needed to show up for the ten o'clock chore. As for the tryst, the possibility of a guest stumbling into the tank room by accident most likely would only add to Ted's thrill.

"I know next to nothing about Tara—or Tiffany, for that matter," Rob said. "And neither do the authorities. Until we have more information, it's hard to even guess what might have happened."

"I'm talking to people on a daily basis, as are you," I reminded him. "More information of some sort will turn up. Even with all the changes in the last few years, it's not that large a community."

"As soon as there's an autopsy report on Tiffany, I'll give you a call," he said.

We ended our conversation. I went to the kitchen and fixed a plate of fruit and cheese, brewed a cup of chamomile tea, and gave Winston a biscuit. We then retired to my suite just in time for the ten o'clock news.

After getting us through the icky national and international stuff, the station treated viewers to a byte about Tiffany's death, including a snapshot of what appeared to be a very pretty and innocent young woman. It was followed by footage of Ted's funeral—caves, people, reception, garish mansion— accompanied by drivel about Ted's contributions (!) to the Oregon wine industry and the controversies that had plagued him regarding land use in Yamhill County.

The latter was interesting in that, to me at least, it provided a couple bits of new information. A group called Water Watch and 1000 Friends of Oregon both were suing Ted because he'd wanted to build a big resort development on some property that had been protected as farm land—at least until Ballot Measure 37 had been passed. What about the eco-terrorists, I thought. That was a group of potential killers I'd never even considered, but what would *they* want with Tiffany? Nothing occurred to me. The anchor concluded by reminding us that Ted's death was being investigated as a homicide, but that no further information was available on Tiffany's death pending an autopsy.

Still very wide awake, I pulled my journal out of the desk drawer, crawled back into bed and began writing. Details emerged from the previous days that enabled me to create a page for each player in the local drama in which I had become a player. Flesh and blood characters emerged, each with different characteristics, backgrounds and desires. There were no patterns of which I was aware, but I found great satisfaction in creating a tangible tool with reference points, and in gossiping about them, even if just to myself. It seemed like a good way to proceed, and was entertaining. I managed to fill several pages before retiring.

I jerked awake to the sound of a deep-throated and very menacing growl from Winston. The darkness was nearly total. I realized that in addition to no moonlight, there was no light from the outdoor fixtures that normally provided a bit of ambient brightness in my room. I sat up in bed, and Winston growled again, this time with considerably more conviction. Not good. I crept from the bed to the window that overlooked the back entrance. From that vantage, I ascertained that the back porch light was indeed not lit. I had just replaced the bulb earlier that evening. The lights along the walks were out as well, including the little solar garden lights near the Chicken House. How in the hell could all those lights have gone out, and why?

No guests were in attendance. Both the Chicken House and the distant Carriage House were in total darkness. And here was I, completely alone except for a dog.

I stood motionless, carefully and methodically taking in those sections of the grounds visible from my window, hoping to catch a sign of something, hoping to hear whatever it was that was causing Winston to be on alert. He heard something inaudible to human ears, and exploded in a staccato of barking. I thought I detected movement reflected in my car's side window. If I was correct in my observation, person or persons unknown were lurking very near or at the back door. The clock on the night stand registered three twenty-three a.m.

In the darkness I pulled a sweater over my head, tucked my nightshirt into my jeans, and slipped into some clogs. Then I wondered, now what? Call 9-1-1 again? I wasn't certain enough that there was cause for alarm. It could be an animal prowling for food, a coyote or a raccoon. Bears were not unknown this near the forest. Someone had even spotted a cougar out here a year or so ago. I'd read about it in the newspaper. Even so, I was sufficiently alarmed that the fight-flight mechanisms had kicked in. Hyper-alert, I scanned the dark room for some sort of protection. No sabers or croquet mallets were in evidence, so I crept into the bathroom and grabbed the toilet plunger. It would keep a varmint at bay.

Winston growled again, and walked quietly to the stairway door. I just wanted him to shut up so I could hear what was going on out there! I grabbed him by the collar and quietly opened the door. Hearing nothing, I let him loose and he trotted down the stairs, grumbling under his breath. I tiptoed down the stairs behind him and paused at the bottom. Nothing was stirring in the kitchen—yet.

Winston was silhouetted at the slider that opened to the deck at the back of the house. His attention was riveted the far corner of the deck, where a cluster of huge ceramic planters in graduated sizes were grouped, filled with the appropriate late summer flora. Gripping my weapon, I advanced to the slider, quietly unlocked it, and slid the door open.

Before I could grab his collar, Winston burst from the doorway in an explosion of territorial fury. He barked and jumped at the pots in that comical straight-from-the-ground leap so typical of Schnauzers. The foliage in several of the pots moved vigorously, and one of the narrower of the tall planters careened onto its side and split open with a crash. Then suddenly, the rapid motion of a dark-clad figure leapt from behind the pots and ran toward the deck stairs. It definitely was not a bear. Winston leapt, and I heard a human scream of pain as the dog's teeth connected to some part of the running figure's anatomy.

The figure stumbled to one knee, dragging Winston who was determinedly hanging on to his or her trouser leg. I raced toward the melee, flailing the toilet plunger over my head. A loud roar seemed to emanate unbidden from inside me. I swung my arm and the toilet plunger connected with the interloper's head. Another bellow from the intruder convinced me it was a man. He fell to his knees. I screamed at him again, and began beating his back with the plunger as he crawled across the deck. Winston had released the pant leg and bit him solidly in the rear. The man yowled piteously.

I ceased my beating, grabbed the dog, and pulled him back. The man, I could see now, wore a dark, hooded sweatshirt. A nylon stocking obscured his facial features. He stood and began backing away. I advanced toward him, dog at my left hand, toilet plunger moving menacingly in my right. He held his hands up, palms toward me, and continued backing across the deck.

"You get the hell out of here, and don't come back," I told him. My voice sounded cold, completely clear, and even. "I've got a gun inside, and next time I'll use it." He turned and ran silently toward the driveway. I pulled Winston in through the slider, closed and locked it, and collapsed into the nearest chair.

Chapter 21

I sat at the kitchen table, Winston panting at my feet, for what seemed like a long time. But when I looked at the wall clock it registered three-thirty. Only seven minutes had passed since I'd left my bed. My heart calmed and ceased its noisy pounding; Winston's panting ended, and he lay down and rested his head on my feet. Silence enveloped us. Since Winston had settled, I was fairly certain nobody was lurking outside.

After waiting another five minutes, I walked into the alcove and dialed 9-1-1. The dispatcher wanted to know if the prowler had been armed. "I don't know, and now he's gone," I groused. "Could you please just send someone over here before he comes back with a weapon?"

I slammed the phone down. "Dammit all to hell!" I yelled at nobody in particular. At least I had clothes on. Fifteen minutes later, a sheriff's deputy pulled into the driveway at the back of the house. I walked out on the deck to greet her.

She introduced herself as Emily Vargas and we shook hands. Her grip was solid and sure. I ushered her into the kitchen.

"Tell me what happened," she said, and pulled out a notebook.

I started at the beginning with Winston's alert, and concluded with the perp limping off into the darkness.

"Can you describe him?" she asked. "Was he tall, short?"

I thought about the dark figure moving through the maze of plants, pottery, and the attacking dog. He'd been hunched over. "I don't know," I said finally. It felt ridiculous to be so uncertain. "He could have been anything. It was dark, he was hunched over running, and on his hands and knees when I was hitting him. He seemed huge. His presence was overwhelming."

"It'll come back to you," she assured me, but I wasn't convinced it would.

Next, we walked out onto the deck. Deputy Vargas unsheathed her flashlight and surveyed the damage. The porch light was broken in its socket. A shiver ran through me. This was not good news.

"I changed that light last night," I told her, as if it made a difference. Then she aimed her flashlight at the shattered planter.

Down in the bushes near the house, Deputy Vargas located footprints. She placed a tape measure next to them and photographed the scene with a digital camera. Then she produced a can of spray from her vehicle and dispensed the spray in several coats over the footprints. "Who else is around here?" she asked me as she stood upright.

"Nobody right now. We won't have any guests until

Wednesday." She taped off the area containing the footprints, as well as most of the deck. "I'll send someone out in the morning when it's light," she said. "If anything else happens, give us a call." And she was gone.

Winston and I eventually returned to bed and managed to get a couple hours' sleep. It was not easy getting back to sleep, however. I did not want to think about somebody coming after me, but the broken porch light had alarmed me. Hopefully the intruder was some low-life meth addict looking to steal a computer, and not a serial killer on the loose—not that the two were mutually exclusive. The idea of this frightening event being related to Tiffany's death was not something I wanted to contemplate, either.

I told myself that my fear was a far-fetched notion borne out of a wild imagination and not enough sleep. There would be a simple and acceptable answer to all this, something that precluded anyone wishing harm to my goddess-like person. On the other hand, it had been in the middle of a room full of people that the drunk, or otherwise indisposed, Tiffany Maxell had first announced to me, "I know who killed my father." If the murderer had heard her, I could pose a threat to him or her. And if this event was related to the murders, it appeared the killer was male.

I awakened to beautiful sunshine and a cold, wet, dog nose in my face. It was after eight and I jerked myself awake. All the horrors of the previous night came back to me. Had I dreamed it? I went to the window overlooking the deck. The tall planter was definitely broken, with dirt, plant parts, and shards of pottery strewn across a section of the deck. And then there was the ominous yellow tape in the flowerbeds below the deck.

There were no guests to feed, nobody to talk to but Winston. I remembered Angel had the day off. What a day to be alone. Winston and I ambled downstairs and I let him out to pee. He snuffled around the scene of the crime, then trotted out onto the back parking area, where he snuffled some more before heading into the bushes for privacy.

Just as I was settling myself at the table with a bowl of granola and the newspaper, a sheriff's car pulled up near the deck. Still in my bathrobe, I looked like the wrath of God, but there was nothing to be done about it. They both came—deputies Haymore and Jeffers, who remembered me from the night Ted died. It was hard to believe that barely a week had passed since that soiree-gone-sour at Cougar Crossing. I poured them coffee and repeated my tale of what had happened in the early morning hours.

"What did the prowler look like?" Haymore asked.

"I don't know. He had something over his face, and he was wearing a hoodie."

"How tall was he?"

I still was unable to answer that one. "I don't know," I admitted. "To me he looked huge."

"Did you think to call 9-1-1?" Haymore demanded.

"Well, I did...."

"No, I mean *before* you went out on the deck and endangered yourself."

"What, and have a big fat argument with the dispatcher about if someone was really there and was he armed?" Then I started to cry. It made me so mad to be crying in front of strange men that I cried even harder. The deputies looked away from me, uncomfortable. "They're hopeless," I whimpered. "And I was scared. I thought it might have been an animal. Then Winston got loose and attacked him." I sucked in a huge gulp of air and tried to quit blubbering. "It all happened so fast."

"Then what did you do?"

"I ran outside and hit him."

"You hit him? With your fist?"

"No, I hit him with a toilet plunger. Like I told Deputy Vargas. Why are you asking me all this stuff again? Don't you read the reports?"

"You whacked this guy who could have had a gun with a bathroom plunger?" Haymore sounded incredulous.

"It's the only thing I had," I explained. "I was afraid he'd hurt Winston."

"How do you know it was a he?"

"He yelled when Winston bit him."

"Then what happened?"

"Then I hit him some more, and Winston bit him again and he crawled across the deck ran off."

"God help me," the deputy muttered. "And then, by any chance, did it occur to you to dial 9-1-1?"

"Well, of course I did," I snapped, then resumed blubbering again.

"I understand," he said, the anger finally leaving his voice. "Now, if you don't mind, we've got a few more questions to ask you."

I took a couple of deep breaths. "Do you think this has anything to do with Tiffany's murder?"

"Who says it's murder?" Jeffers demanded.

"Is it?"

"Yes, I'm afraid it is."

"Just so we're clear, I need to know did you touch or remove anything from Tiffany Maxell's house Saturday night?" asked Deputy Haymore

"No," I replied. Discreet snooping didn't count. I really hadn't touched anything except Tiffany's leg to make certain she was beyond human help. I'd just looked a bit more than I should have.

"Did you know she had allergies?"

"No I didn't. I saw the inhaler, but basically I know nothing about Tiffany other than what I have observed the couple of times we've had reason to be together." Just answer the question, I told myself

"And what were those times."

I recounted how she had picked me up for the interview with Ted Maxell that didn't happen the previous week, and how I'd seen her at the Cougar Crossing dinner the night of Ted's death. "She didn't even speak to me then," I said.

"And why was that, do you think?"

"It was nothing really. She was angry because she doesn't—didn't—like to be told what to do." I told them of the cigarette butt incident, and then added, "In my opinion, Tiffany Maxell was a spoiled brat with a drinking problem. That is based on a three face-to-face meetings with her. I came here knowing nothing about her, and I still don't. We really didn't have any use for each other."

The men were silent. Deputy Jeffers scribbled in his book.

Then he looked at me. "Tell us again about those phone calls."

"Last Monday she called here and left a message for me about the funeral. I couldn't have been more surprised, frankly. Then on Tuesday morning she called again, and we talked briefly. She said she had something important to tell me, and she wanted me to be at the funeral."

"Did she say what it was about?"

"No. She said she couldn't talk, and hung up."

"Did you have any idea why she wanted to talk to you?"

"I asked her why she wanted to talk to me because she obviously didn't like me. She said she thought she could trust me, or something to that effect. It was pretty odd."

"Why do you think she said that?" This from Haymore.

"I have no idea. I thought she was nuts."

"And when did you see her again?"

"It was after the funeral, up at the Maxell house. She didn't look well. She came down the staircase, fell into me, and said she knew who killed her father. She was so drunk she couldn't walk, so I just wrote her off. Then she called me again on Saturday. I was just returning from some interviews down the valley. She said she was scared and that she needed to talk to me. She said again that she knew who killed her dad. I told her to call you guys, but she wouldn't. And she wouldn't call her mom or her stepmom, so I told her to wait for me at her house and I'd get there as soon as I could."

"You went there, and then what?"

"I thought she might be drunk again, but at least I could get her to you guys and you could sort it out. There were no lights on in the house when I got there. Her car was parked in front. I knocked, and when she didn't answer I went in and found her on the floor. I saw the needle in her leg, and immediately thought the worst—that she'd overdosed. Then I saw the inhaler and figured she was asthmatic."

"Did you take anything with you to give to her? Did you take her anything edible?"

"No and no."

"Did you know she was very allergic to peanuts, so allergic, in fact, that just a small amount could send her into anaphylactic shock and kill her?"

"I didn't know anything about her." Seems like the questions kept repeating themselves, just phrased differently.

"Did you know that she gave herself injections of epinephrine when she felt an anaphylactic reaction coming on after exposure to peanuts?"

"Oh, God no. Is that what happened?"

"We're fairly certain that's what happened. The shot she gave herself Saturday night was supposed to be epinephrine, a stimulant that would counter the effect of her allergic reaction from ingesting something that she shouldn't have. There were small medicine vials in her refrigerator and one on the counter. All of them contained a saline solution. We are going on the assumption that person or persons unknown wanted her dead and tampered with her medications. We don't know how this was done. She ate something containing peanuts, almost immediately went into anaphylactic shock, and tried unsuccessfully to give herself an injection and counter the effects. Basically, she suffocated. That's why her lips were blue," said Jeffers.

"Whatever she ate hit her fast. She got the needle into

her leg, but not soon enough. It didn't help. She didn't have a chance even to make a phone call," Haymore said.

"Was that why she fell on me at the reception? Had she eaten something then that could have made her ill?"

"We have no way of knowing. It could be, because one of the symptoms is dizziness. At a buffet like that, she should have been carrying her hypodermic just in case. We don't know everything she had in her Saturday night, but epinephrine wasn't in the mix," said Jeffers. "We won't have a full toxicology report for several days."

"And the peanuts were in what?" I wondered. My mind flashed to the plate of biscotti on Tiffany's counter. It was the only recognizable food I'd seen in the house.

"We're not certain yet. We've taken several items from the scene for analysis," said Haymore.

We talked a little more, mainly rehashing the same stuff. The deputies had not seen anaphylactic shock, but when EMTs arrived at the scene they had rightfully concluded that's how she died.

Finally, after poking around a little more, the men left. Before departing, they located where the intruder had cut the wires to disconnect the outdoor lighting. The solar lights had simply been pulled out and thrown into the bushes. Nothing was broken that couldn't be fixed, but it would have to wait until after someone else came out and looked for more evidence. They took some photos of the mess on the deck. They searched in the bushes, and examined the footprints sprayed by Deputy Vargas in the damp soil. Then, apparently satisfied with their observations of the scene, they prepared to leave.

"Don't talk about this," Haymore told me before leaving. "We're not releasing a cause of death for several days. We'll send someone back for the footprints." There was the ritualistic passing of cards, and I was to call them if I thought of anything. At the moment I was thinking of a nap, but it was not to be. I still had two afternoon interviews ahead of me.

It was nearly noon and my first appointment was at one. Thankfully, it was at a nearby vineyard. I grabbed a bottle of water and an apple, gathered notebook and camera into my tote, and carefully locked all the doors before leaving.

At my second interview that afternoon, I met Nestor Pullman, a grizzled vintner who looked older than his probable sixty years. He'd grown up in the Willamette Valley. Two previous generations of Pullmans had been involved in raising turkeys, but Nestor had always hated turkeys. In fact, he hated them so much that when his tee-totaling parents had died some ten years previously, off came the turkeys' heads, down came the turkey sheds, and up—on a loamy, well-drained southerly slope that had been fertilized by generation upon generation of turkey poop—went a vineyard.

Since Nestor was a lifelong farmer and commanded one of the best locations in the valley, the Pullman Family Vineyard thrived. Its grapes commanded top prices from nearby wineries, including at one time, Cougar Crossing.

Nestor was more than happy to walk me through the vineyard. His greatest joy was that section of land planted to the Dijon clone of chardonnay. "I was one of the first to plant it here," he said as he gently fingered a cluster of translucent chardonnay grapes. I appreciated his humility, and even more his willingness to step out of the once-restrictive family mold. "I watched for years when they first came here," he said of the early Oregon vintners. "It seemed like such a good use of the land—to create something that makes people happy."

I briefly thought of Carolyn and myself. Fortunately, most people do not have our wiring where alcohol is concerned, and when I reminded myself of that fact, then it was true, wine does make people happy. It had made me happy, or what passed for happy, for quite a long time.

Nestor was big and bald, and he wore bib overalls. I followed his large, lumbering form downhill between the rows of ripe grapes. "We're picking these tomorrow," he told me. "Conditions couldn't be better. It's our best vintage to date."

"If you sold grapes to Cougar Crossing, you must have known Ted Maxell," I ventured when the conversation lulled. Whereupon Nestor's kindly face reddened and his eyes began to bulge.

"Yes I did, and damn him to hell!" was his immediate response. "Dead or alive, that fat bastard's winery is getting no more Pullman grapes."

"Did he try to cheat you too?" Of course this was none of my business, but I asked anyway. There seemed to be a pattern to my inquisitiveness.

"That would be the best thing he could have done," Nestor fumed. "But no, the bastard raped my daughter."

In a nutshell, Monday had proved exhausting. The previous night's events had left me shaken. By the time I returned to my base of operations from my interview with Nestor Pullman and his wife, the sun was setting and the grounds were falling into deep, ominous shadows. Since Angel had the day off and I don't speak Spanish, the lighting situation had not been corrected. I was too brain dead even to change the porch bulb. I figured if the damned intruder wanted to come back, let him, and I'd quickly devise some way to kill him—with a toilet plunger if need be. But I didn't think he'd be back. More likely he was laid up somewhere taking antibiotics and putting hot salt water compresses on those parts of his body where Winston managed to penetrate the skin.

I ate a bowl of granola for dinner and reflected on my continuing conversation with Nestor, which had stretched late into the afternoon, and eventually included some really bad coffee and delicious cookies served by his wife in their farmhouse kitchen.

The Pullmans' daughter Rebecca, twenty-one at the time, was hired when Cougar Crossing finished its tasting room. It seemed like an ideal arrangement to Nestor. As the Pullman Vineyard grapes enjoyed a separate bottling from the other Cougar Crossing chardonnays, Rebecca was the perfect person to talk about those wines with visitors to the new winery—when Ted actually deigned to admit them. She also had taken an interest in the winery chores, topping barrels and doing basic cellar work when needed. She was going to school and needed the money for tuition.

It had seemed like a win-win situation, according to Nestor. He had even, selfishly, hoped she would take an interest and learn more about the wine business. None of the other Pullman children were interested in farming, or even staying in the area. If Rebecca proved the exception to the rule, who knows, maybe they'd have their own winery someday.

That had been nearly three years ago. Ted was transitioning from the log cabin he'd stayed in when the winery first opened—the same one that was until recently occupied by Tiffany—to the monstrosity on the hilltop he'd named for his new bride.

As Nestor explained it, "Rebecca was studying interior design. That's how Ted got her up there to the new house. He said he'd hire her—he'd be her first client—and he told her that with his house on her resume she'd get jobs all over the valley." I could see what was coming. "He got her up there alone. He'd paid her a large deposit, and he was the perfect gent the first few times they met there. And then one afternoon, just for the hell of it, he raped her."

Nestor had been out of town at the time, he said. He was spending several days in Corvallis at Oregon State University learning about the new grape clones coming into Oregon and perfecting grafting procedures. "Maureen noticed Becca was acting strange," he said. "But those two have never been close. Like oil and water, they are."

Within a few days of the incident, she had quit her job at the winery and abruptly quit working on Ted's decorating. She refused to give her parents a reason for her behavior. Ted, of course, demanded his deposit back. She refused to give it to him. Her parents never would have known about the rape, Nestor said, except that Rebecca discovered she was pregnant. She would not have an abortion. And she did not report the rape to the police.

"She knew she didn't have a chance against Ted Maxell

in court. She knew that from the get-go. It was her word against his, our money against his." Instead, he said, "She told Ted Maxell to stuff it where the sun don't shine, that she was keeping his blankety-blank money, and he had better be thankful he got off so easy. The hell of it is, until last week I shared a grandchild with Ted Maxell."

Rebecca moved to California so she would never have to see her assaulter again. "Her sister lives down there, and she seems to have adjusted. But if we wanted to see her and the little guy, we've had to go down there." He scratched his head. "Maybe now she'll come home once in a while. She's a good kid, but she's gotten hard. I don't think she'll ever be the same."

As I munched my granola, I thought about resentments and revenge. Here was the perfect motive for Ted's murder. Were I Rebecca's father, I'd have killed the miserable goat myself. I'd asked Nestor about how he felt about it today. "I hated the guy," he openly admitted. "There was a time I wanted him dead. But I've got the cutest little grandson, and he looks just like Becca. Maxell got what he deserved, and I didn't have to lift a finger. What goes around comes around."

To me, this seemed a little too glib given his earlier ranting. I wondered where he had been the night of Ted's murder, or Maureen for that matter. Being a parent myself, I'd never underestimate the resolve and guile of an angry mother when her child has been harmed. But even if one of them had killed Ted, I couldn't see them having it in for Tiffany. Unless she had seen one or both of them in the winery that night. Unless she knew too much. Once a person actually had killed another human being, things very quickly became complicated.

I tried to remember if I'd seen either of the Pullmans anywhere else—for example in the Cougar Crossing parking lot, or at Ted's funeral. So many people, plus Tiffany's little drama that day. I couldn't remember—but I was pretty sure the answer was no. Nestor was the size of my former husband, and of a much gruffer appearance. I'm certain I would have noticed his lumbering form.

About seven-thirty Rob called and wanted to talk. "Only if you come over here," I said. "It's completely dark outside, and I'm not leaving here and coming back alone. There's nobody else even staying here." Within half an hour he was at the front door.

"This is amazing," he said as he entered the house. Walking through the rooms to the kitchen, he gaped at the art, the grand piano, and Melody's style, which managed to be at once overstuffed and edgy, punctuated with wild colors and pieces of art which pulled everything together beautifully.

I brewed us each a double latte from the house espresso machine, and we sat at the round table near the sliders to the deck. With a flashlight, I pointed out the remains of the previous night. "I don't know what to think about it," I said. "I guess it could just be a random incident."

Rob sipped his latte. He then said, "We know it couldn't have been Axel. He's been under house arrest at his mother's since he was released to her custody."

"I don't think if she lost the bail she'd blink an eye," I said. "But they all have an alibi, so he obviously didn't kill his sister. He couldn't have. And he certainly wasn't out here trying to scare me. There is so much meth around Yamhill County; I suppose it could have been any punk looking for cash or something to sell for drugs."

"That's true," Rob said. "But the fact is, these incidents have happened more than coincidentally close to each other. There were no other break-ins or related activities on Sunday night. I checked all the law enforcement incident responses for the weekend. Except for situations where you were directly involved, it was a quiet weekend."

"Oh, that's great news," I said.

"Still, we can't eliminate random."

We both were quiet for a couple minutes contemplating the possibilities.

"I don't think he was after me," I said. It was denial, and a poor attempt at that.

"Usually with drug-related burglaries there is more than one event. And there usually is more than one person involved. They travel in twos or threes, and they'll do several break-ins in a night—unless somebody catches them in the act and law enforcement people are looking for them. Then they go to ground. You say this guy was alone?"

"As near as I could tell."

"Then I don't think it's a coincidence. I think the guy was after you, to scare you or whatever."

"It's the 'whatever' that worries me."

I told him about my interview with Nestor Pullman. "Do you know this guy?"

"You know I've never had much to do with the wine scene. If his daughter's rape was never reported, I'd have no reason to even know who he is," Rob said.

228 ◊ Judy Nedry

"Well, it certainly adds another dimension to the story, doesn't it? Ted seemed to like the sweet young things. I wonder if there are any others out there who, like Rebecca Pullman, knew they'd be wasting their time trying to fight him."

"They could still nail him if they wanted to," Rob muttered. "All it would take is a DNA test."

"That is pretty moot at this point, since he was cremated."

"There is still stuff around with his DNA in it."

"She wanted the child, I guess. And at the time she obviously wanted the money," I concluded. "If she wants more, they could probably do the DNA test now." Unless she's a suspect too, I thought. It was getting pretty complicated.

"Speaking of children, there is something I forgot to tell you, said Rob. "The autopsy revealed that, among other things, Tiffany was ten weeks pregnant."

Chapter 22

Melody called again on Monday night after Rob left. I never figured out the time change exactly, except that for her it was a different day. God knows what time it was in Brisbane. When Melody gets determined about something, the time of day doesn't matter.

"I wonder who the father is," she said when I told her the news about Tiffany's pregnancy.

"Any ideas?"

"None. I have no idea who she ran with. I would think, though, that someone of her age would have enough sense not to get pregnant."

"Maybe she wanted to get pregnant," I observed. "Little lost, screwed-up girl needs something to love, that sort of thing?"

"Yes, and maybe the father didn't want to be a dad."

"Which would mean the murders are unrelated?" My question hung in the air. "They have to be related, because like Rob says it's too much of a coincidence to really be a coincidence. Just like the prowler the other night was too much of a coincidence."

"*That* gives me the creeps," said Melody. "How are you doing with all this?"

"I'm fine in the daylight. Until those lights are back on, though, I won't step out the door after dark."

"Smart woman. I'm sorry I got you into this."

"It breaks the monotony," I told her, and she laughed.

I told her about my visit with the Pullmans. She didn't know them. Then we chatted about their trip and B&B business, then rang off. Melody's long-distance assignment was to see if she could come up with any potential fathers to the recently deceased's child. At her age—and this goes for me as well—it was an extremely long shot. What could we possibly know about the social lives of the Gen Ys? Some days I found it difficult to decode the mores of the Boomers, and I'd been one all my life. I probably needed to get out of my comfort zone and do a little investigating in that arena.

We also agreed to find out whom, if anyone, Ted had been poking—besides his wife. Melody said she would search her brain for rumors and possibilities, while I agreed to apply my energies during my interviews. If rumors abounded regarding a liaison between Tara and Jess Spears, there would be plenty of rumors about old Ted, providing he was up to no good. Given that they had normal human curiosity, coupled with extreme dislike, people in the wine business out here would have been looking for things to stick on Ted. If Ted had a woman or women on the side, this part should be if not easy, at least doable.

Angel arrived Tuesday morning as I was brewing a pot of coffee. "Oh my God! What has happened to the duck?" were the first words out of her mouth.

"The deck, Angel. It's the deck." Quickly I filled her in on the details. "All the grounds lights were disconnected or broken."

"I will have Salvador fix them immediately," she said as she buzzed around the kitchen in preparation for the day's cooking. Several parties were scheduled to check in on Wednesday, and we needed to get ready. "Ay-yi-yi, Senora Melody will have a fit!"

"She already knows. I talked to her last night."

As it was my official day off, I left immediately after breakfast for my abode in Lower Hillsdale Heights. With me was a list of things to pick up on the way back to Dundee. Once home, I located some black silk slacks that would go with my taupe shell, and a lovely silk duponi jacket. It seemed properly funereal, subdued and ladylike. Then, driving like a crazy woman, I made it to the Episcopal Church in Lake Oswego and was seated a full twenty minutes before Tiffany's memorial service was slated to begin.

I positioned myself near the rear of the church so I could watch people as they filed in, convinced that somewhere in the throng was a murderer—perhaps more than one murderer, although my gut feelings told me we were looking for one person. And if my Sunday night visitation was related to the murders, that person most likely was a male.

The church filled with many souls I remembered from my time in wine country. Axel walked in with his mother on his arm and Zephyr beside him. Zephyr, her hair in a French twist, sported a striking pinstripe pantsuit. With her spike heels, she was taller than he.

Pamela wore a lovely dark plum suit, probably a St. John. When she entered the pew she hugged two women and an elderly couple who already were seated. They bore such a striking family resemblance I guessed they could be her sisters and parents. Once Zephyr was seated, Axel greeted the four with kisses. The old lady began crying, and he sat down next to her and put his arm around her. He was attentive and calm, the ideal son and grandson, at least to my mind, further dispelling any idea that he could have murdered anyone.

Across the aisle sat the ever-more-pregnant Widow Maxell attired in the same dress she'd worn at Ted's funeral, ample bosoms amply displayed as usual. Beside her was her suspected lover, Josh Spears, looking appropriately somber in a pale grey Italian suit tailored to fit his stocky, broad-shouldered frame and trim waist. She leaned toward him to whisper something. He nodded and smiled. It seemed inappropriate that he should be sitting next to her at her step-daughter's funeral, but I realized that probably had more to do with my old-fashioned notions than anything to do with the real world. I made a mental note to find out more about him.

Rob slid into the pew next to me. "What are you doing here?" I whispered to him as strains from the church organ broadcast Bach above the heads of the mourners and the curious.

"Same thing you are," he replied. "Paying my respects and watching people." He nodded to our right. Across the aisle and a couple rows behind us, sheriff's deputies Doug Haymore and Dave Jeffers were seating themselves. In blazers and slacks, they blended with the other mourners. "Whoever killed Ted and Tiffany is here today," Rob said. I nodded in agreement.

There were the usual formalities—music, words from the minister in his funeral vestments. And then Axel stepped to the podium. He began speaking, and the words that came out of him were not words from the Axel I knew. His voice was clear and filled with a certainty I hadn't known he possessed as he remembered Tiffany as a delightful, happily independent, small child who somehow morphed into a withdrawn and troubled adolescent who acted out and began using drugs and alcohol. As a young adult, he told the audience, his younger sister became angry and selfish to the outer world and distant with her family. And she continued to self-medicate.

"The girl I knew, my sister Tiffany, was not the woman most of you knew when we came to Oregon," he concluded. "Most of the people in this room never saw the beautiful soul she was as a child. My little sister, the Tiffany I will always remember, was sweet and generous, and hopeful as only a child can be. Her untimely death was not an accident. My promise to her is to discover where and how she came to be the wounded creature she was during the second half of her life, to discover why she had to die, and to see that justice is served.

"Tiffany and I loved each other. We fought like brothers and sisters often do. She said terrible things to me sometimes, most often when she was impaired by whatever demons haunted her. But she also told me, 'Someday Axel I will be myself again.' I now will honor her with some of my music, which, she always told me, made her feel 'like myself'."

He stepped to the baby grand piano on a platform behind the lectern, sat, and adjusted the bench. And then his fingers touched the keys. With his first selection, George Gershwin's "Summertime", he accompanied a female soloist who sang the challenging piece beautifully. When they were finished, she resumed her seat and he launched into a medley of jazz tunes, some of which I recognized and others not. His final selection, he told the gathering, was a piece he'd composed for his sister. "This is how I always will think of her," he said.

The music that came out of the piano was unlike anything I'd heard before. It began as a soulful ramble up and down the keyboard, a tuneful and mellow meandering of lilting rhythms that gradually grew into an angry and dissonant war between treble and bass. As the piano's chords filled and shook the church, so did Axel demonstrate his complete mastery of the instrument. His grief and anger poured through him and out of him, the notes rising and falling, the chords smashing into each other like waves on a storm-pounded beach. And then it was over. His right hand softly caressed the treble keys, the bass answered. His hands chased one another down the keyboard then up again, and came together into a graceful and harmonious finale.

Axel sat back, hands in his lap, and waited silently. I didn't know whether to cry or applaud. After several seconds of absolute silence, the minister began clapping his hands, and the mourners followed suit.

No other remembrances were offered. The minister made closing remarks. The organist again worked her keyboards and pedals. Then, gradually we all filed out of the church and into the church's well-appointed reception hall for a light buffet.

Rob and I expressed our condolences to Pamela and Axel and then traversed the buffet. Once fortified, I located Axel standing alone and approached him. "I need a bit more information on the winery for my book," I told him. It was crass, but in my mind necessary, to have an urgent need to know more. My need had nothing to do with the book. "I realize this is a terrible time, and of course it can wait a couple weeks."

"Talk to my stepmother," he said, nodding in her direction. "I am finished with the winery business, and have been since my father died."

"Your music was inspiring. I hope you continue with it. But what about crush?" I asked innocently, although I already knew. "Who's going to finish the job?"

"Tara re-hired Josh Spears, our former winemaker. He was only gone because of his falling out with Dad. I am not a winemaker, and I never wanted to be a winemaker."

"Do you plan to follow a career in music?"

"I plan to have a life now, soon" Axel said. "I'm grateful that I'm out of jail. I didn't kill my father. We had a pretty good argument the night he died, and I'd owed him that for a long time. I'm glad he left us life knowing I have at least a bit of backbone. As soon as his and Tiffany's killers are brought to justice, I can get on with my life. I hope that answers any other questions you may have of me. Oh," he added as an afterthought, "and I'm sorry I was such a boob the first time

I met you at the winery. I really don't know anything about that stuff." Then he nodded at me and I moved on.

My, my.

"I'll talk to him," Rob said, a few minutes later. "Maybe he'll do an interview. We could use some public sentiment going in his direction. The sheriff's department needs to keep investigating this thing."

I made my way across the room to where Tara Maxell was sipping tea and chatting with her winemaker. They seemed joined at the hip. I reintroduced myself to make certain she was tracking. I clearly was not a person of significance in her eyes. "It would be most helpful if I could interview you and your winemaker so that I have the most current information on Cougar Crossing before the book goes to press."

An ironic smile played at Tara's well-painted mouth. "I've already introduced you to my winemaker," she said coyly, with a nod toward Spears.

He extended his hand as he took my inventory with his eyes. Again it was the mushy paw rather than a real handshake. I was certain there was more to him than that limp excuse for a greeting acknowledged. His eyes were very dark, and his chiseled features handsome. His temples showed tiny flecks of silver. His well-tanned complexion sported furrows at the forehead and deep laugh lines. He was quite a specimen of *Gentlemen's Quarterly* manhood. But as I looked at him, his perfect smile appeared forced and cold, and the eyes that bore into me showed no expression. A chill swept over me.

"Happy to see you again," I somehow managed to say. "When can we get together?"

He considered for a moment. "How about Friday morning?

That gives me a few days to get caught up." Again, the straight teeth, the smile like ice.

"Perfect. I can be there as early as ten." He nodded.

That established, I refilled my water glass and took a quick survey of the room. People were beginning to leave. I turned to have another browse at the refreshment table and found myself face-to-face with deputies Haymore and Jeffers.

"Have you had any more excitement at the B&B?" Jeffers queried.

"It's been quiet," I said. "Melody's crew will have the place completely back to normal and lit up by the time I get back. Have you found out anything about who may have been hiding in the bushes?"

"We checked the area emergency rooms for cases with dog bites in the buttocks, but so far nothing," said Haymore. "We did send out forensics people to pick up casts of the footprints and anything else the perp may have left behind. They gathered some fibers from the shrubbery. Something will turn up."

"Does the shoe size match Alex's?" I wondered.

"No, his feet are smaller than our prowler's," said Jeffords. "We checked that first thing. But don't worry. We'll get your man."

"Hopefully before somebody comes after me again," I said.

"What makes you think he was after you?" This from Haymore. "It could have been a simple burglary. We see plenty of those at secluded homes."

"It's a feeling I can't seem to shake. Intuition? Paranoia? Your choice."

"We've got patrols in your area nightly now," said Jeffers. "Unmarked cars, of course. I want you to call us immediately if anything else unusual happens. We'll get to the bottom of this."

Maybe so, maybe no, I thought. They'd already made a big deal of arresting the wrong man. But then I hadn't come up with anything better. "Will do," I said.

"Remember, not a word about this case," Haymore cautioned. "By virtue of being first at the crime scene, you know more than we are releasing to the public."

As I continued my way in the general direction of the buffet table, I noticed my former husband Dwight crossing the room. Was he limping? I looked again, but he'd stopped to talk to someone, smiling and slapping the other man on the back. As he hadn't noticed me watching, I observed him for a few seconds before he laughed with his friend and then moved on. And yes, by God, he *was* limping, and in quite a lot of pain judging from the way his jaw was clenched.

I veered away from the healthy food and walked straight to the dessert table. If he was the prowler, I needed sugar and chocolate, and I needed it now! I grabbed a plate and quickly piled three tiny chocolate éclairs onto it. As I turned away from the table, I almost banged into him.

"Eeek!" I squawked.

"Emma, what the hell is wrong with you?" He dwarfed me by more than a head. Was the prowler that tall? I couldn't remember. All I could remember was a hunched over, dark form scuttling across the deck.

"Dwight, you scared me to death. Why are you hovering?"

"I'm not hovering. I saw you and came over to say hi. What's wrong with you?"

"Nothing! Does it look like something is wrong with me? What's wrong with you? You're limping."

"I fell off a ladder."

"When?"

"When? Who cares when? A couple of days ago. Why?"

"Did you go to the doctor?"

"No. Of course not. I only fell off a ladder. I mean, Jesus! Are we going to have another one of those conversations?"

"What conversations?"

"Calm down. Forget it." His face was contorted with frustration and anger. "I just came over to say I'm sorry about the other night."

"You mean it *was* you?"

"Of course it was me. Who else could it have been? You were there."

"Oh my God! Why did you do it?"

"Do what? Pick a fight? Because that's the way I am. You always said I was an asshole."

"Pick what fight?"

"Earth to Emma. We were both there at Tina's, for chrissakes. I'm sorry, that's all. I'm trying to be better." His face had reddened. He looked miserable. I suddenly realized we were talking about different things. What was *wrong* with me? Was I losing my mind?

"It's okay Dwight." I set the plate of éclairs on the table behind me. My bladder had chosen that precise moment to fail me. He'd managed to scare the pee out of me! "Don't worry. Just forget about it. I'm sorry too. Gotta run." I scurried toward the restroom.

When I emerged, Rob was looking about the nearly deserted reception hall. "Where were you?" he demanded, walking up to me.

"Middle age problems. It's OK now." Thankfully he had no idea what I was talking about. "Dwight was limping," I moaned. "It was him. He killed Ted, but hopefully not Tiffany. But if he was after me, that means he killed her too."

"He couldn't have killed Ted."

"You don't know. He hated Ted."

"Lots of people hated Ted. You'd have to look under rocks, Emma, to find someone who didn't hate him."

"He's never been violent," I muttered, more to myself than to Rob. My eyes swept the room. "Forceful, but not violent."

"Emma, get a grip here." Rob touched my arm and I looked at him. "There are several people who had more motive and more opportunity. Dwight didn't kill Ted."

"You don't know him," I said. "He has a mean streak. And he'll do damn near anything to get his way. That's how he got where he is. We didn't have any money or connections, but he has the will to do anything. And he's always right."

"Did he abuse you?" He gripped my arm tightly and looked me in the eye.

"No, not physically. But if I, or anyone else, was in his way, he'd walk over us, around us, or through us. He is very strong-willed, very *forceful*." Dwight did shake me once, right before I left him. I decided not to mention that incident.

"Listen, I know this is awful for you. But we don't have

any facts. Dwight is not the kind of person who goes around murdering people. He's got too much to lose."

I inhaled deeply. Breathe in, exhale slowly. Breathe in, exhale slowly. "OK, I am going to put this out of my mind for now," I said finally. "I'm going back to headquarters to take a nap."

Chapter 23

Angel was cleaning the kitchen when I returned to inn late that afternoon. Winston pranced around me barking, and I handed him a dog biscuit, hoping it would keep him quiet until I could change clothes and walk him.

"You are tired, Senora," Angel said as I tossed my handbag and jacket in the alcove. After turning around the desk chair so I was facing her, I plopped into it with a sigh.

"I am," I said. "Tired and confused. Tiffany's service was nice, but I didn't learn much. Your daughter, by the way, looked beautiful. And I finally heard Axel play his music."

"You see it is true, then. He has the gift. And thank you for my daughter." Her face momentarily flushed with pride.

"Definitely."

"The lights, they are repaired," Angel said, all business once again. She moved gracefully from the refrigerator toward me and handed me a glass of iced tea. "The crew has worked all day on them. They were very damaged, some of them. But now everything is ready for when the guests arrive tomorrow."

"Thanks, Angel. It makes me feel a little safer, too. This place wouldn't function without you." I took a long drink from the frosty glass. "Ted Maxell," I continued. "Did he have a girlfriend?"

Angel expression quickly registered dismay. "I would not know that Senora. How would I know such a thing?"

"Do you know anyone who would know?"

She eyed me warily, then turned her head away. But I saw her lips purse before she turned. She disapproved of my asking—my prying, more accurately. She would know darn well who knew such things because she was one of them. They were the people in positions such as hers, people who worked for other people—like the house maid at Pamela Fontaine's, and whomever worked or had worked for the Maxells. The housekeepers, gardeners, and other helpers in the wine community came almost entirely from Angel's Latino community. And like all of us, they talked. They observed the goings-on of their employers. They raised their eyebrows at the goings-on of their employers. And they gossiped and swapped information. Of course they did. It could help them do their jobs better; it could amuse them. Such things are universal.

"I only ask because if he did, it may be a motive for someone to want him dead—such as a pissed-off husband," I continued, in an attempt to soften my request. "Axel is still on the hook for Ted's murder, even if he's out on bail. The authorities know he didn't kill his sister, but they still believe they have strong evidence linking him to the death of his father."

"Many people dislike Mr. Maxell. I do not know."

"Well, think about it," I said, not wishing to upset her further. "You may know someone who knows someone. Obviously you're in a better position to hear local gossip than I am."

"Perhaps, Senora," she said. "I will ask." She removed her apron and hung it in the pantry, gathered her handbag and sweater, and with a forced smile and a wave she exited through the sliding door and onto the spotless deck.

I turned my chair toward the alcove desk and checked the day's messages.

The next few days passed uneventfully. Guests—three couples—arrived on Wednesday afternoon, the same day I decided to move the late afternoon wine and cheesy bits into the sun room permanently. Though still beautiful outside, it had grown a bit chilly for gathering on the front porch. We closed the swimming pool for the season. And, I continued in as disciplined fashion as possible with my interviews. When I wasn't running around the valley accumulating information for the book, I worked at the laptop or did hostess detail at the Westerly.

I gathered and compiled notes from interviews and observations, and organized the book's chapters into a meaningful sequence of information. And from this work, a theme of growth and change evolved. The wine industry that had existed when Dwight and I bought our vineyard property twenty-plus years previously had all but vanished.

Certainly many of the industry's original pioneers were still going strong, but most were in their sixties now. They would be thinking of retiring soon, or at least slowing down. For some of them, passing the baton to younger family members was an option. For others, it wasn't—which meant they would be selling their vineyards and wineries when they retired.

Meanwhile, new wineries were springing up like mushrooms despite the fact that land prices had escalated, along with everything else. I realized that people like Dwight and I could never do today what we had done twenty years ago. We wouldn't be able to afford it. That that went for everyone here who started out before Oregon had a reputation for making world class wines.

Our industry had been started by driven, determined, passionate men and women of middle class means. In just a few short years, it had evolved into a rich man's game. As in France, Germany and California, Oregon's wine industry had become elitist. As the state's wine quality had gained stature on the international market, demand had become greater than supply. At this point in time, we were still on the rising curve, and probably would be for several years.

Now, the place was reminiscent of Napa Valley the first time I'd visited there more than twenty years ago. The pioneers were still alive and well, and were finally even living comfortably and easily as a reward for their years of hard work. But the newcomers starting the wineries in the northern Willamette Valley now, for the most part, bore little resemblance to them. The majority of the newcomers had serious money, be it from fortunes made in the pharmaceutical industry, high tech, real estate developments, or a fortuitous invention. Some of them, like Pamela Fontaine, had the sweetest of all money—old money. And the sharks were circling. It was only a matter of time before corporations moved in and purchased Oregon wineries. I dreaded that day, which would truly mark the end of the personalized, down-home ambience the industry had thrived on for so many years.

I tried to tell myself that the new face of the industry was neither good nor bad. It was what it was—different than it had been. It was part of Oregon's continuing story, a natural progression. Through my writings, going back two decades, I had been part of that story. Gradually, as the wines became more available, other writers had gotten on the bandwagon, attracting more players. As a result, the wine industry had grown in quality and quantity until it was no longer recognizable to those of us who'd helped start it. For what it was worth, we'd all contributed to the growth and change.

Now it was different. The taste was bittersweet—but probably more sweet than bitter to people like my former husband, whose bank accounts continued to grow. These folks certainly had earned whatever rewards came their way now. The changes naturally resulting from their successes were out of their control.

That I had become extinct really didn't matter. I hadn't stayed in the wine writing game. Had I not removed myself from the business I'd be dead by now. I knew that to be true. It had been a conscious choice, one I'd made in order to survive. But that too was bittersweet. Each day since I'd left that life, I had awakened with the hangover of regrets. I missed the old days. No book contract was going to change that. I had loved it all too well.

Yet here the days continued, and I was immersed in each one. Like the changes in the industry I had observed over the past three weeks, it was neither good nor bad. I was completely engaged, and where I belonged for the moment. When it was over and I returned to Portland, I'd be extinct again. But I was determined to move forward with my life. This time, I'd figure how to go home and leave the regrets behind.

How ironic that I would not stay here. The familiarity I was experiencing had a beginning and an end. The work I now was doing was the work I'd been created to do, and yet it could not and would not continue. In just three weeks I would return to my little house, and my life in Lower Hillsdale Heights. And in a year or so, the book's proceeds would pay a few bills.

Friday morning at ten I presented myself at Cougar Crossing Winery for what I hoped would be the last time. From the outset, it had felt like a place where I didn't belong. The same grouchy bitch was holding forth in the tasting room. When I asked for Josh Spears she asked my name and my business. "I'm Emma Golden and he is expecting me," was all I said. My business, indeed!

Josh arrived in the tasting room within two minutes, a good indication that at least something was working again. He wore a flannel shirt open at the neck and a fleece jacket sporting the winery logo. A heavy gold chain circled his thick neck. We did the mushy handshake once again, then he led me into the tank room and up a flight of stairs to his office. One entire wall consisted of windows which overlooked the tanks. I took a seat, suddenly wondering if anyone had been in this room on the night of Ted's murder. It provided a great vantage point from which to view goings on in the entire tank room. I looked directly across it to the very tank where Ted's body had been discovered.

"We haven't been able to locate anyone who saw anything," Josh said, as if reading my thoughts. I turned around to give him my full attention. All the while, the shit fairies in my brain kept telling me that something or someone was at my back. It was most unnerving, and it was all I could do not to turn around again and look at that tank.

With a great deal of effort, I started through my standard list of questions. We began with practices in the vineyard, covering such topics as pruning, canopy management, irrigation, crop levels, and so on right up to grape sugar levels versus acidity, and how long Josh allowed the fruit to hang at the end of the season. Skin contact for the reds, fermentation temperatures, malolactic fermentation for the chardonnays, the use of new versus older French barrels, and other topics dominated the winemaking part of the interview.

Spears was aiming for a very big, ripe, forward style of wine, and with his expertise, based on many years as a winemaker in California, plus several back-to-back dry, warm growing seasons in Oregon, he'd been able to achieve this style consistently. While his style was not the typically sought-after one among Oregon pinot noir traditionalists, Cougar Crossing's pinots had developed a passionate following. They also were at the top of the price range for Oregon pinots, due to probably no reason other than Ted Maxell's insatiable ego.

"There are rumors around the valley that Cougar Crossing

will be for sale in the coming months," I said as we wound up the technical part of the interview. "Would you care to comment on that?"

Spears gave me the chilly, hard look I'd seen in his eyes at Tiffany's funeral, but he grabbed the bait anyway. "Don't believe everything you hear," he said. "I plan to be here and running this winery for a very long time."

Chapter 24

Two more couples had checked in on Thursday afternoon and by Friday night the Westerly was full again. Housekeepers ran around tidying rooms and laundering linens. Gardeners mowed, raked leaves, and cleaned the flower beds of withering annuals. Angel and I kept busy in the kitchen, where we had reached a comfortable détente, going about our respective tasks and not talking about what was undoubtedly foremost in both of our minds.

Nothing that could be tied to the murders or a possible suspect had caught my attention in any of my recent interviews. No more bigger-than-life characters like Nestor Pullman had sprung fully formed onto my pages, replete with horror stories about the villainous Ted Maxell. Oregon vintners were unanimous in their delight over the quality and quantity of the grape harvest. And they unanimously were looking forward to the end of it so they could get caught up on their sleep. I marched through each day, one foot in front of the other, reminding myself that my job included writing a book and running a bed and breakfast inn, not solving murder mysteries.

Meanwhile, the sheriff's department had found no new suspects in the county's two recent murders, nor had they located the Sunday night prowler. My thoughts were plagued with things known and unknown. Ted Maxell had brought about his own demise. Who had been bold enough, desperate enough, angry enough, and able enough to kill him? And where did Tiffany fit into the puzzle?

I talked to Rob and Melody nightly. On Rob's part, the sheriff's department had made a big meth bust in rural McMinnville. He informed me that most of their energies were focused on it, and as it had made the national news, said energies were likely to stay focused there for a while. Nothing was pending immediately as far as a trial for Axel. At least he wasn't locked up. I wondered what he was doing, but in the aftermath of his sister's death decided not to take immediate action to find out.

Melody regaled me with tales of Dan's and her adventures in Australia. They spent a few days in Brisbane before heading to Fiji. She had not been able to come up with any more ideas that would point to a successful solution of the local murders or who might be the father of Tiffany's baby.

Both of my confidants did sit up and take notice, however, when I told them of my interview with Josh Spears. More than being interested in him, they were interested in the location of the office and what it portended.

"Anyone could have been up there watching," Melody breathed into the phone.

"Anyone with a key," I replied. "They probably keep that part of the building locked."

"Well, that narrows the field doesn't it?" Excellent point.

"Spears wasn't employed at Cougar Crossing at the time of Ted's murder, so that eliminates him."

"Unless he held onto his key. In the heat of the moment, Ted may have forgotten to get it back," she reminded me. "Or Josh may have gotten one from Tara. He could have gotten in there and just lay in wait for Ted to show up." I nodded in silent agreement. "Did he limp?" she wondered. Unfortunately he did not.

"There remains the problem of the pants, not to mention the *estagieres*, whom everybody familiar with winery practices knew would be showing up at some time late during the evening in question to do punch-down," I said. "Either the killer was lucky, or he or she knew there would be that window of opportunity exactly when no one else would be in the tank room." Yes, I was a broken record regarding the pants. Especially with so many avenues to be followed, the pants helped narrow the field a bit. Or at least I thought they did.

"It could be how Tiffany knew who killed her father," Rob said when I ran it by him on Saturday morning between breakfasting with the guests and going out for my first interview of the day.

Neither of us could remember seeing Tiffany during the dinner intermezzo that fatal night. "You're right. She could have been the watcher," I said. "She could have been anywhere. And she wasn't at our table, so we don't know when she returned to the dinner party."

"Or it could have been Tara. As one of the owners, her presence in the winery wouldn't attract attention," he added.

"Nor would Tiffany's. But Tara didn't come back. Somehow one of us has to talk to her."

"She wasn't feeling well that night," Rob reminded me. He'd been sitting next to her at the table. "She squirmed all through dinner until she left." As far along as she is in her pregnancy, she'd had good reason for leaving early. We rang off, as I had to get to an interview.

Tanager Vineyard and Winery was another splashy operation, and was located in one of the valley's newest designated American Viticultural Areas, Chehalem Mountain, about five miles as the crow flies from my base of operations. I took the shortcut over the Dundee Hills, bouncing up and down steep grades on washboard roads and dodging potholes. The way was scenic, but curvy and demanding of a driver's attention. One did not want to miss a turn and make a downhill dive into an important vineyard.

The Tanager family had made its fortune in a small pharmaceutical company located in upstate New York, where they still lived most of the year. Thus, none of the family members were in attendance to be interviewed the day of my visit. Alas, you say. However, as they were absentee vintners on the best of days, and as they had hired Zephyr Lopez to be their winemaker and general manager, it was the best of situations for me.

Tanager was not the biggest kid on the block, but it appeared, at first observation, to have been done right. No expense was spared, I realized, as I took in the banks of solar panels on a series of roofs that cascaded down the hillside. In keeping with the practices of the day, Tanager had been built following the contour of the hillside on which it perched, with crush pad at the top, flowing downward to the tanks, and from there downward into the barrel room. The bottom level was home to bottling line, warehouse, and distribution. In this case, the offices and adjacent tasting room were located on the third level. I parked in the small parking lot and followed Zephyr's directions through the tasting room, which was closed for harvest, and down a corridor toward her office. It was quiet, all the harvest activity underway on the levels above us.

The office door was open when I arrived; Zephyr was deep in concentration, absorbed with her computer screen. I rapped gently on the lintel and she jumped and turned toward me. "Good morning," I said.

"Oh, it's you. Hi." She smiled, then quickly exited her screen to give me her full attention. "Coffee?"

"Sure."

She walked to a credenza at the back wall of the office, which housed a coffee pot and mugs, a jug of fresh flowers, and several tidy stacks of various wine magazines. She poured me a mug of coffee. I declined the condiments. She gestured to a pair of leather chairs near the window. I settled in a chair and she settled in the other one, setting her coffee on the table between us. "How can I help you?"

Our interview took an hour. At least the formal part of it—the list of questions I asked everyone, plus the winery tour that took us up and down stairs, across catwalks, and between barrels. All of it was la-di-dah and wonderful, a totally green operation, plenty of money for all the things a new, state-of-the-art winery needed.

People who could afford to be in the wine industry were popping up wineries as fast as buildings could be erected, each one better than the one before it, as quickly as barrels could be built in the remote hills of Burgundy and shipped across the Atlantic Ocean, as many as were needed, no matter the cost. It was boring, if you ask me. These folks had never had to make the choice between paying the electric bill or paying the vineyard crew when they lined up on Saturday afternoons, tired and dirty. When you knew there was money in the bank to cover the checks, where was the damned adventure? Where was the so-called "romance of winemaking"?

At our house, Dwight always had paid the crew whether we could afford it or not. Now that, my friends, was an adventure. While I'd understood that people who worked needed to be paid, it had frustrated me. I always had wanted to go more slowly, to grow as we could afford it. Our day jobs couldn't begin to keep up with the amount of money consumed by a young and barely producing vineyard.

Over my protests, poles were driven into the ground and more wires strung, more plants purchased, and more workers paid whether we had the money for it or not. For me, it became just one more really good reason to drink. And Dwight had won. He'd grown his dream, and kept it alive and vital, because slowing down and behaving like a sane person was not in his DNA and quitting was never an option.

We all get to where we are supposed to be by a different path. It was not my concern any more.

Back in her office I looked at Zephyr Lopez—a beautiful young woman in her designer jeans and sheepskin vest, high-heel boots, and perfect make-up. She was in the early stages of her big adventure, but based on what little I knew about her, many extraordinary things had happened in her life to get her to where she was now. I asked her what had been the most difficult thing she'd gone through in getting from where she began to now.

Her dark eyes flashed. "Watching my parents work in the fields and do without so I could go to college? Watching my siblings struggle and do without so I could go to college, not because I deserved it more, but because I was the oldest and the one most likely to succeed? Oh, and did I mention prejudice? Which appeals to you most for your book?"

I scribbled the words into my notebook, my face burning. No way was I going to tell her about how my former husband had paid the vineyard workers first over my drunken objections. I felt ashamed for entertaining that bitter memory even though it was the unvarnished truth. While I had experienced gender discrimination at times during my career, it had been insignificant enough to be ignored. It would have been nothing like what a Mexican-American woman must have gone through.

Zephyr had the resolve of my former husband, no doubt about it. I could see it in her eyes, in the way she carried herself. For her, quitting was never an option. She also harbored a full reservoir of anger. I fleetingly wondered if she was capable of murdering the man who had obstructed her path to marriage, the man who had tried to shame her for being who she was. I put the thought aside for further consideration.

"I'm sorry," I said. "I work with your mother and love her dearly, but I know nothing of your history—only your accomplishments and how proud of you she is. I'm certain you have a remarkable story to tell, and I'd love to hear whatever parts of it you're willing to share."

She appeared to relax a little. "I'm sorry too," she said. She treated me to a little smile. "I tend to be a bit passionate. Yes. And there has been publicity about me. First Latino winemaker in Oregon, and a woman at that. Imagine. What shit! Blah, blah, blah, until I could scream. So I am an oddity? So what? Get over it. This is not the circus, this is business. Talk about the real stuff. Who is this woman? What can she do? I've dealt with the other for my entire twenty-seven years, and I'm sick of it."

She walked to the credenza. "Have another cup of coffee," she said, and then laughed at herself. I accepted more coffee and resumed my seat. Instead of sitting, Zephyr paced the room, coffee mug in hand, as she told me of her life.

"It's a pretty simple story," she said after a moment of pacing. "I was born in Parma, Idaho. My parents worked in the fields. They made us learn English, even though they were not proficient themselves. We lived in a very small house, ten of us, one bedroom. But we had enough. We lived near where we worked. Our neighbors were, without exception, people just like us. We were poor, but we children had no particular awareness of that.

"Until I began grade school when I was seven years old, I had not encountered prejudice. My parents shielded us from it. We were among our own people, you see. And then, with school, my life changed. Other children mocked the Latinos.

We wore hand-me-down clothing. We brought our Mexican food for lunch. We were not the same. Can you believe this was still happening in the 1980s?"

I shook my head, but I could believe it. I'd grown up in a similar environment.

"But, you know," Zephyr continued, "that is how I learned to be a survivor. I could no longer be shy if I was to survive this stupidity. Instead, I decided I would win. I would become better than they. I was graduated Valedictorian of my high school class. I was the homecoming queen and the prom queen. Who cares about that? Not me, but I did it anyway. I was student body president. Not because I am Latino and somebody helped me. Because I am smart, you see?" She stopped pacing for a moment and tapped her head with her forefinger. "I had figured out how to do it. My parents, so undereducated themselves, taught me to love learning. It was a game for me. When it came time to go to college, I chose a good school—University of California at Berkeley. I asked for—and received—a great financial aid package."

She sat, finally, across from me again, still wound very tight.

"How did you choose to be a winemaker?" I asked.

Her answer was one I'd heard before. "The science and the art. Before my father was killed, he worked in a vineyard in Idaho. He knew the work from California, from before I was born, and in Idaho he became a foreman. He died in that vineyard, you know; his tractor rolled on him on a steep slope. He loved the vines. I loved them because he did. He understood them. I loved the science, too. But as a little girl I wanted to be a famous artist."

At Berkeley, Zephyr majored in chemistry and excelled. But she also enrolled in many art classes. She enjoyed hanging out with the art students, taking in the Bay Area cultural scene and the late-night political and arts discussions, listening to music, and drinking the local wines. "But you know, I learned about the wine. It was easy there, the wineries were so close. I knew very soon what I would do with my chemistry degree. Then one day my senior year, I attended a student piano recital with friends."

"And you met Axel?"

"Yes, I met Axel." Zephyr softened visibly. The anger washed out of her.

"And then?"

"He was a junior. His music was brilliant, but he was such a sad little man. We were not in love instantly, you see. I loved the artist, but not the man. He was so lost. It took many months for me to learn that the artist and the man were one, and that lost part—well, I met his family. Who would not be lost?" She shrugged.

After graduation, Zephyr pounded on winery doors all over Napa and Sonoma counties, and was hired for crush at a winery in the Carneros district. "By then, Axel and I were involved, and I could work and be near him," she said. She lived in a house near the vineyards with three other winery workers, and saw Axel on weekends and holidays. When the winery hired her full-time, she decided to work another year and apply for the master's program in enology and viticulture at University of California at Davis.

Axel, meanwhile, finished his bachelor's degree, but stayed

on at Berkeley to begin working toward a master's degree in music.

"Getting into Davis took a year longer than I thought it would," said Zephyr. "But I was able to intern at a winery in Australia during their crush, and at another in Oregon. The Davis people saw I was serious and admitted me. I knew I wanted to go to Oregon when I was finished there."

Meanwhile, she said, Ted learned that Axel was seriously involved with the daughter of Mexican field workers. "He was starting to build Cougar Crossing and decided that Axel needed to become its winemaker. He ordered him to move to Davis and enroll in enology courses. Of course, at the time Ted had no idea that's where I was going to be." Zephyr laughed humorlessly. "Axel and I rented a house together. He showed up for classes—sometimes—composed, and played music on the weekends."

"And then he went back to Daddy?"

"Yes. Daddy summoned and Axel jumped." Zephyr's coldness returned. "I never understood the hold that man had on his children. Both of them were terrified of him, but also subservient. Axel came north as soon as he could. For some reason, he was terribly worried about his sister. It didn't matter that he left me, because I'd already secured a job in Oregon and was planning to move here. When I got here, Axel was a mess. We found him a good counselor. That's helped, but it's going to take a long while for him to work through his issues with his parents.

"I take it you would have married in spite of Ted." This was not a question now that I had spent some quality time with Zephyr Lopez.

"No matter what he tried to do, there is no way on earth that dirty little man could have stood between us. He insulted me, he berated me, he spread rumors. He threatened and huffed and puffed. He played dirty tricks and made me cry. He made life hell for me and Axel and everyone around us. But now he's dead. He ultimately was of no consequence, because we've won."

"...Because we've won." Zephyr's parting words repeated themselves in my head all day and into the night. She was so certain, so icily certain. Had life made her so hard that it was all just a game for her? I'd seen a glimpse of softness when she spoke of meeting Axel and their early days together. She loved him and trusted him, and she was comfortable with being the stronger of the two. She would marry him, no matter what. While he may have lacked the resolve to murder his father, I had no doubt that pushed to the wall Zephyr could efficiently do the deed, dust off her hands, and walk away.

How far had she been willing to go? Would Ted Maxell have found it amusing to tryst with the woman who wanted to marry his son? He would have found it very amusing indeed, I decided. He would have intended to take her down a notch, and relished every moment.

Back at the Westerly that Saturday night I took a huge, deep breath, made a big bowl of buttered popcorn, and plugged a DVD into the television. Then Winston and I settled in for the evening, relaxed. No one else had died. I was exactly halfway through my stint in wine country.

Chapter 25

Sunday dawned crisp and cold. October colors had displaced the dusky glow of Indian summer, and a chilly breeze riffled the rose bushes and other shrubbery when I let Winston out. It was the time of year that made my pulse quicken in anticipation of something, I knew not what. Perhaps holidays, perhaps warm fires or images of days gone by that had little to do with present reality—or past reality, truth be told.

The forecast called for rain, I noticed, as I flipped through the *Sunday Oregonian*. The Ducks had won, the Beavers had won. At that Oregonians could rejoice. Meanwhile, body parts had been discovered in a vacant lot in southeast Portland, and our president was doing his best to put on a happy face about so-called "progress" in Iraq. People were still out there killing and maiming each other—even in Yamhill County, I reminded myself.

Angel let herself in through the slider from the porch. "Ooh, it is cold," she said as she hung her sweater and handbag in the pantry. I looked at Angel differently today. I had learned so much about her from Zephyr. One always knows when there has been hardship, but for me her life was now more fleshed-out, defined. She had triumphed where many had simply given up. And she and her late husband had sacrificed much for their children. To me Angel was a hero. She didn't know that. She turned on the oven and mixed the muffin batter while I set to work on the breakfast trays. To be working beside her felt comfortable and real. Somehow my life was better because I knew her.

The visit with Carolyn loomed. I was excited to see her and learn of her progress. While she did have telephone access during parts of her day, it was limited, and pay phones were always in high demand with the Serenity Estate residents, whose cell phones were taken away when they were admitted. She could have called me, but I expected that what phone calls she made during the limited allocated times were to Michael and the boys. They had a lot of work ahead of them.

Breakfast over, I loaded the dishwasher, then took the ever-demanding Winston for his walk. After four of our guests checked out, I picked some late tomatoes in anticipation of the change in weather. "Tell the crew they can clean out the garden," I told Angel when I returned to the kitchen. "This is the last of the tomatoes."

"Senora, I have something to tell you."

I set the basket of ripe tomatoes on the counter and looked at her. Her eyes were unsettled. "What is it?" My mind started racing. Had another terrible something happened to someone?

"It is not an emergency, Senora. Do not be afraid. I have

learned something that may help Axel." She wiped her hands on a clean towel, and then folded it neatly.

"Well, what is it?"

She looked around the room, obviously uncomfortable. "My cousin Lucila, she works for Mrs. Maxell. She cooks, she does the laundry, she cleans the house. She lives at the house during the week and goes to her family on Saturday night and Sunday."

"Yes?" This seemed to be taking forever.

"She was there the night Mr. Maxell was killed. She says Mrs. Maxell, she come in very late."

"How late is very late?" I felt my pulse quicken.

"She say after ten. She comes in and she is all dirty. She is in a fancy dress with no sleeves. She has scratches on her shoulders, and her hair, oh my God! Lucila says the hair, it is sticking out everywhere. She looks awful and she is acting scary."

"What did she tell Lucila?"

"She say a man grab her outside the winery as she is going to the car. She does not know this man. He wears a mask and he tries to pull her into his pickup. She say she fight him and he scratches her and she kick him in the man parts and he yells 'ai-ai!' and get in his pickup and drive away."

What a load of crap! "Did Lucila believe her story?"

"I don't think so. But Mrs. Maxell, she run upstairs and take a shower, and she fixes her hair and puts on her bathrobe. She say, 'Lucila, don't tell Mr. Maxell. He will be so angry.' And then the sheriff's deputies arrive to say that Mr. Maxell is dead."

"What did she tell the deputies?"

"I don't know, Senora. When they arrive, Mrs. Maxell, before she answers the door, she send Lucila to her room and tell her she doesn't need her any more tonight."

So now we allegedly had a masked stranger running around the parking lot along with all the other people who were at the Cougar Crossing that night. It was disturbing news.

"Thanks Angel," I said. "I think this is important, but I'm not certain how yet. Did the deputies talk to Lucila?" There were all kinds of different ways this could play out.

"Oh yes, but not that night. Later they ask her about Friday night and she says Mrs. Maxell came home very tired. The police ask are Mr. and Mrs. Maxell happy together and she say yes. Mrs. Maxell say to her, 'You know what to say Lucila. You want to stay here working for me.'"

"And were they happy together?"

"Oh, no, Senora. Mr. Maxell was a very bad man. He did bad things."

"What kinds of bad things?"

"I don't know, Senora. Lucila hear Mrs. Maxell accusing him of bad things."

"Why did Lucila tell you this?"

"I ask, like you say. She is always so nervous, and I ask her what is going on. She is afraid to talk to Mrs. Maxell about that night. Mrs. Maxell has a very bad temper."

Indeed, women in late pregnancy often do have terrible tempers. Hormones are often awry; husbands often behave like imbeciles. It's surprising there aren't more homicides attributed to women in late-stage pregnancy. Why would Tara tell Lucila to keep her mouth shut unless she had been the one tussling with Ted in the tank room? One would think she'd want her assaulter caught, provided there even was a stranger in the parking lot that night. It seemed unlikely, but possible nonetheless. I definitely wanted to run this by Rob, but in the meantime I needed to change and get over to see Carolyn.

Once again I met Michael in the Serenity Estate parking lot as he was leaving and I was arriving. He'd had lunch on campus with Carolyn and spent two hours with her. "How's she doing?" I wondered.

"She's clear. She's conscious. In that regard she's better than she's been in years," he replied guardedly. I knew him well enough to know he was holding on to something.

"But what?"

"I don't know. She seems fine. She's still that awful color."

I didn't want to think about the color part or what Carolyn had told me about her liver. Michael probably knew the worst case scenario. "Are the boys going to visit her?" Like my daughter, Carolyn and Michael's sons, Archie and Blaine, were as far as they could get from *loco parentis* and still be in the continental United States. Both were successful in their given careers, and living in Virginia and New York City, respectively.

"They each told us they'd come home for a visit Thanksgiving week. Carolyn has been on the phone with them and has talked them into it. We'll do Family Week here, and then, if all goes well, she can come home for the holiday weekend on a pass."

I nodded. Family Week is when all the patient's family members gather at the treatment center to learn about alcoholism and other addictions. Then, under counselor supervision and in the presence of peers, everyone in the family tells the patient how her disease has affected them personally. It is a humbling experience, and not for the faint of heart.

"This is certainly a pain for the rest of us when she's the one who caused all the trouble," Michael muttered.

I silently counted to ten. Yes, it was a pain for everyone concerned. I wondered if he would say the same thing were Carolyn suffering from diabetes and the family had to meet to learn what to do when she went into a diabetic coma. Instead of a lecture, I merely told him, "It will help you all, and will make things easier in the long run. Once it's over, you'll be glad you were there to support her."

He shook his head. "Telling her how much and how often she fucked up doesn't seem real supportive. I'd just as soon not think about it anymore." With that he got in his SUV, turned on the key and revved the engine.

When I located her, Carolyn was recumbent in what seemed to be her favorite Adirondack chair on the women's deck, cigarette dangling from her fingers. "How ya doin' honey?" she drawled as I handed her a large bunch of dahlias from Melody's garden and kissed her cheek.

"I'm doin' great." I bummed a cigarette. Probably not the smartest move, but my nerves weren't very good. I needed one. "When are you going to quit these things?" I asked as I lit up and felt the nicotine go into my lungs and straight to my brain.

"One thing at a time," she said. "No alcohol. No caffeine after lunch time. I don't want the shock of all this healthy stuff to kill me!"

"How's it going here? Are you getting smart?" I kept the conversation light. Her color was appalling, her skin a greyish green, the whites of her eyes still dull. She looked terribly tired, small, and old. "Are you getting enough rest?"

"I guess. I seem to spend a lot of time lying awake, thinking about how I managed to mess up my life completely." She looked away from me, her jaw set. "And I know how awful I look. You don't need to dance around that part."

"I'm sorry." I was sorry. I couldn't hide the shock I felt when I saw her, even though I had seen her looking much worse. "It takes time. The good thing is, you've got the time, and you've got nothing better to do here than take care of yourself."

"Let's talk about something else besides me."

"How about murder most foul? Let's take a little walk and talk about that."

"That works for me. What *has* happened since I saw you last?"

As we followed the asphalt trail around the Serenity Estate grounds, I brought Carolyn up to speed, including every possible detail. When I was finished she pursed her lips. "Do you think Tara did it?"

"I don't know yet, but she certainly is hiding something. Since Tiffany's funeral, my greatest fear has been that Dwight did it. At least Ted's murder. He'd have no reason to kill Tiffany, except if she saw him he wouldn't want to get caught. He has never let anyone get in his way for long. Oh God! My brain gets hold of this stuff and it spirals out of control. It's just too much!"

"You know a great deal, but there also is much you don't know," Carolyn reminded me. "There are as many people unaccounted for as not. We've got Nestor Pullman. I know him, by the way. A good man—as is your ex-husband."

She held up a hand and touched her first finger. "Then there's Dwight. Hell, let's throw Michael in there too. He hated Ted." Three fingers. "Then Tara, and who did you say that guy was? The one at the dinner?"

I had no idea who he was. I described him.

"Short guy? Big gut? Fake-and-bake tan? Big nose? That sounds like our old friend Johnny Cardoni. We call him Guido around here."

I laughed. "I'm serious," Carolyn said. "He's one of the principals in C&C Imports and Distributing out of New Jersey. He's a slime ball, and there are rumors hat he has gang connections."

"What would he be doing at that dinner?"

"Perhaps he and Ted were doing business. You should check him out. Johnny wanted us to do a private label for him. He wanted a lot of wine, but he didn't want to pay what it was worth. Maybe he made Ted an offer he couldn't refuse."

"And then Ted changed his mind?"

"Or the terms became less favorable for Ted. Or for Johnny. It happens. If they were working together, each was getting what he deserved. However, Ted liked to mess with people—he just couldn't seem to stop himself—and if Johnny felt wronged for some reason, or disrespected, he'd find a way to get even. You can believe me on that."

Based on that information, I didn't doubt it. I looked at my watch. It was four o'clock. Carolyn looked exhausted, but she was sharp. It was amazing what two weeks sober plus regular meals and rest could do. As for the rest of it, we'd just have to wait and see. We walked back toward the residence hall.

"Any idea when you're going to get out of here?" I wondered as we approached the deck. "Not that you're ready, yet."

"The kids will be here for Thanksgiving. I'll get a pass then if I'm a good girl. Then they want me back here for at least another month—so I can figure out my living situation, and how I can manage and be comfortable with where I'm going."

"Any thoughts?"

"Nothing firm yet. I have to talk more with Michael."

"That sounds hopeful."

"I don't know. It could be. Right now, it's just one day at a time."

I hugged her and returned to the Westerly, where I set up for the late afternoon refreshments and resumed he seemingly endless job of playing hostess. Once the remaining guests were happily on their way to dinners in various restaurants, I called Rob.

Chapter 26

Rob and I made progress on our little investigation during the course of our telephone conversation. We agreed that he would do some investigative reporting regarding Johnny Cardoni and C&C Imports. One of my tasks involved calling the Yamhill County detectives to update them on what we had learned. At the very least, they could check out Tara Maxell's alibi, and I knew they'd be glad to get the information on Cardoni. I also was assigned the job of finding out who Tiffany hung out with—in other words, who was the likely father of her child? And would he have reason to kill her?

I called the sheriff's office after breakfast and spilled my guts to Dave Jeffers. The only thing I failed to mention was Dwight's limp at the funeral. I'd decided to handle that one on my own. Jeffers was polite on the telephone. "Thank you, Ms. Golden, for this information. We'll definitely look into it. However, you should know that we don't put a lot of credibility to hearsay evidence."

Of course I took immediate offense. It wasn't necessary, but I did so anyway. "How can you call this hearsay? Someone close to the Maxells actually saw Tara Maxell in a highly disturbed state on the night of Ted's murder—and that was before anyone even knew about it!" Good grief! Did I have to spell it out for him?

"That may be," Jeffers said. "But you heard it from a housemaid, who heard it from another housemaid, and no one has come forward. We don't know if they're reliable. Plus, we already have a signed statement from the Maxell housemaid. As I told you, we'll check it out."

"When?"

"That's not your problem."

"Someone just did come forward. That's what I'm telling you. She was scared out of her wits, but finally, thank God, she talked to her cousin. This is a good lead. This is important!"

"Mrs. Maxell's response to her husband's death was what we would have expected, and was entirely credible. We certainly will recheck the facts with her and talk to the housemaid, but I'll tell you right now, these stories have a way of changing when we're the ones asking the questions. What seems like a drama between two women often turns out to be nothing."

I couldn't believe my ears. "You guys told me to call you if anything unusual came up. This seems to me to be exactly the kind of thing you'd want to know."

"Yes, we did, and it is. We appreciate your call. But that doesn't give you license to go running around and playing detective for us. We're the ones trained to handle this type of investigation."

"I'm writing a book," I sputtered. "I run around. I *hear* things. That's what I *do.*" Then I added, "Is Tara Maxell the one who pointed the finger at Axel? Is that why you're so protective of her?" I was completely insulted, not to mention out of line.

"I'm afraid we aren't at liberty to give you that sort of information. But thank you for your call. We'll certainly look into this." And then he hung up on me. Thank you indeed! I'd just been blown off!

Be a big girl and get over yourself, the good angel on my right shoulder said. *This is not about you.*

You show 'em, said the little shit fairy on my left shoulder.

Why stop when you're on a good, dry drunk roll, I asked myself. And to whom did I listen? Why, the shit fairy, of course.

When I finished with my morning interview, which was just outside McMinnville, I called Yvick Robin. "Can you meet me for lunch? I'm buying."

"Sure thing, Emma," he said in his delicious French accent.

We pulled into the parking lot of Martha's Tacos just as it started to rain, and dashed into the place together. The droplets messed up my glasses and my hair, but it didn't matter. The harvest was pretty much over. Rain felt good.

"I have to ask you something, and you have to keep it to yourself, okay?" I said as soon as we had ordered.

"I like this, Emma, this drama, this secrets. I will tell no one, I swear it." Yvick laughed out loud. He reminded me of an otter; everything was a game to him. He dipped a tortilla chip into Martha's fiery salsa and popped it into his mouth. Then he folded his hands and smiled at me across the table. "What is on your mind that is so serious?"

"Tiffany Maxell," I said. "Can you think of why anyone would want to kill her?"

"I do not know. I did not know her so very well."

"You're close enough to the same age. Didn't you go to parties together? What was she like socially?"

"Alex and I, we have the children. We do not go out very much. But yes, we see her a little bit here and there, and I think she is the alcoholic. She is always drunk."

"Always?"

"Yes, and you know, she is very weird. She says stories that aren't true."

"How do you know they're not true?

"Just because.... She lie a lot about everything. She lie about what day it is."

"Did she have a boyfriend? Anyone special? Did you see her with guys?"

"Nobody special that I know about. She slept with many men. I know this because she talks about this one and that one. These were men from Portland, or they come here from somewhere else for business. Generally older. She says they are swingers."

"She said this to you?"

"Mostly to Alex. She says they buy her things, they give her drugs. Alex is shocked that Tiffany tell her these things. But you know, Emma, we don't see her very much. We have not much in common."

"Why did you believe those stories if she lied all the time?"

"One time, Alex and I are having dinner in Portland. We see her with a man, an old man."

"How old were these men she slept with?"

"Oh, they were old, Emma. At least fifty!"

That's why women my age can't get a date. The geezers are hanging out with chicks in their twenties! "Gross!"

"Very gross!" Yvick agreed. "Think about it—the wrinkles, the loose skin, the bellies. Ugh! All that fat rolling around. It's disgusting!" He laughed.

"I beg your pardon!" I sputtered. Had he completely forgotten to whom he was speaking? It was too much to bear.

I paid for our lunches, thanked him for his help, such as it was, and returned to the Westerly. On the way up the stairs to my lair, I felt more than a little diminished by our conversation. At my advanced age, I decided, I probably just needed a good nap.

It didn't make sense, I told myself, as I drifted off into what would end up being two hours of deep sleep. A young woman with her good looks, money, and that thong underwear could have any cute guy she wanted. Why did she hang out with old farts? I wished she was still alive so I could ask her.

I'd just cleaned up from the cocktail hour, and was rummaging in the refrigerator for something to call supper, when the phone rang. It was Henry Siu from San Francisco.

When I identified myself, he said, "Oh, Emma, you're still there. Will you be around for Thanksgiving? Frank and I are coming up for a week. We're going to spend time with friends in Portland, but we want to stay in the Chicken House if it's available." It was, and I penciled them in.

"We heard about Ted Maxell's death," he continued. "It was all over the papers down here. Have they found the murderer yet?"

"Not conclusively," I said. "They booked Axel Maxell, but he's out on bail. Meanwhile, his sister, Tiffany, is dead." I filled him in on the details.

"So Axel is on the line for two murders, then?"

"No, it's not that simple. He was under house arrest at his mom's when his sister was killed, so unless we're dealing with two different murderers, he can't possibly be guilty unless his mother is in on it too."

"It's totally different MOs, you say? So it could be different murderers, right?"

"I'm not so sure." I explained the layout of Ted's office overlooking the tank room. "I think Tiffany might have been up there that night and seen something. She told me she knew who killed her dad. Someone had to shut her up before she got up the courage to tell the authorities what she knew."

"I'll pass the news on to Frank. He actually knew the family." For what that was worth.

Two hours later, the phone rang again. This time it was Frank. "Solving a little mystery, are we?" he cooed. "How delightfully decadent! One wishes one were there to wallow in the intrigue."

"It's good to hear your voice, too," I said.

"Bring me up to speed, darling. I may be able to help."

I told him everything that had happened since he and Henry had returned to San Francisco, including the most recent developments with Lucila, the sheriff's department, and my conversation with Yvick.

Frank hummed and squeaked and exclaimed throughout the report, but didn't comment until I'd finished. "And Henry says you knew the family," I concluded.

"I was known to hang out with them a bit in olden days," said Frank. "You know, the occasional opening at the art museum, a benefit here or there. That sort of thing. And I actually *was* invited up to the manse once or twice, but that must have been at *least* ten years ago."

"So you all must have been fairly close by that point."

"Not really *close*, per se. I enjoyed Pamela. The woman is impeccable, such a patroness, don't you agree? But I never could stand Ted. He was a very nasty *little* man. He completely bullied Pamela and those divine children. And, you know, I had the oddest feeling that he abused Tiffany. In fact, I'd bet money on it."

"That's horrible!" I said.

"It's much worse than horrible, my dear. The man was a *monster.* That poor little girl. She was so beautiful and so lost. Just a little shell, really. Sometimes I'd look at her. Hopeless."

"Did you report him?"

"No I didn't. I couldn't. I had no evidence, you see. I once mentioned to the divine Pamela that I felt Tiffany must be depressed, that she was such a sad little girl. I suggested that Pamela might want to take her to talk to someone. I even gave her a name of a very reputable child psychiatrist in the city, a fellow practitioner and former *close* friend. Pamela couldn't see it. I'm afraid she didn't want to."

"Do you think that's why Tiffany went for older men? Because she was looking for a father?"

"Perhaps that. Perhaps looking for a father figure, but also because a man thirty years her senior is what she knew. And you say she was angry?"

"Every time I saw her. Angry, fearful, drunk, stoned. Pathetic, really. I guess it was that pathos that hooked me into going to see her the night she died. She was so frightened and alone. Alex was at his mother's, and therefore not available. She wouldn't talk to Pamela or Tara, she wouldn't call the authorities. She said she didn't have anyone. I wish I could have gotten there sooner. I didn't have a clue."

We were silent for a moment. "I doubt you could have done much for her," Frank said finally. "You weren't in a position to be able to get through to her. You could have been killed, too."

"Do you think *she* might have killed Ted? Was that what she wanted to tell me?"

"It's always a difficult call. Was she angry enough? Was she strong enough? If she attacked him with that paddle and knocked him in the head, I suppose it's possible. You've got to remember that this abuse, if it happened, occurred at a very formative stage of her development. As a result, it arrested her emotional development. It's more than likely that she still felt a lot of guilt and shame about being abused, and she blamed herself for what happened to her.

"She wasn't my patient. Judging from your description of her recent behavior, however, she never got the help she needed to deal with the awful events in her life. She was twenty-four years old, but emotionally she'd not matured much beyond the age of eleven or twelve. My best professional guess is that she did not kill her father. In some sick and confused way she was in love with him."

"I still wish I could have helped her."

"It's unlikely anyone could have helped her," said Frank. "When girls are messed with at such a young age and don't get the help and support they need early on, the prognosis is not very good. Most of them self-destruct. Even if she hadn't been murdered, I doubt she would have lived much longer."

Chapter 27

Shaken, I hung up the phone and paced around the house. I let Winston out and had a big drink of water. Then I called Rob and told him of my latest gleanings. The unsolicited ones interested him the most.

"What are we going to do about it?" he wondered.

"I need to talk to Pamela. I'll figure out a reason," I said. "She must have known what was going on—if Ted indeed was molesting Tiffany. We've got the motive."

"Why did she wait so long?" Rob lamented. "*That* doesn't make sense."

"She very likely was in denial." I'd certainly had plenty of experience in that realm, both in treatment and in my own life. "But maybe they patched things up when she learned Tiffany was pregnant, and one thing led to another, and the first thing you know it was true confessions, mother and daughter all warm and fuzzy again, except for the fact that Pamela had learned the truth about Ted. It would have been easy for Pamela to lure him into a tryst for old time's sake. I'm convinced, after all I've heard about him, that he would screw anything with legs and he didn't need a reason. And then Pamela exploded into rage and killed him. I would have done it years ago."

"What if it was Ted's baby?"

"That is the grossest thing I've ever heard of! Tiffany was an adult. She had other relationships. Even if she'd been his victim in the past, she'd have had a choice now. Who wouldn't get away from something like that the minute she was able?"

"You just answered your own question," Rob pointed out. "She didn't get away. She and Ted were joined at the hip. Everybody says so. She worked at the winery doing God-knows-what. She didn't have any education to speak of, no visible skills. It was not usual. Now who's in denial?"

I brushed him off by saying, "Nothing about *any* of this is usual. I'd bet money Pamela is the key. I just know it," I said. "What did you find out about C&C?"

"I called them this morning," said Rob. "Talked to Johnny Cardoni himself."

"*And*?"

"We had a very informative talk. He had both the motive and the opportunity." During their twenty minute telephone conversation Rob established that Cardoni had known Ted Maxell since Ted had purchased that now-legendary bottle of wine at the Napa Valley Wine Auction many years ago. They had been bidding against one another, it turns out, and after Ted finally outbid him, Johnny had walked over to his table to congratulate him.

The two soon discovered their interests involved more than wine. They did business together, sometimes traveled together, overate together, and partied together. "They were both at the strip joint where Ted met Tara," Rob said. "In fact, Johnny let it be known to me that he'd had an on-again, off-again, cross-country relationship with Tara before Ted met her." I wondered if Ted was aware of that fact. "Oh, he knew," Rob assured me.

"Is that what the argument was about the night Ted was killed?"

"No. That was about business, which always rates way above women with these guys. Ted reneged on a contract. He made Johnny look bad. It was a respect thing."

I felt I was watching an episode of "The Sopranos".

Soon after Ted opened Cougar Crossing, Johnny Cardoni had approached him because he wanted to add an Oregon pinot noir to his portfolio, he told Rob. His plan was to create a private label in the mid-price range—an everyday wine—not plonk, but a wine that aficionados could enjoy during the week at home, thereby saving their big money wines for entertaining and showing off. Maxell had a good winemaker in Josh Spears, one who not only could negotiate contracts with young but promising vineyards, but also could blend judiciously and skillfully the wines that didn't make the cut for the more expensive bottlings. Such a wine could be made inexpensively, and in enough quantity each year, to fulfill C&C's requirements.

"They signed a ten-year contract," Rob continued. "It was a lucrative deal for Cougar Crossing, but then Ted realized he'd been stupid to commit for such an extended period of time. Plus, he fell in love with his own, less expensive wine—or at least the idea of it—and decided to cut back on supply to C&C, do his own second label for Cougar Crossing, and make even more money by entering the more popular price range himself."

That sounded just like Ted, based on what I knew about him. "So, Johnny came to Oregon to sort things out?"

"Exactly. Only Ted wouldn't budge. In fact, he took great pleasure in embarrassing Johnny by sending him home empty-handed."

"So on the night in question, Johnny follows Ted into the winery and bops him, then pulls down his pants before he dumps him in the vat?"

"It sounds very plausible to me."

"Me too. But what about Tiffany?"

"Emma, c'mon. Those guys don't care. What is she worth to them? Nothing. Especially once Ted was gone. Johnny even admitted he slept with her once. In fact, one of her assignments under the auspices of working at the winery was to find female companionship for Johnny and Ted's other cronies when they were in town."

"He *told* you this?"

"Yeah. It was a real *mano a mano* conversation. Tiffany was a piece of meat to him."

"So you're one of the boys now? Isn't *that* nice. What happened to Johnny after their big argument the night of the dinner?"

"Cardoni says he stomped out of the winery, drove to the airport, and traded his ticket for a red eye to Newark. That will be easy for the sheriff's department to confirm, so he's probably not lying about it. The question is, what if he killed Ted before he caught the red eye? Did he somehow figure out that Tiffany was on to him—maybe she called him and told him, or tried to blackmail him, whatever—and send someone back to deal with her? That would be a little harder to trace since we don't know who we're looking for."

"As goofed up as she was most of the time, it's very likely she threatened him in some way."

"That's possible, but it would take someone with more pull than me to find out if Cardoni's bunch did send someone out here to shut her up."

"Which reminds me, have you talked to anyone at the sheriff's office, told them all this?"

"Not yet. I had a deadline today."

I told him how Jeffers had blown me off. I found myself getting pretty steamed.

"Calm down," Rob said. "Jeffers is the hard ass in the department. I'll take Doug to lunch tomorrow. He'll listen to me. He's a little less territorial."

By the time we rang off, I was squirming with excitement. I finally felt like we were getting somewhere. It was too late to call Pamela. What was I going to say to her anyway? I let Winston out for his late evening dash around the yard, then we retired to my eyrie where I sipped a calming mug of peppermint tea and brought my journal up to date.

I called Pamela Fontaine next morning as soon as my hostess duties were behind me. She really didn't want to see me. "Why can't we just do this on the phone?" she wanted to know when I pressed her.

"Pictures, ambience. I really need to come back to the estate. It's hard to get a feel of the place over the phone. I usually make two visits minimum," I lied, staring out the alcove window at the grey skies and drizzling rain. "And I need to take a couple photos because my editors may want to send a photographer out later." Another lie.

She reluctantly agreed to see me at two o'clock that day. "And I won't be able to give you much time."

"I'll make it work," I assured her. Since I had only one other interview that day, I was looking forward to spending some quality time upstairs with my laptop. Meanwhile, Winston was agitating for his walk so I grabbed a jacket from the mud room and found his little doggie raincoat. Thus attired we spent half an hour trudging through the mizzle.

"What did the deputies say? Did you tell them about Lucila?" Angel asked me when we returned. Something—who knows what—made me tell another lie. There was no reason really, I just did it.

"The deputies are very interested in Lucila's story," I said. "And I'd really like to visit with Lucila myself if she'd agree to it." Until that moment, I hadn't thought for a moment of talking to Lucila.

"I will talk to her," said Angel. "Something will be arranged."

I knew I'd also have to talk to Tara sooner rather than later. Perhaps Lucila would have more useful information about the Maxell household when we got together. And, I reasoned, seeing her would give me a better sense of her character and the veracity of her observations. Then I'd think about what to do about Tara.

At promptly two o'clock I drove through the gates of Fontaine Vineyard and up the drive to the turnaround in front of the house. Pamela answered the door almost as soon as I rang the bell. She looked me up and down and gestured for me to enter.

"I really don't feel like talking to anyone," she said as we walked through the house to the living room. "I'm certain you can understand."

"Of course," I murmured. "I'm sorry I had to barge in on you like this. I'm working on a very tight deadline and am trying to get all these loose ends tied up before I return to Portland."

"I guess it can't be avoided," Pamela sighed as she sat on her expensive leather sofa and gestured me to a chair. "How can I help you?"

I asked several detailed questions about the vineyard, planting density, crop load, and so forth. To her credit, Pamela was no fool. She knew precisely what was going on in her vineyard. Then I switched gears.

"I am very sorry about your daughter," I began. "She called me the evening she died. She wanted to tell me something, but I got to her home too late to find out what it was. Do you have any idea what she might have wanted to share with me?"

Pamela gazed at me for a few seconds, her expression unreadable. "How unusual," she said, even though I was certain she knew the circumstances of me finding Tiffany and why I had been present at her home that evening. The authorities would have given Pamela those details. She paused as if deep in thought. "No," she said finally. "I can't imagine why she would have wanted to talk to you."

"It must be very troubling to have Axel involved as a suspect in Ted's murder. I'm very sorry about that as well."

Pamela looked confused. "Yes, it is troubling."

"The entire situation is unusual, wouldn't you say? Your ex-husband and your only daughter both dead in a little over a week. I keep thinking there's a link between them—a reason someone would have wanted both of them dead."

"Why are you talking about this to me?" Her voice took on an edge. "I fail to see how my family is any of your business."

"I've heard they were very close, your ex-husband and Tiffany. Do you think that might somehow have something to do with her death? He molested her when she was just a kid, didn't he? Perhaps if the authorities knew the truth about the two of them, they'd leave your son alone and start looking for the real killer."

Pamela's mouth opened and closed. Her complexion had gone very white. Then she regrouped. Her eyes flashed with fury and she leaped from the sofa. "It's time for you to leave! Get out of here right now!" She almost spat the words.

"Come on, Pamela. It was right there in front of you for years—her behavior, how she suddenly became distant and disturbed when she reached puberty. You tried to pretend that nothing was going on, but you knew. In your heart you knew. And you finally divorced him, but that didn't save Tiffany. She told me she couldn't talk to you. Instead, she wanted to talk to me, a stranger, because she thought I'd listen. She was hoping I'd believe her."

"You have no business talking to me like this. We were a completely normal family. Normal in every way except for Ted's adulterous behavior. He was a womanizing bastard. I divorced him. That's the best I could do. Now get *out*!"

"Did his womanizing always involve girls your daughter's age? Did Tiffany tell you who was the father of her baby? Was it Ted?"

"Shut up! Get out of here!"

"You abandoned your daughter to that monster, and now you act like it's my fault. That poor girl. She didn't have a prayer."

"Get out of here!" she shrieked again. "I'm calling my lawyer. I'll have you flayed!" Several expletives have been deleted from our actual conversation, but let me tell you that woman could swear!

I stood up. "What nice sentiments," I said. "Have a good day."

She screeched some more, unintelligible things mostly, but her words were at my back. I'd tucked my notebook under my arm and was already on my way to the door. She'd answered almost all my questions, but it was a hollow victory. Angel was right. These people were disgusting.

Chapter 28

While I spent the rest of the afternoon in front of my laptop, the time was not productive as far as my book was concerned. I was too agitated from confronting Pamela about her daughter. The fact that Pamela suspected all along about Tiffany's abuse and wouldn't admit it was sickening. Ted's behavior was beyond belief. In my mind, he was an evil man—just as Angel had alleged. He'd exploited his own daughter to feed a soul sickness so revolting it was beyond human comprehension.

Somehow, in spite of or as a result of it all, Tiffany had stayed near him, worked for him, and been forced not only to find prostitutes for his friends, but to be one herself. How much more degrading could it get? Often in literature I had read about despicable people committing despicable acts. I couldn't remember anything as vile as what I'd learned during the past twenty-four hours. The fact that he may have fathered her child made it even worse.

I felt we were getting closer to knowing who had committed the murders. In my mind, Dwight was still a possibility for Ted's murder, but I couldn't see him killing Tiffany. Johnny Cardoni and company, on the other hand, seemed far more qualified to pull off a double homicide without getting caught. Cardoni would have exacted his revenge with Ted, and as Rob had observed, Tiffany was a completely useless commodity in Cardoni's eyes. If she had observed Johnny in the act of murdering her father, and he somehow had become aware of it, it was certain she'd have to be eliminated as well. Had she been stupid enough to actually call him and try to shake him down? If she was drunk or high, she might have done anything.

Nestor Pullman certainly had the motive. He was a grouchy old fart, and physically strong. He also was an honest soul who loved his daughter and her young son, never mind that the boy's father was the vile Ted Maxell. Nestor seemed a man rooted in reality, a man who knew himself and behaved as a hard-working, honest human being ought. I truly believed him to be above committing murder, except to protect himself or a family member. If nothing else turned up, I'd revisit my decision, but for now, in my mind at least, he was not a suspect.

Until our interview, I'd not considered Zephyr as a contender, but now there certainly was a slot for her as well. Of all the possible murder suspects, with the exception of Dwight, she was the smartest. She knew what she wanted from life and how to get it. She was capable of fine and deep feelings, but she also was a realist. Axel was a mess because of Ted. Ted was determined to foil their plans to marry.

And Zephyr would not be foiled. Get him to agree to meet, get his pants down, ruin a vat of pinot noir? No big deal. Could she really be *that* cold? I couldn't be certain. Her fierce protectiveness of Axel possibly could drive her to such an act. Or, they could have worked together. But she'd never kill Tiffany, no matter what. Would she? Certainly not if Axel knew about it.

Which brought me to Pamela Fontaine. Much of Pamela's existence depended upon her look good. Society matriarch, old money, a serious player in a glamour industry, patroness of the arts—her entire way of life was based on appearances. If she finally had been forced to look at the incest that had transpired under her very nose for years, she would have faced some tough decisions. Would she hold her head up and get her daughter the help she needed? I'd seen no sign of compassion or empathy when I told her I knew about Tiffany's abuse—only outrage that I'd found them out. "I'm calling my lawyer!" she'd screamed between expletives—and somebody had really taught that woman to swear. With both Ted and Tiffany out of the way, Pamela never would have to face her role in their family tragedy.

Indeed, perhaps she had killed Ted—for revenge or to keep him from polluting the family reputation. He'd hardly been the jewel in her family's crown. But that done, would she have the ability, the absolute cold bloodedness, to kill her own daughter and thereby cover up the entire sordid business? And why would she want to? By all indications, she and Tiffany had had a difficult relationship. Tiffany did not trust her mother, but that did not make her mother a murderer. It only meant that she would not tell her mother what she felt she needed to tell me. Big question, that one.

As a mother, I could not picture another mother committing such an act. Perhaps that was naïveté on my part. On the plus side, she had stepped forward with one hundred thousand in cash to get Axel out of jail. According to Rob, they both had been at her house having dinner at the time Tiffany had died.

Tara was still an unknown. Obviously, as the sheriff's deputies were not ready to talk to her again, I hadn't been very effective in stating what I believed to be a legitimate case for further investigation of her activities. As I hadn't yet had a real conversation with the woman, I felt it my duty to the prospective readers of my upcoming book to ferret out whatever information I could about her views of the wine business. And, if I found out more about her life, her relationship with Ted, her plans for the future...well, hell, so much the better. In my book, something would have to be said about the grieving widow. After all, she was now owner of one of the state's more visible wine properties.

With Ted out of the way, Tara would have complete access to Josh Spears if that is what she wanted. Was that affair enough to justify a murder? Was she that calculating? They seemed entirely too cozy to be enjoying a strictly business relationship, though what he could see in her was beyond me. Spears seemed a fairly bright man, and certainly easy on the eyes. He'd have his choice of any number of attractive single women.

Why would Josh Spears want someone like Tara? I had to think about that one for a minute. It must have something to do with oral sex, I reasoned finally. A male friend had once told me, "A man will do just about anything for a good blow job." Perhaps Spears was the person Ted had gone to meet in the tank room that night. Or had Tara lured Ted out there so her lover could kill him?

We were back to the original murder scene in Cougar Crossing's pinot noir tank. A blow job, promised or otherwise that fateful night, was at the bottom of the case. Had the murderer staged it to render Ted helpless? Was the murderer the person giving the blow job, or was someone coerced into doing it so the murderer could have easier access to the victim? Once Ted dropped his drawers he was at the mercy of whoever happened to be on the catwalk with him. The sexual favor didn't have to be performed. The promise would be enough for the murderer to get Ted where she or he wanted him.

Or was Ted killed simply because the person giving him the blow job was someone else's lover or spouse? Was it a simple crime of passion that had escalated, for one reason or another, into a double homicide? Or were the two murders unrelated? To me, it seemed the most likely murderers were Johnny Cardoni and friends or Tara Maxell. Johnny had a plausible motive. Tara's, if it was indeed she, was less clear.

It was driving me crazy, and continued to do so as I set out wine and chatted with the Westerly guests.

However, the next logical thing to do, it seemed, was talk to Tara Maxell and see if I could shed further light on anything connected with the two killings. After making a couple of dinner reservations in the kitchen alcove, I looked up the number and dialed the Maxell estate. "She is not here," said the woman who answered the phone. "She is having the baby. The ambulance take her to hospital just an hour ago."

"Is this Lucila?" I asked.

"Yes, this is Lucila." Bingo! This was almost too good to be true.

I identified myself. "Lucila, I need to talk to Mrs. Maxell about some things, but since she is not available I wonder if perhaps I could come up and visit with you." I had no idea what I was going to say to this woman, mind you. But since I had her on the phone, I wasn't going to let the opportunity slip away without at least asking if we could meet.

"Oh, I don't know," Lucila said faintly. "I don't know what to do."

No, she had no idea whatever what to do because nobody was there ordering her around, poor dear. And she was scared of her boss—so scared it seemed impossible that she would do anything without making certain it was all right with Tara. "When do you get off work?" I wondered.

"I stay here until Saturday at noon. I must stay here even when she is gone."

"May I drive up and just visit with you for a few minutes?"

"I don't know, Senora. Mrs. Maxell, she not like me to have the visitors."

"She's in the hospital," I reasoned. "They'll keep her there overnight at least."

"I already tell Angel all I know."

"Right, and she told me what you said. It is very good information, but I need to talk with you just for a few minutes and clear up a couple of details."

There was what seemed like a lengthy pause while Lucila

digested this information. I strained to keep my mouth shut and let her cave in without prompting. What I was asking her to do was risky, and we both knew it. It put her job in jeopardy. But who would know? *Absolutely no one*, the shit fairy whispered in my ear. *Once you talk to Lucila, you'll know what you need to do next.*

"Please, Lucila," I said finally. "This is very important. Two people have died."

Her sigh was audible. Then I waited and allowed the silence to float between us.

"Okay, you come visit," she said finally. "I do not like this, but I will try to help."

I set the telephone receiver down gently, and then jumped around the room as Winston dodged for cover. "Yes! Yes! Yes! *Yes!*" I ran to the car, hopped in, and drove up the hill before Lucila would have a chance to change her mind.

It was six-eighteen when I arrived at the estate. Daylight was going to dusk, and was muddled with a soft and friendly autumn rain. I got out of the car and stood for a moment and listened. No birds sang. It was so quiet I could hear the raindrops patter gently on the ground. I could smell wet, dying leaves. Notebook in hand, I trotted up the stairs and onto the ridiculous veranda, then rang the doorbell. She opened it so quickly I felt as if she must have been waiting behind it for my arrival.

"Lucila, I'm Emma." I stuck out my hand and she took it unenthusiastically.

"Come in, Senora. It is very wet." She whisked me inside the door and took my jacket and hung it the entry hall coat closet. "I will make us tea," she said, and I followed her across the foyer with its wide, open staircase, down a long hallway and into the kitchen. The rooms seemed much larger now that they weren't filled with the funeral throngs. The kitchen was palatial, with a huge informal dining area and sliding doors that faced a large, well-lighted deck. I pulled up a stool and sat at the granite island while Lucila busied herself filling the tea kettle with cold water and turning it on.

"How is Tara doing? Have you heard anything?" I asked, by way of making conversation.

"I have not heard anything," said Lucila. She opened a tin on the counter and began placing biscotti on a fused glass plate. I watched her. I'd seen a nearly identical plate somewhere not long ago. "She will call me when the baby is born."

"That's good," I said, as my tired brain worked on what to say next. "Are you the biscotti chef?"

"I learn to make them from Senora Maxell," she said. "She eat them all the time. The senorita liked them also." She stacked them into a perfect tower—just like the one I'd seen on Tiffany's counter the night she died. I stared at the tidy stack of biscotti on the beautiful plate. Lucila had made biscotti and given some to Tiffany, who ate them and *what*? Had they killed her? I didn't know how she'd gotten peanuts, but someone did.

Lucila handed me a cup of tea. Then she came around the counter and sat on the stool next to me. "I already tell Angel all I know," she said miserably.

"I'm sure you did," I said, hopefully sounding calmer than I felt. "I just wanted to be certain on the time. You see, the dinner began about seven-thirty, and it was about nine, maybe a little later, when we had a break. And that's when Mrs. Maxell told someone she wasn't feeling well and went home. And yet you told Angel she didn't come home until after ten."

"Yes, and she say there was a man in the parking lot."

"And there was a scuffle, she said, right?"

"Yes, and she was very scrat-ched and dirty, and her hair is like this, and *this!*" Lucila pulled her hair out and up to demonstrate. "The front of her dress is wet, and she smell like wine, and she is scrat-ched here and here." More theatrics, in which Lucila pointed to her neck and her upper arms. "I ask her what happen and she say a man attack her."

"Did you call the police?"

"Oh, no, no. She say no police. She say Mr. Maxell will be very angry, and no police. He is not to know about this. She say she is okay, and she will take the shower and go to bed."

Something moved almost out of my range of peripheral vision and I turned my head automatically. There, in the doorway to the butler's pantry, stood Josh Spears. He had entered through the front door and dining room. Lucila squawked. I hoped my gasp wasn't audible.

He surveyed us with those cold, dark eyes, expression revealing nothing. "Good evening, ladies." He nodded to us and smiled. It was a very taut, strained smile. "It looks like you're having a fine visit. I stopped by to pick up some of Tara's things."

"How's she doing?" I asked brightly as Lucila opened and closed her mouth like a dying fish.

"Doing just great," said Spears, equally brightly. "She was

delivered of a seven pound, six ounce baby girl just over an hour ago. Mother and daughter are both well."

"Tell her congratulations," I said, smiling. "I dropped by to see how she was doing and Lucila said she'd been taken to the hospital."

"I'll be sure to pass that on. I'll just go get those things now," said Spears and left the room. We could hear him moving up the staircase, and listened as his boots clomped on the floor above us.

"Oh my *God*!" Lucila whispered. "What will I do? She will kill me. I am not to have the visitors. I need this job." Her face was drawn and ashen.

"Snap out of it!" I said sharply. "Get a grip! Nothing happened. We don't know what he heard. He couldn't have heard very much. And you weren't having visitors. I came here to see Tara, and that's your story. Don't change it. No matter what anyone says to you, stick with that story. It is *the truth*. You don't know anything else. Tell them I brought a gift for the baby. I'll get something early tomorrow. You tell her that the doorbell rang and there I was, and that you invited me in to be polite. Tell her I will bring it back so I can see the baby. Can you remember to do that?"

Lucila nodded. Then she shook her head. "She will fire me."

"Stop it. She'll do no such thing. I'm going to go now. Walk me to the door and try to sound normal."

We paraded back through the house, me in the lead chattering about the excitement of new motherhood. I almost made myself sick just thinking about how sore everything had been after the birth of my children, but I kept blabbing.

Lucila was murmuring and helping me on with my coat when Spears descended the staircase with a well-stuffed gym bag.

"Be sure to call me when Mrs. Maxell gets home," I said to Lucila.

"Yes, Senora."

"I'm really sorry I missed her." I looked at Josh Spears as he opened the front door and held it for me to pass through.

"Thanks, Josh. Give my best to Tara."

He nodded but said nothing. His eyes were like nuggets of coal—velvety, black, and expressionless. I walked slowly down the front steps to my car. Once inside, I fiddled with my seatbelt, got out, pretended to look for something in the back seat, and then got back into the driver's seat. Those eyes. Call it paranoia, but I didn't want the bastard behind me. By the time I started the car, Spears was on his way down the driveway. I followed him all the way down the hill. He turned left toward Newberg, and I turned right toward the Westerly.

Chapter 29

"I talked to Lucila last night," I said to Angel as we were preparing breakfast.

She looked at me, alarmed. "You talk to her on the phone?"

"Yes, and then I went up there." I repeated our conversation and what had happened. Angel stopped working and glared at me.

"You know she will lose her job. I did not want this to happen. You make her lose her job. This is why I don't want to tell you these things."

"Angel, relax. I made it look like I'd just dropped in. And I'm going to Fred Meyer this morning to get a card and buy some baby stuff. I'll go up there when Tara is back from the hospital. Then, if there is a problem, I can do damage control."

"But he hear you talk about her, this man."

"Josh Spears. Yes, he showed up, but I don't think he heard

much of anything. And if she or he didn't kill Ted, then so what if he heard us? There's nothing to hide."

There was the matter of the peanuts. Nothing had been mentioned in the media regarding exactly what had contained the peanuts that had killed Tiffany, or that peanuts had even been the cause of death. It had been more like allergic reaction, suspicious circumstances, that sort of thing. That led us to the small matter of the biscotti, and I needed to talk to Rob about it as soon as possible. Based on what I had seen in Tara's home, the biscotti seemed to be the trail to follow.

"I worry, Senora," said Angel. "There is a bad stink in Denmark." Someone had been reading Hamlet to Angel. I laughed out loud.

"The boys are coming for Thanksgiving week," I told her to change the subject. "They're going to be in the Chicken House."

Angel flushed with pleasure. "I like the boys. They tease me, and they always give me the big tip."

"That's sweet," I said, then headed for the dining room carrying a platter of sausages and a basket of homemade cinnamon rolls.

After breakfast, I made a list and went to Fred Meyer to pick up a few things for the kitchen, plus the baby gift that would get me readmitted to the Maxell mansion. When I returned, I phoned the hospital. Tara and her baby had just checked out. I called Rob on his cell phone.

"Yo," he said.

"Yo, yourself. We need to talk."

"So talk," he said.

"Not on your cell phone. Let's do lunch."

302   ◊   Judy Nedry

I met him half an hour later at a wonderful little Mexican restaurant in downtown Newberg.

"You probably know this and just forgot to tell me," I began as platters of *carne asadas* tacos were set before us. "Were the peanuts in the biscotti?"

"Yes, but that's top secret information. I wasn't supposed to tell anyone until they tracked down the source and had some hard evidence."

"So why haven't our servants and protectors arrested Tara Maxell?"

"How do you know the biscotti came from her?"

I told him about my interview with Lucila, and about Tara's and Tiffany's abiding love for biscotti. "It's probably the only thing Tara and Tiffany had in common. Tara taught Lucila how to make them. She easily could have gotten peanuts into the batter without Lucila noticing. Their version is full of hazelnuts, so Tiffany wouldn't even have tasted the peanuts. They're delicious, by the way."

"Well, well," was all Rob offered in response.

"Yes, so I stuck my neck out to get that information. Now what?"

"The servants and protectors, as you call them, are very excited about the Cardoni connection," he said. "They are on top of it, talking to law enforcement personnel in New Jersey, the whole deal. The entire department's shook up. I took Haymore to lunch yesterday, and he's a happy man." He looked so pleased with himself I wanted to hit him.

"You better tell him about *this*, then," I sputtered. "If Tara is involved, Josh probably is too. After last night, they're on to us."

"Tara isn't very smart," Rob observed. Still in his own world, he was oblivious to my seething. "Besides, anyone with access to that kitchen could have made the biscotti."

"And who would that be, Rob, besides Tara and Lucila? Listen to me. Tara's already killed two people, or had someone do it for her. She no doubt has very complex reasons, motives as of now only surmised, for doing so. Thus far, she's proven herself to be smarter than the people who are looking for the killer."

"Emma, she's a stupid girl. She's not much more than a teenager—a stripper, a bimbo for godssakes. And now she's got a new baby to worry about. Even if she did it—and it looks as if that's possible—she's not thinking about it now."

"Do you want to make a bet? She is hormone-fucking-crazy! If she's not completely drugged, she's thinking about who she can kill next! Remember the times when Janine gave birth. We females are not rational human beings at such times."

Rob appeared to give this some thought. "Janine is a very calm woman," he said finally. "A natural mother, in fact. With her, the craziness usually sets in quite a bit later."

"What does that mean?" It was a bunch of crap, that's what it meant. And I could feel myself growing angrier. Mentally, the part of me I worked with every day to keep things functioning on a rational level in that scary neighborhood between my ears had just stepped aside and given the shit fairy her head. It was time for Rob to come around to my way of thinking quickly, or suffer the consequences. He marched bravely forward, opting to play it his way, the fool.

"Briefly, it means that I'll talk to Doug this afternoon and pass along your information," he said. "I'm sure he'll want to go up and talk to Tara when the time is right."

"And *you* don't think the time is right?"

"I didn't say that. What I am saying is that she is a new mother. She gave birth less than twenty-four hours ago. Let the sheriff's department get its rocks off chasing mafia in New Jersey. Who knows what they might find? And cut her some slack. She's not going anywhere."

"And how do you know that?" I screeched. "You have no idea what she might do or where she might go!"

People turned around in their booths and looked at us.

"Calm down, Emma."

"I'm calm," I hissed. "And *you* are a *rat*. Silly me. I thought we were on the same page. Do you think one of Johnny Cardoni's mafia buddies baked a batch of biscotti with ground up peanuts in them? That is *not* what happened, and you know it! They wouldn't have done it that way. Meanwhile, Lucila and I are caught in the perpetrator's kitchen, if you please, *talking* about the goddamned biscotti. Someone will be after us next! Clearly, this conversation has gone far enough."

I stood up. I wiped my arm across the table. Tacos, salsa, chips, and two medium-size diet Pepsis went into Rob's lap. He looked up at me, stunned.

I bent down and hissed, "Goodbye, you horse's ass," then walked out the door of the restaurant seething with rage. *That will teach him to mess with a post-menopausal woman,* said the shit fairy as I got into my car and turned the key in the ignition.

The big question looming, I realized as I drove out of Newberg, through Dundee and up the hill to the Westerly, was what to do next. I'd lost my partner. Why could he not see the urgency of the situation? Was he so enamored of his own part in the investigation that he wouldn't take a hard look at the evidence I'd gone to such pains to unearth? I couldn't believe the ego of the man! The condescension. It was impossible to fathom his arrogance and deceit! But I was wound up like a crazy woman, and the minute I figured out what to do next I was going to set things right.

I walked into the kitchen and flung my purse into the alcove. At the sink, Angel was washing utensils. She turned to me with terror in her eyes. I went to her and grabbed her hands. "What's happened?"

"Senora," she blurted, "I can't find Lucila." She burst into tears.

My mind raced. "Can't find her? What do you mean?"

"She does not answer the telephone at the Maxells' house. She is not at her house. They have killed her!"

"No, no. It's nothing like that," I said. "It's all right. She's out running an errand for Mrs. Maxell. It's nothing bad, Angel."

"You do not understand," Angel wailed. "She is so afraid of that woman! And she always, always answer the phone. She carry it with her in her apron always." She cried great wailing sobs. This was crazy-making.

"I'm sure it's something with a very simple explanation. She probably got the day off. This is not a normal time, you know. Mrs. Maxell just got home from the hospital. She probably turned the phones off. I'm sure everything is fine."

Actually, I was not certain about anything, especially anything concerning Tara Maxell. As far as I knew, she'd

306 ◊ Judy Nedry

already killed two people. I didn't know how or why, but it was my tacit understanding, having read hundreds of mystery novels, that once someone killed another human being it became easier to kill the next one. Easier and easier. Bodies popping up everywhere.

The light on the alcove phone flashed but I didn't give a rip. Let it flash. Angel was bawling as if she'd lost her best friend—which, for all I knew, she had. I slowly breathed inward and outward, wondering what to do next. My gaze settled on the Fred Meyer bag containing baby clothes, a card, and wrapping paper that sat on the desk where I'd dropped it earlier.

"Angel, help me with wrap this gift, will you? We'll get this stuff together because I'm going to pay Tara Maxell and her new baby a visit."

It worked. Angel's braying ceased. She wiped her eyes and followed me into the dining room.

Chapter 30

It was nearly two when I arrived at the Maxell estate, beautifully wrapped baby gift on the car seat beside me. I was beginning to re-evaluate the situation. My behavior at lunch had been deplorable. Sure, it hurt me that Rob hadn't kept me up to speed on the investigation. That violated our agreement. However, it could have been as simple as his forgetting to mention something. At any rate, his behavior was his problem. As a designated grown-up, my reaction had been completely crazy. And when I listened to the shit fairies I was not a grownup—a lifelong struggle, alas. I owed him a huge apology. I decided I'd call him as soon as my meeting with Tara was over. By then I'd have more information anyway.

As far as Lucila was concerned, I tried not to be insane with worry. She doubtless would answer the doorbell. The new mother no doubt had instructed her to silence the phones so the baby wouldn't be disturbed. I got out of the car and walked across the damp pavement and up the stairs to the front door. I rang the bell. No answer, no approaching footsteps, not a sound. I rang it again. I began to feel a bit concerned.

The door was unlocked. I opened it as quietly as I could. The shit fairy was back on my shoulder and running my life again. She told me it would be all right if I just walked in like I was going to leave the gift. I really needed to know what was going on. Since Lucila was not present to answer the door, where the hell was she?

"Hello!" I said. "Knock, knock, anybody home?" I said it quite loudly.

Not a sound. Not a ticking clock, no music playing, nothing. I retraced Josh's steps of the previous night, through the dining room and butler's pantry and into the kitchen. "Is anybody home? Tara, are you here? I brought a gift for the baby."

Nothing. Perhaps Tara and the baby were sleeping. I looked all around me. The kitchen was spotless. There was no indication that anyone had come home or was in residence. It occurred to me that Tara may have gone to Josh's place to take it easy for a few days. It seemed like a good idea, but what about the unlocked front door?

Then the shit fairy and I remembered the fused glass plate of biscotti. If only I could lay hands on that plate, so similar to the one found in Tiffany's kitchen, it would prove that the biscotti had come from Tara's kitchen. And who'd be the wiser?

I stood at the counter where I'd sat the night before watching Lucila. I visualized how she had bent down to get the plate before opening the cookie tin. Excellent. The house was empty and cold. I'd find that plate and get out of there and come back later with the gift. Tara had so much stuff she'd never miss the plate.

I walked around the island and stood where Lucila had stood the previous night, trying to remember where she'd found the plate. I opened the wide cabinets to the right and voila! There on a convenient pull-out shelf were an array of ceramic and glass pitchers, bowls, and platters. On top of a stack of smaller plates I found what I was seeking—the elusive biscotti plate, or one almost like it. There were several others obviously by the same artist. They were really cute. I wondered where Tara had found them. I reached for the plate and brought it up to the countertop, where I examined it in the ambient light. It was a lovely piece.

Now to get it out of the house. I removed my suede jacket and wrapped it around the plate, lay it across my left forearm, then set the gift on top of it and headed toward the butler's pantry and dining room.

"Turn around." It was Tara's voice, sharp as broken glass. I jumped, and dropped my jacket. The plate fell free and crashed to the floor. Glass shards flew in all directions.

I turned slowly to face Tara. She was standing at the French doors that led from the informal dining area to another part of the house. In her hand was a pistol. It was pointed at me. "What are you doing here?" she demanded.

"I came to see you," I managed to croak. She did not radiate the sweetness and joy of new motherhood. In fact, she looked downright menacing. "I rang the bell but nobody answered, so I came in to see if you were okay. Where's Lucila?"

"Why do you care about Lucila? Who's Lucila to you? And what made you think you could just walk into my house uninvited?"

"I didn't think that. The door was unlocked. I brought you a gift. I was hoping to see the baby, but if you weren't here I'd just leave the gift." I slowly lifted the package from the wreckage and held it out to her. "Here. You can open it now if you'd like."

"Put it down." She gestured with the gun. It was a small gun, but a gun nonetheless. I don't particularly like them.

I set the gift on a large table to my left. "The baby's asleep, but *you* didn't answer my question. Why did you break into my house?" She shifted her weight from one foot to the other. "As for Lucila, I sent everyone home at noon—gave them the afternoon off with pay—because I knew you were coming." Her voice sounded very hard to me, but there was an edge to it that hinted at excitement? Hysteria? I couldn't be certain. The gun was still pointed straight at me. Arms free, I stood very still facing her.

"Why are you pointing that gun at me?" I asked. "You're safe. I'm not an intruder." The gun remained where it was. It occurred to me that things weren't suddenly going to go my way here.

"I was napping in the den," she continued. Her voice adopted a sing-song rhythm. "And I heard a noise. Someone had broken into my house, and I found her going through my desk in the kitchen where I keep my cash for the month, and several of my credit cards." I felt the hair on my arms tingle. "I said something to the burglar. I told her to stop. But she didn't stop. She turned to me. And then I noticed the knife

in her hand, the big one from the block on the counter..."
She waved her pistol in the direction of a small desk located
to my left.

"Tara, knock it off. I'm here to help you. Put the gun
down." Clearly she'd lost her marbles. Just as clearly, I was in
deep ca-ca.

She gave me a fleeting smile and took the gun in both
hands, holding it out in front of her. She looked like she knew
what she was doing, but how should I know? I'm not a gun
person.

"You bitch!" she shrieked. Her hands began shaking and
she walked toward me. "You're not here to help me. You know
what happened. ...And I told her to stop but she ran toward
me with the knife. I warned her to stop but she wouldn't. So,
bang bang! I shot her!!"

She hadn't lowered the gun, but her hands were shaking
so hard I wasn't sure she'd be able to fire it. I hadn't wet my
pants. Yet. Things were looking worse with the passing of
each second. My mind didn't seem to be working, but words
automatically came out of me. "Tara, please, think of your
baby. Think about your little girl. Let's just sit down and talk
about this. Something's really screwed up here."

"Yes it is, thanks to you," she said flatly. "And I *am* thinking
of my baby. What good am I to a little girl? What can I do for
my little baby if I'm in jail for the rest of my life? Tell me that,
you damned bitch."

"What are you talking about?"

"Don't you bullshit *me*! Do you think I'm *stupid*? I'm
not stupid, and you aren't either. You know exactly what I'm

talking about. You know I killed that fat bastard and his slut of a daughter. That's why you're here."

"You killed Ted." It was not a question.

"Yes, I did." She smiled at me, sweetly, innocently, but the expression in her eyes was ferocious.

"Was there a particular reason you killed him?"

She snorted and the smile disappeared as quickly as it had come. "Of course there was a reason. I don't just kill someone for no reason. He was fucking the slut."

"Which slut?"

"You're right, in the time Ted and I were together there were a number of them. But he was fucking the slut Tiffany."

And suddenly it made sense. I drew my breath in sharply, and she noticed. "I think you may have that wrong. I believe he molested her when she was younger, but surely..." It was a lame attempt at best.

"You are *not* that stupid, so don't act like you are. Listen to me. I caught them right here in this house."

"I don't believe you." Actually, I *did* believe her. Based on what Frank had told me just a couple days before, it suddenly made perfect sense. In fact, it explained everything.

"It's true!" she screamed. *"It's true!"* Her hands were shaking again, and she tried to steady them. In a far-off room, the baby began crying.

"Ha, ha," I said. "That's funny Tara. You didn't kill anyone. Let's sit down and have some iced tea. You can get the baby and tell me what really happened."

"Don't lie to me. All he did was lie and lie and lie. 'I didn't do it, Honey. How can you accuse me of something like that?' Even when I caught him, even when I caught them together.

'She's my daughter,' he'd say. 'Of course I kiss her, Tara. Get a grip.' His whole life was one big lie—and so was hers.

"At first I thought *I* was the crazy one. I saw how he looked at her sometimes. I sensed something, you know? I'm not dumb. Everybody thinks I'm dumb, but I'm not. I could feel it when they were in the room together. But I ignored my gut for a while because thinking about that kind of stuff made me sick. I was so happy up until I figured him out. Ted could be really fun, you know. And I loved him for a while. He took care of me. He really took care of me. I didn't know there were so many ways to be taken care of. Trips, expensive hotels, fancy dinners, whatever I wanted. Stuff I didn't even *know* I wanted."

All this she told me staring down the barrel of a gun. I wondered how long she could stand there like that, so recently delivered of a child. She was young. She was tough. She'd been a dancer of sorts. I stood still and waited, hoping like an idiot that she would faint, or perhaps just want to sit down and have a chat. It didn't happen.

"I wanted to believe him up until that last time. The night of that dinner is what did it. I saw him say something to her at the dinner after he was pawing you under the table. I was already mad about that, and I followed them. He left first and a couple minutes later she followed him across the parking lot and up to the tank room.

"I used another entrance and went up to Josh's old office. They were in plain sight. They each did a line of coke on the railing, Then down came his pants, and he was hanging his old thing out there, and she was blowing him."

She peered into my face looking for some sort of reaction.

Apparently she saw one. "Shocked? Aren't families a gas? I saw my sister blowing Uncle Ricky once. Icky Ricky, we called him. She was a lot younger though. She was really just a little girl. It wasn't her fault. Tiffany was old enough to know better."

"I'm very sorry," I said.

"Oh, don't be sorry." She gave a toss of hair and a shrug. "It happens. I just thought I'd gotten away, that's all. I thought I'd finally reached a time in my life where those things didn't happen like they'd been happening all the time I was growing up. I thought I had escaped that degrading shit, and then there it was all over again, with my fucking husband in charge of it all, causing misery everywhere.

"They heard me come out of the office and clomp down those metal stairs, you know. They heard me and I didn't care. Tiffany completely freaked and ran off, but Ted just stood there waiting for me. He was grinning, and he was so drunk and stoned he didn't even bother to pull up his pants. I grabbed one of those paddles and busted him across the side of the head. Then he quit grinning, the son of a bitch.

"I beat him with the paddle. He got a hold of me once and tried to fight, scratched me a little, but I backed off and hit him again. Then he begged. He begged me to stop. He kept hanging onto the railing somehow. He wouldn't let go no matter how much I hit him. When I stopped, he still was standing, but I'd knocked him senseless. I went up close to him, and shoved and heaved, and finally I managed to get him over the rail and into the vat, but he kept hanging on. I beat on his fingers until he let go, and then I got the paddle and shoved him under."

She held her gaze with me. "Do you believe me now?"

"Yes I do. I believe you," I said, not looking away.

She brightened and smiled a satisfied smile. The baby's crying had ratcheted up to a hefty scream, but Tara seemed oblivious. "That's good. I'm glad." She sounded almost happy now, as she walked a little closer to me, still pointing the gun. She got within about seven feet and gestured with the gun.

"What do you want?" I said.

"I want you to go out through those doors behind you and onto the deck," she said and gestured toward the patio doors. "I don't want to mess up the kitchen."

"I need to know something first."

"What?"

"Did she tell you about the baby?"

Tara's chin jutted up and out. She held the gun higher. It was pointed at my face. I wanted the answer. I could think of nothing but her answer.

"Yes," she said, her voice lower now, and husky. "Yes, of course. She told me she was carrying his baby. She told me she was going to *have* his baby, and she would make me sorry for what I'd done."

"But you knew she was crazy. She was bonkers."

"So what? She knew I killed him. Or she thought she knew. She told me the day after the funeral—all of it—how I'd be in prison and my kid would go somewhere and I wouldn't get any of the money. She planned to *live* in my house because it was her father's house. Her lover's house. She knew enough to ruin my life forever. Now get outside."

"I'm not going anywhere. You'll have to shoot me here."

"But then Josh...."

"Oh, is he in on it too?"

She smiled. "Of course he is. Who do you think was out there messing around at your place that night? Me with my big belly? Now get outside!"

"Why? What was that all about anyway?"

"Oh, we thought it would be fun just to mess with you. Like maybe you'd just get the hint and go home. Yeah, Josh will do anyth--...."

We both heard it at the same time and turned toward the butler's pantry.

"Sheriff's deputies! Drop your gun and freeze!" Deputies Jeffers and Haymore stepped into the room, followed by four men in riot gear.

In one smooth movement, Tara swung her body around and fired the pistol at them as I dropped to the floor. Several guns exploded at once. It was over in seconds. I lay on the floor in the fetal position, drenched in Tara's warm, sticky blood. For a moment there wasn't a sound except for the screaming infant.

Chapter 31

Haymore had his cell phone out and was pressing in numbers. Jeffers walked toward me as I pushed myself to a sitting position. Blood was everywhere and I was covered with it. It was not a tidy shooting. Tara lay on the floor next to me, what was left of her. One quick glance was all I could muster, and I couldn't look at her again. I lifted my hands to my face. They were slippery with her blood. I began to scream.

Sirens in the distance. Two uniforms, one on each side, picked me up by the elbows and led me to the front door. I couldn't have walked without them holding onto my arms. I couldn't stop sobbing, and yes, I had wet my pants.

As we came out the door, Rob was running up the steps with a photographer. He was met by Jeffers, and they started talking and gesturing. Jeffers turned him away from the house. The noise around me was babble. Rob saw me and stared, mouth open, as the deputies hustled me down the front steps. I rode to the hospital in the ambulance since Tara had no use for it. She was going to the county lab in a body bag.

At the hospital, some nice people cleaned me and checked me all over. There was no physical damage, not a scratch. They gave me Librium and put me in a room for observation overnight. Rob showed up about seven. I'd been dozing, but jerked awake when he entered the room.

"I'm sorry," I mumbled. My mouth felt like it was stuffed with cotton, and I had trouble forming words. "Sorry I called you all those names."

He pulled up a chair and handed me a latte. "You had every right to be angry," he said. "In fact, after I got cleaned up, I drove up to the Westerly to apologize. Angel told me where you'd gone, and she was hysterical. She'd finally caught up with Lucila, who said she'd been sent home that morning when Tara came home. Angel didn't like it at all that you'd be up there with Tara by yourself."

I was too groggy from the drugs to say much, but Rob was content to talk. He'd called the sheriff's department from the Westerly kitchen and told Jeffers and Haymore what I'd learned from Lucila the night before. I'd already told them, of course, but it probably sounded more convincing somehow when backed up by someone they knew and trusted. At Rob's urging, they quickly mobilized a team and headed for the Maxell estate. Meanwhile, Rob figured there would be an arrest at the very least, and called a photographer from the newspaper to meet him there.

Everyone who had entered Tara's house wore protective vests. Although Tara's bullet hit Haymore at the left side of his stomach, the Kevlar vest had done its job, and the damage was limited to bruising. Tara had taken five bullets and died instantly. Her next of kin in California had been notified. In the meantime, as he was her closest relative, Axel had stepped forward to care for his infant half-sister.

I was released from the hospital the next morning, there being nothing visibly wrong with me. The pictures in the newspapers and on the television news showed little more than the outside of the Maxell estate and crime scene tapes. By the time I was back at the Westerly, Josh Spears had been arrested, having been charged with abetting a murderer and hindering a murder investigation. And he had been the prowler at Westerly. Tara had treated the dog bites, and for some reason they had not gotten infected.

The deputies talked to me and then they went away. I wanted nothing more to do with anything involving the murder case. I was done with all of them and just wanted them to leave me alone.

Back at Westerly, Angel fussed over me as if I was going to break. I did very little for the next few days except eat, sleep, and walk Winston. Angel very capably ran the bed and breakfast, including all the reservations and staff supervision. I wondered why Melody ever thought she'd needed me. Then a small idea gained purchase in my mind. Perhaps she had wanted me there so I finally would pull my head out of the sand and try to help Carolyn. I knew Melody wanted to help me with the book to any extent possible, but as the days wore on, I was certain that Carolyn's well-being also had been part of her overall plan.

The weather continued cool and soggy. Angel and I went about our daily tasks, but the tourist season was basically finished for the year. Except for a small flurry for Thanksgiving, there were only a few bookings. After my walk each morning, I'd set up in the solarium in front of a lovely wood fire and work on the book. I invited girlfriends out from Portland to have lunch or dinner. I even began reading fiction again. On Sundays I'd drive over to Serenity Estate and visit Carolyn.

Melody and Dan returned home six weeks to the day from when they had departed. I met them at the airport. When I saw Melody in the airport, I began crying again and bawled all the way back to Dundee. Dan drove while she sat with me in the back seat and let me cry on her shoulder. After a couple days of catching up, I returned to the relative calm of Lower Hillsdale Heights and planted tulip bulbs. The rains had set in for the winter.

Chapter 32

Thanksgiving was held at Westerly that year. It was a wonderful reunion in the huge dining room. Michael and Carolyn attended with their sons, Archie and Blaine, Carolyn looking weak but happy. She had put on a little weight, gotten a good hair cut, and was wearing makeup. Although frail, she looked smashing. Her sense of humor had never been better.

Frank and Henry, who'd rented the Chicken House for the week, were invited to dinner and were in attendance with two female doctors from Portland, old friends of Frank's from medical school. I brought my friend Cate, who lives up the street from me at the uppermost reaches of Lower Hillsdale Heights. The Delaneys left early because Carolyn was tired. The rest of us played games and laughed far into the night. It was pouring rain so Cate and I spent the night.

We had just finished breakfast on Friday morning when the phone rang. It was Michael Delaney. Carolyn, he said, had died at about five that morning. He'd discovered her when he awakened. They had known she didn't have much time left, he told Melody on the phone. They'd agreed not to share that information outside the family, and had made the best of every day she had left. Her heart had simply failed, and she'd died in her sleep. She hadn't made a sound, he said, and when his time came he hoped it would be that easy.

We held a memorial the following Sunday in Dan and Melody's home. Angel, Melody, and I had cooked tirelessly for two days to prepare for Carolyn's send-off. Everyone I'd ever known in the valley was there remembering Carolyn's wit and humor, her talent, and her tireless contributions to the good life. The urn with her ashes was placed in front of the painting where everyone could pay tribute. Axel and Zephyr arrived with Angelina Maxell, and announced their plans to marry before Christmas and adopt the baby. It was the sort of occasion our friend would have enjoyed.

Carolyn had died happy and at home with her family. So we celebrated. People brought their favorite foods and wines, and we ate, drank, reminisced, and talked about the good times when it was just a few of us and the center of our universe was that little half-timbered house on the side of the hill that was the beginning of the wine industry as we knew it.

The End

LaVergne, TN USA
27 August 2009
156191LV00009B/21/P